THE CAGE

THE CAGE

Radu Herklots

Matador
Unit E2 Airfield Business Park,
Harrison Road, Market Harborough,
Leicestershire. LE16 7UL
Tel: 0116 2792299
Email: books@troubador.co.uk
Web: www.troubador.co.uk/matador
Twitter: @matadorbooks

ISBN 978 1800465 626

British Library Cataloguing in Publication Data.
A catalogue record for this book is available from the British Library.

Printed and bound in Great Britain by 4edge Limited
Typeset in 11pt Adobe Garamond Pro by Troubador Publishing Ltd, Leicester, UK

Matador is an imprint of Troubador Publishing Ltd

For Lucinda

THE RHYME CHANTRY

Iron and steel structure. Established in 1445 in first bay from west end South Nave Aisle as burial place of Charles, Lord Rhyme and his wife Jane St Budeaux and as chantry with Altar. After dissolution of chantries permission obtained in 1783 to move structure to present position as Rhyme family pew used by consecutive Earls of Rhyminster. Known as "'the Cage'", the roof inside painted with series of motifs showing lineage of Rhymes and Woolfords.

From *Notes to Guides in Rhyminster Cathedral*, first published in 1958.

ONE

The obtrusive ring of the landline cut through the peace and quiet of another Rhyminster morning.

"Hi, Sally. It's Barbara. Well done for *Children in Need* at the weekend – must catch up soon. Either of them in?"

Barbara Battershill: secretary to Robert, 78th Bishop of Rhyminster, and arch diplomat.

Sally Munks glanced around the tiny open-plan outer office.

Aside from her, it was populated by a prone border terrier and his master, a cheerful-looking man who had arrived at his fifties in generally good nick.

He wasn't vain, as a rule, but was proud of his thick thatch of grey hair, which offset a slightly ruddy skin tone.

The man looked up from his work, smiled at his PA and gave her the thumbs-up sign.

"Barbara – John's in. And Barker, of course. I'll feed you through."

Tedesco took the call.

"Barbara. Lovely to hear from you. Now? I see, I understand, it must be urgent. Tell Bob I'll be over in ten minutes."

1

"Come on, Barker," he said to the terrier, "let's go for a woof down to the North Canonry. I'm sure Sally can hold the fort."

*

John Tedesco had taken early retirement from a career as a provincial solicitor in the south-west.

After completing his training in his home city of Plymouth, he joined a partnership in the tiny cathedral city of Rhyminster.

Within a matter of days, he realised that this was it – he'd found his perfect place, and he'd never leave, and so for two decades he combined his day job – dealing with routine conveyancing, divorce and writing wills – with the post of Diocesan Registrar, or Bishop's legal adviser.

But as he approached the age of fifty, Tedesco surprised his colleagues – and himself – by taking the decisive step of leaving his practice to form a small, word-of-mouth private detective agency with his friend and former divorce client Lynne Davey, formerly of Devon and Cornwall CID.

Although no longer the Bishop's official adviser, he remained on call for anything particularly delicate, or out of the ordinary.

He was rarely idle.

*

Attaching Barker to his lead, he led the dog down the narrow stairway from 4A Minster Precincts into the outer Cathedral Close.

Barker stopped to cock his leg by the Victorian lamppost, and then they continued their circuit of the most glorious open space in England.

The North Canonry, or Bishop's Palace, was at the far end of the Close.

As Tedesco stopped at the office entrance and keyed in the security code, Barbara Battershill came down to greet them, wearing her trademark navy blue bandbox-fresh suit.

"Come on, Barker," she said. "You can help me with some paperwork. The Bishop is waiting for you in the study, John."

As Tedesco nudged the oak study door ajar, Bishop Robert slowly rose from his partner's desk, an item of furniture that existed in a constant state of tension between the Bishop's inability to file paper away and his secretary's obsessive tidiness.

The Bishop was of a similar vintage to his informal adviser. In brief, if there was such a thing as a typical bishop from Central Casting then Robert Dwyer wasn't it.

Short and stocky, resembling a human Oxo cube, he was built for the scrum rather than the pulpit.

Rhyminster had been the culmination of a sometimes controversial career in the Church of England – apart from being one of the early advocates of women priests, and subsequently bishops, he had been outspoken on race and gender issues, and was firmly established as one of the leaders of the liberal wing of the C of E.

The two friends and erstwhile colleagues moved to a small table overlooking the Cathedral, where Barbara had already laid out the coffee and pastries.

"Thanks for coming at such short notice, John," said the Bishop.

"My pleasure. Barker needed a walk, and I needed a break from Sally and her latest fund-raising mania," Tedesco answered.

3

Bishop Robert leaned in, quasi-conspiratorially.

"Another tricky one, I'm afraid. You know Ollie Canford? My lay assistant?"

Tedesco had seen Canford around and about the Close but didn't really know him; they had never spoken.

"Anyway," the Bishop resumed, "he is supposed to attend the monthly staff meeting. He is invariably late but has never completely missed one until two days ago.

"He isn't returning calls or answering emails, and there has been no sign of him in the flat."

Canford occupied the small service flat in the Canonry, which had variously been the home of chaplains, gardeners and visiting clergy from abroad. During World War Two, it was used to house a refugee couple.

"John," Bishop Bob went on, "Oliver does spend rather too much of his time in London – which wasn't in the Diocese of Rhyminster when I last checked – so he may have gone AWOL up there. He has form."

He paused, as if about to deliver a legal judgement. "But something doesn't sit right. I don't think we should be alerting the authorities yet, as it is still less than forty-eight hours, but could you and Lynne have a discreet look into it?"

Tedesco nodded to signify agreement, and then Bishop Bob made a surprising admission.

"To be frank, I've been regretting his appointment since the moment he started here."

Tedesco looked out over Cathedral Green before turning to face the Bishop again.

"Of course, Bob. Lynne and I will see what we can find out. Can I start with background? Does Oliver Canford have any family?"

"That's the odd thing," replied Dwyer, "he's never mentioned any living relatives. His late father was a vicar, and I assume that his mother is no longer with us.

"And before you ask, he doesn't have a partner that we know about, although he has developed a following among the Ladies of the Close – something I have warned him about more than once."

"Interesting. What about his interests? Hobbies and so on?"

"He jogs – if that's a hobby – mainly around the Close. He has mentioned the Park Run, so it might be worth asking Lynne about that."

Tedesco's colleague Lynne Davey was a very keen runner, and a regular at the Saturday – morning communal jog.

"Let's see," the Bishop added, "he drives a rather ostentatious little car, so he may be part of an owners' group."

"I've seen him in a red Triumph Stag," said Tedesco, "and he must be a skilled mechanic or have access to one to keep that beauty on the road. It's a seventies classic – but I agree, maybe a little out of place for a bishop's lay assistant. Anything else come to mind?"

"Oh, yes, there's his singing. This may be significant, John. He is part of a very refined London choir – in Chelsea, I think – called the 'Tuneful Company of Minstrels'. You can only imagine what Charles Tantum calls them."

Tedesco smiled knowingly. "That gives us plenty to start with," he said.

TWO

Venice, one year earlier

"*Pronti!* Let's be having you! All members of the Honourable Order of Titianites – *Andiamo!*"

The young tour leader, strikingly blond, held his yellow flag proudly aloft as he led the bedraggled group of pension-padded senior citizens from the *vaparetto* stop onto the waiting boat.

Once they were safely aboard, he made a further announcement.

"Don't get too comfortable, people! We need to get off at the next stop, then it's Culture a Go-Go at Santa Maria dei Frari, where we will encounter Titian's *Assumption*, you lucky lot!"

As the boat approached the next landing stage, the tour group – the usual mix of Home Counties Gin and Jag and Booths Food Market Northern Affluence – shuffled and stumbled awkwardly, the young man making sure that they were all safely ashore before the *vaparetto* chugged away from the Toma stop.

He undertook a swift headcount – none of them had fallen in this time – *Grazie a Dio.*

*

The Bishop of Rhyminster, Robert Dwyer, and his wife, Hilary, were staying at the Ca' Rafael, a medium-sized hotel on a curve of the Grand Canal. They seemed to be the only guests who were not part of the Bel Paese Tour group.

They arranged, with the eye-rolling connivance of the management, to be seated in a quiet area of the restaurant so they could enjoy their breakfast at a safe distance from the retirees.

This avoided two dangers – overhearing predictable moans about the weather, the Italians and Brexit, and the very real threat of recognition should anyone from the Diocese form part of the group.

Once the members of the Order of Titianites were safely out of sight, the Bishop and his wife took the next *vaparetto*, then changed to a number 52, getting off at the Madonna dell'Orto.

Hilary was passionate about the works of Tinteretto, and so the visit to his parish church was the highlight of this, their 30th wedding anniversary celebration.

Neither of them had been to Venice before, and so the anticipated week of church crawling, gallery hopping and people watching, with the added bonus of some uninterrupted time together, had just about kept their spirits up during a difficult few months in Rhyminster.

The Bishop had been assailed on all sides.

The *Daily Mail* had laid into him for his 'liberal' views on a variety of issues.

An awkward clergy discipline case, with possible safeguarding implications, was about to blow up – and he needed a new chaplain.

7

The previous incumbent was Sarah Dillon – his protégée and an obvious future star in a none-too-glittering firmament.

She had, naturally and rightly, been fast-tracked into a coveted London parish, and should be a shoo-in for a bishop's mitre before long.

Hilary was a ward sister on the cardiac unit at Rhyminster General, and so she had more than enough of her own stress to deal with, let alone coping with the lonely role of bishop's wife, with its attendant and outdated assumptions – and they both worried about their adult daughters, Grace and Sophia, loaded with student debt, bravely navigating a world screwed up by their parents' generation.

So Bob and Hilary could hardly be blamed for lingering for several hours in the spacious and miraculously tourist-free Madonna, marvelling at the delicate gothic façade, the unexpected little cloister, taking the opportunity to spend time with the 'Little Dyer' and his masterpieces.

After a quick plate of *cicchetti* for lunch, Bishop Bob and Hilary took an early-afternoon *vaparetto* back to Rialto and, as the sun was about to break through, decided to stroll back to the Ca' Rafael.

They had a busy twenty-four hours ahead of them, so the chance to grab a siesta was more than welcome – their plan was to make an early start the next day, so they could take a boat out to Torcello before the hordes arrived.

Charles Tantum, the Master of Musick at Rhyminster Cathedral and self - proclaimed gourmand, had insisted, rather than recommended, that they visit a particular seafood restaurant. Tantum had raved about Alle Testiere, a tiny place in Castello which was 'impossible to find' without his hand-drawn map, and he had taken it upon himself to secure them a table using his 'famed contact book'.

They were due there at eight that evening. Hilary was convinced that they would never find it, while Bishop Bob shuddered at the likely cost. And he knew it wouldn't hold a candle to the Harbour Fish Bar in Brixham, the best chippy in the Diocese.

*

Hilary nudged the Bishop awake. It was gone six, so she suggested they go down to reception to see if they could ask for some better directions, as Tantum's map really was impossible to follow.

After a quick shower and change of clothes, they took the rickety lift down to the ground floor, which had been engulfed by a newly arrived tour group from China.

"Hiya!" It was the Bel Paese tour guide. "Off for some dinner?"

Hilary explained the situation and her attendant anxiety over finding the place in time – never mind navigating their way back in the dark.

The young man introduced himself as Oliver Canford, adding that he was enjoying a rare night off from 'The Crumblies'.

Having packed his geriatric group off to a tourist concert, 'Vivaldi and so on', he would be delighted to take his new friends to the *osteria*.

Canford reassured them that they would be in for a treat but that Alle Testiere was, indeed, exceptionally difficult to find, even with Google Street Maps.

Bob and Hilary still had plenty of time before their reservation, so they accepted his enthusiastic invitation to join him for a drink in the bar, the tour guide insisting on 'Bellinis all round', which he ordered in his fluent but showy Italian.

Canford, seemingly elated by his release from his middle-brow charges, relished the chance for some educated conversation, becoming quite garrulous in the process.

Bishop Bob and Hilary swiftly learnt that Oliver worked for Bel Paese for the major part of the year, sharing his passion for art, architecture and opera with a not-always-responsive audience.

As well as Italian, he spoke fluent French and Spanish, but his degree was in Theology.

The Bishop raised an eyebrow, before asking, "Where did you study Theology, Oliver?"

"I'm a Cambridge man," Canford replied, somewhat pretentiously in Hilary's view. "Trinity Hall."

He continued: "I had considered training for the ministry, but I struggled to find a real vocation.

"Now don't get me wrong – I love this job, and it gives me a congregation of sorts, but trying to interest a group of nineteenth-hole philistines in the wonders of the Italian Renaissance does have its limitations."

Hilary sought to open up the conversation, drawing out of Canford that his father had been a priest, rising to the rank of archdeacon. Despite sharing the ambiguous relationship with the Church common among children of the clergy, Oliver said that he missed his connection to the 'dear old C of E'.

Hilary hoped that he hadn't noticed her grimace at this point, but Canford, clearly oblivious, ploughed on.

"I can't decide if I do have a vocation after all, or whether I'm just another nostalgic Anglican – you know, savouring the early-evening light in a Saxon church, the smell of the hassocks, the Mothers' Union banner, Betjeman."

At precisely what point, thought Hilary, *is Bob going to reveal his identity to this charmless fool?*

As if he had read her mind, Canford asked Bob what he did for a living.

"Let me guess. Surgeon? Academic?"

Bishop Robert broke into a broad smile.

"I'm the Bishop of Rhyminster, and Hilary works for the NHS. And I think we need to find this hidden restaurant."

Canford was momentarily lost for words; the moment soon ended.

"It's an absolute pleasure to meet you, Your Grace," he burbled. "People like you give hope to those of us who are terrified of the fundamentalists. Wow, this is incredible!"

"Look. I know this is fascinating, but we need to get moving," interrupted Hilary.

Canford proceeded to guide them to their supper venue with a practised expertise, knowing which *vaparetti* to hop on and off. He led Bob and Hilary from San Zaccaria through the tiny, narrow *calle*, ending up at the welcoming light outside the restaurant.

Having successfully navigated their way there, he insisted on going inside with them, fussily checking their reservation and arranging for one of the waiters to take them back to the landing stage when they had finished, then he turned at the door, bowing theatrically, and gave them a mock salute as he left.

The seafood was simple but beautifully cooked – Tantum

clearly knew his sea bass from his John Dory – and they both welcomed the stark décor of the place as a contrast from the overstuffed Ca' Rafael.

"What do you make of our new friend?" asked Bob.

"I suppose he was all right."

"Come off it – you were giving me your 'Shania Twain look'. What was that song called?"

"*That Don't Impress Me Much*," Hilary said. "Honestly, it took a nanosecond for him to drop Cambridge into the conversation. And all that gushing nonsense about Betjeman, old maids cycling through the mist to communion, or whatever he was going on about."

"Oh, I don't know, I rather liked him. An enquiring mind, searching for truth, on our wing of the church. It may be the wine talking, but this could solve my chaplaincy problem."

Hilary took a gulp of the excellent house white.

"You have got to be joking. Apart from anything else, he isn't ordained. He isn't even sure if he has a vocation!"

"Several of my colleagues have lay assistants these days instead of chaplains. Anna Lichfield has a wizzy ex-banker, and Stephen Winchester has a Theology graduate, not unlike young Oliver, in fact.

"It works well for them – the job is largely admin, so you don't really need an ordained priest."

The Bishop paused while the main course was cleared away, then he continued, warming to his theme.

"As you know, most of the chaplain's work is taken up with organising parish visits, liaising with Barbara over the diary, a bit of media, the odd bit of driving.

"Hilary, I think God may be working a bit of his magic in Castello tonight."

"Definitely the wine talking," was her swift reply, followed by, "and, if you remember your Trollope, Slope was a bishop's chaplain."

"So perhaps I need a lay assistant then."

"Time to leave, I think," said Hilary. "I'll get the bill – *il conto, per favore.*"

THREE

Barker, with his master in tow, ascended the familiar winding stairs that led to the office of Tedesco and Davey.

Once inside, he made straight for his day bed under Tedesco's desk, strategically placed to render whatever canine assistance was required.

Before Sally could badger her boss for some sponsorship for her latest charity stunt, Tedesco asked her to find Lynne – "It's urgent."

"She's in Taunton – keeping tabs on that lawyer who keeps bonking his clients."

"Delicately put as ever, Sally," he replied. "Could you text her please, and ask her to call me as soon as she can?"

Tedesco retreated to the stationery cupboard and removed a fresh counsel's notebook.

These pale blue pads, with a perforated edge to each ruled page, had been a beloved staple in barristers' chambers, and classier solicitors' offices, for as long as he could remember.

He wasn't a complete technophobe – you couldn't practise law these days if you were – but he still found it comforting to write up his case notes by hand.

Always using the same ink pen, the one he had been given when he qualified, he inscribed his entries in immaculate copperplate.

As he delicately turned over the pale blue cover, he ran his finger down the spine and wrote in capital letters, *THE CASE OF THE MISSING LAY ASSISTANT.*

Canford was his first subheading.

He carefully recorded the Bishop's initial comments, underlining the reference to his regret at the appointment.

This was followed by a few preliminary actions:

Lynne – Park Run tomorrow, ask around, see if Canford was missed, what people made of him.

Actions for JT – call sister, get her insight. Go to Cathedral, gentle digging.

Sally interrupted his inscription.

"Lynne's on the phone!"

She managed to transfer the call without losing the caller – something of a collector's item, thought Tedesco – and he was put through to his fellow detective.

"Lynne. How was your bogus consultation with your randy litigator? Are you still in one piece?"

"I got an hour's free divorce advice, about half of which was taken up with shameless flirtation. And boy, was he handsy!

"I'll need a run around the Close followed by a long shower when I get back.

"Anyway, it's all recorded on my phone, so I'll be arranging a meet with my client to look at next steps."

"Good work. He sounds like a class act. In an ideal world he'd get struck off, but I won't hold my breath."

Tedesco had always upheld the highest of standards,

and was surprised and disgusted by those who put his old profession to shame.

"Lynne, do you think you can make it back by three?"

"More like half past, just joining the M5 now," she replied.

"Okay, let's meet in the Cathedral refectory. I'll make sure I get there by then."

"Sure – you've got me intrigued now."

Tedesco replaced the receiver then he texted his sister. He thought he'd invite himself round for supper.

Nicky rang him straight back, another rare event.

"Short notice, Bro, but good timing. How about 7.30? Chag will be late back – another of his bloody sales dinners – but Jack and Ella will be made up to see you. Actually, they'll be more thrilled to see Barker. I assume he's your plus one?"

Tedesco laughed politely. "I will ask him to check his social diary."

Ending the call, he got down to some routine correspondence with the aim of clearing the decks before the weekend – then before he knew it, the Cathedral clock struck one.

"Just popping out for lunch, Sally. Come on, Barker," he called, as he did on a daily basis at this precise hour.

Tedesco's long-established lunch routine started with a quick stroll to Jenks Bakery, located just behind the Butter Cross.

"Another week nearly over, Mr T?" said Joan, as he reached the front of the queue.

Joan had worked there since his early days in the little city.

His Monday sandwich choice would invariably be a boring one, like cheese and tomato, but his selection became progressively more indulgent as the week progressed, culminating in his Friday bonus of a sweet treat: a delicious yoghurt and blueberry flapjack, or, if he were feeling a touch louche, a millionaire's shortbread.

Sandwich and flapjack duly purchased, his next stop was WHSmith to pick up a copy of *The Times*, then he headed back to the office with Barker, for what Sally annoyingly and persistently referred to as his lunch *al desko*.

Once back behind his desk, he allowed himself half an hour to skim the main paper, eat his lunch, then complete the easier of the *Times* crosswords, always remembering to check if Sally had filled up the dog bowl – after all, a border terrier needs feeding after a swift woof around town.

Sally Munks, by way of contrast, had spent her break on Facebook, swapping hilarious video clips of the *Children in Need* curtain-raiser, held a good two months before the main event in late November.

She had been dressed as a scantily clad fairy and had spent the day terrifying the residents of the Close – and the still impressive number of tourists – into donating to the cause.

Tedesco soon brought her back to reality.

"Sally, I need to pop over to the Cathedral and I won't be back till after four. Could you keep an eye on Barker for me, please?"

He strolled across the Green towards the main visitor entrance, then studiously ignored the woman at the donations desk as he made his way into the central nave.

FOUR

He'd given plenty to the Cathedral over the years, both of his precious time as well as by regular giving, so he was unfazed by the woman's look of disdain.

As ever, several visiting tour parties were being coaxed around the building by volunteer tour guides.

The guides were easily identifiable, their sashes making them appear like superannuated Thunderbird puppets, but Friday's lead guide stood out from the others – Tedesco recognised her immediately.

It was Liz Gerrey, her crimson sash setting off an elegant skirt suit combined with a cream blouse.

Liz had moved all the way down to Rhyminster from Edinburgh about two years ago.

Her late husband, Roddy, had been appointed as the lead cardiac surgeon at Rhyminster General, but with a horrible irony, he succumbed to a massive coronary after a mere six months in post.

This had been a terrible shock; he was only in his early fifties, scrupulously followed his own advice to his patients, and was an active sportsman.

Hilary Dwyer, the Bishop's wife, had been his ward sister, and she became close to his widow, offering her both Christian support and practical help.

Liz had wondered about moving back to Scotland but found a new purpose in tour guiding and soon became a leading light in the Cathedral's volunteer community, to the extent that the Cathedral marketing team made shameless use of her elegant features in their brochures and on their website – picturing her with groups of attentive tourists, or maybe sharing a staged joke with the Dean over a coffee in the Refectory.

Tedesco approached her at the end of her tour, which had clearly gone down well with her group of Rotarians.

"It's Liz, isn't it? You won't remember me…"

Without missing a beat, the only blonde among the tour guides replied: "Of course I do! Who could forget the distinguished Mr John Tedesco!

"We met at the Dean's drinks do last Christmas. Where have you been hiding? It's so lovely to see you in the Cathedral."

So this is what a charm offensive feels like, thought the lawyer turned investigator.

"Actually, Liz, I'm here in a professional capacity. Is there somewhere we can go for a quick word?"

"How intriguing! I've got half an hour before my next tour – a group from Texas, can you believe it! Why don't we find a quiet place in the cloisters?"

She led him out via the transept door.

As it was warm for early September, it was still pleasant to sit out there, protected from any wind by the cloister roof.

Once they had found an unoccupied bench, Tedesco came swiftly to the point.

"Liz, do you know Oliver Canford, the Bishop's lay assistant?"

"Of course! Everyone knows Ollie! I shouldn't say this, but he's such a terrible flirt. I wasn't at all sure about him at first, but he has grown on me."

Tedesco took careful note – this tended to corroborate Bishop Bob's comment about Canford's pin-up status with the Ladies of the Close.

He moved things on. "Does he spend much time here in the Cathedral?"

"He certainly does. He's a regular at Evensong, and he has been known to help us out when we get overrun with visitors. Did you know that he is fluent in several European languages?"

Choosing to ignore this, Tedesco ploughed on.

"When did you last see him, Liz?"

"It would have been at Evensong, a week ago. As guides, we all cover one day a week, so it would have been last Friday. He should be here again tonight."

Tedesco paused then reached into his inside pocket for his silver initialled business card holder, a qualification present from his late uncle.

He flipped it open, produced a card and gave it to her.

"Could you call me when you see Oliver again?"

She looked puzzled.

"Let me explain. He hasn't been seen for a day or two, so I am asking around for His Grace the Bishop. Just *sotto voce*, you understand…"

Liz frowned. "You don't think anything has happened, do you?"

"I doubt it very much. I gather that he goes to London quite a bit, so he may have just stayed up there and not thought to let anyone know how long he was going to be away."

As they rose to leave, another guide suddenly appeared, as if he had been teleported.

Tedesco didn't recognise him so assumed he must be a new recruit, although he was hardly memorable – rather cold expression, though, he noted.

Liz made the introductions. "Richard Swain – John Tedesco. Richard joined us a year ago, and John here works for the Bishop."

She barely paused for breath before speaking to Swain.

"You took early retirement just so you could move down here and join our super special team, didn't you, Richard?"

Swain barely acknowledged Tedesco, seemingly anxious to move Liz away from him as quickly as he could.

Once Liz and her anonymous-looking sidekick had returned to their guide duties, Tedesco decided to lurk around the cloisters for a while, taking in the tourists with their selfie sticks, vainly hoping that they were appreciating something of the beauty of this 900-year-old building, rather than ticking it off on some 'Been There Done That' bucket list.

Noticing that Liz and Swain were now huddled in conversation by the Treasury door, he took care to avoid them and ambled off in the general direction of the vestry.

Blatantly ignoring the *No Visitors Beyond This Point* sign – having spent years upholding the law, he rather enjoyed ignoring signs – he strode into the vestry with an air of insouciance.

He wanted to see if the Head Verger was around.

Roy Baird occupied a candlelit cubby hole to the

left of the vestry itself, a spot that suited his hobbit-like appearance.

Tedesco had known Roy's father, Jack: Jack Baird had been an old-fashioned legal clerk at the court office when the young John Tedesco had first pitched up in Rhyminster as an idealistic, wet-behind-the-ears, freshly minted lawyer.

He had learned a lot from Baird Senior, not least how to be patient with younger members of the profession. Jack was a thoroughly good man.

His son, Roy, rose from his leather club chair and ushered Tedesco into his little cave, indicating the only other seat.

"Mr Registrar," he said.

He always addressed Tedesco thus, and probably always would.

"What a pleasure. How are you and Lynne finding the private eye game? I don't expect you miss the law."

"You're not wrong, Roy. I can pick and choose what I do and when, no more Law Society breathing down my neck, no more fee targets.

"Roy," he added, "bit of a strange one. I expect you know the Bishop's lay assistant?"

"Indeed, I do. Never understood why His Grace hasn't got a proper chaplain. This fellow isn't a patch on Sarah Dillon."

Tedesco laughed. "Not many of us are, Roy. Anyway, what do you make of him? This won't go any further."

It was Baird's chance to laugh.

"Chatham House rules, eh? Okay. Here's what I think. He's a smooth bugger, spends far too much time here when he should be out and about in the Diocese. Between you and me, there are some in this place who think Canford is being used by the Bishop to keep an eye on us."

"I very much doubt that, Roy," responded Tedesco, brushing the comment aside.

"No one at North Canonry has seen him for a couple of days, and he isn't picking up. Liz Gerrey has just told me that he is a regular at Evensong."

Baird sighed. "If young Ollie isn't driving His Grace around the country lanes of Merrie England, you'll find him up in the Quire, regular as clockwork at 5.15, then he hangs around afterwards, chatting up the great and good, flirting with the choir mums."

"When did you last see him, Roy?"

The Senior Verger stroked his magnificent beard.

"Wednesday it would have been. Two nights ago.

"I remember it well – he was taking an age to leave, and I had to let him out via the Dean's Door."

The Dean's Door was a discreet, largely unknown entrance to the Cathedral, originally designed for the personal use of the office holder.

Clearly enjoying himself, Baird carried on: "He was having a proper heart-to-heart with poor little Ginny Tantum, looked like he was a shoulder for her to cry on."

"Interesting," said Tedesco. "Listen, Roy, I'm running late, but let me know if you see Canford, would you, or if anything comes to mind about him.

"By the way, we haven't met up for a pint for ages – how about the Rhyminster Arms after Evensong one night?"

"Not 'arf, as Alan Freeman would have said. Do you think Canford's done a runner?" asked Baird.

"Too early to say, Roy. I'm just having a quiet look for him before we think of involving Bloomfield."

DCI Jimmy Bloomfield of the Devon and Cornwall

constabulary. Former colleague of Lynne Davey. He and Tedesco had graduated from a brief period of wary suspicion to a solid state of mutual respect.

"Anyway, Roy," added Tedesco as he got up to leave, "you be careful about mentioning Alan Freeman. It's what my nephew calls a Boomer reference – makes us sound past it!"

"We are past it, Mr Registrar."

"Yeah, but we had the best music... I will be in touch about that pint."

Tedesco hotfooted it from the vestry to the Cathedral Refectory – Lynne Davey wasn't someone to be kept waiting.

Five minutes late, he found his business partner tucked away in their usual alcove, checking her messages; he saw that she'd already ordered them a pot of 'Minster Blend' tea.

"Sorry, Lynne. I've just been having a chin wag with Roy Baird. Could be useful."

Lynne Davey was a good decade younger than Tedesco. She had the brisk efficiency and athletic build of the ex-CID operative, but this was softened by her hazel eyes, stylish black bob and her Dutch doll complexion.

He had always vehemently denied his sister's insistence that he fancied his colleague – although he did once let slip, after a surfeit of Christmas claret, that Lynne was 'hardly unattractive, to put it mildly'.

Nicola Tedesco had taken this as the nearest she would get to an admission from her dyed-in-the-wool lawyer brother.

Having asked Lynne about the Friday – afternoon traffic, and having received an update on her investigation in Somerset, Tedesco outlined the delicacy of their latest mission from the Bishop.

Lynne, intrigued, agreed to ask around at Park Run the following morning.

"The après-run coffee at Starbucks is always a good source of local gossip. Why don't I ask around at 'Rhyme in Rhythm' as well?" she added.

"Good idea," he responded.

Lynne was a mainstay of the local choir with the ridiculously impossible name.

It was conducted by Charles Tantum, the Master of Musick at the Cathedral.

"How on earth do you put up with the maestro? An evening with Charlie Tantum doesn't sound like my idea of a relaxing night out."

Lynne gave an involuntary giggle.

"Okay, so he's an awful human being, but as he's such a brilliant musician, we have all learned to put up with his outbursts. We're used to them."

'Tantum's tantrums' were the stuff of local legend.

"Any road up," Lynne continued, "Ollie Canford came to one of our rehearsals shortly after he deigned to land among us, and he and Tantum almost came to blows. Canford considers himself something of an authority on the English choral tradition, and was questioning Tantum's baton technique or something."

Tedesco agreed that it would be worth Lynne keeping an eye on her choir, and he made a mental note to add a summary of Roy Baird's description of the scene between Canford and Tantum's wife to his casebook.

FIVE

4A Minster Precincts was locked by the time Tedesco and Davey got back from the Refectory.

Sally was about to hop on her bicycle, but she held back in order to reassure Tedesco that Barker had been duly walked.

The detectives let themselves back into their modest premises, and Tedesco was soon busy filleting his inbox – but within half an hour, he had left Lynne typing up her notes on *The Case of the Amorous Lawyer*, telling her not to stay too long.

"Home time, Barker!"

The terrier and his master meandered back through the Close, exiting via the South Gate, which led directly into St Budeaux Place, a small row of cottages situated just outside the Close but within its ancient 'Liberty'.

The properties remained in the freehold ownership of the Dean and Chapter of the Cathedral, and that august body had generously granted Tedesco a medium-term, non-assignable lease of number 17.

His brother-in-law thought him mad to live in a rented house with no prospect of making a killing on a resale, but Tedesco couldn't have cared less, as he loved his bijou bolthole, which reflected how he saw his life – involved in the life of the Cathedral and the Close, but standing slightly apart from it.

After a quick bath, watching through the skylight as the sun began to sink down behind the Cathedral tower, he changed out of his work clothes, bundled Barker into the back of the Lancia and drove out to Woolford.

Good, Friday evening at last, he thought to himself, *time for some Nick Drake, or Françoise Hardy perhaps.*

On balance, he decided that Drake was more in tune with the perceptible early-evening feel of September melancholy in the air, so he gently slid his prized copy of *Five Leaves Left* into the CD player.

The Cathedral would sink into its foundations before he streamed his music – where were the liner notes on a download?

The village of Woolford is about a fifteen-minute drive from the Close, but a world apart from the comparative bustle of Rhyminster.

It is really two villages, the first a long main road of Victorian cottages, then, once over the bridge, the other side of the river reveals a run of twee chocolate box thatched dwellings interspersed with the usual mid-eighties barn conversions.

Nicky lived in one of these, Crane House.

The five-barred gate was wide open so Tedesco drove through, his wheels scrunching on the gravel just as Nick Drake began to sing *Day Is Done*.

It will be lovely to start with that on the drive home, he thought to himself.

Tedesco released Barker, who, right on cue, started to wag his tail, throwing in a couple of trademark barks for good measure, which immediately attracted Nicky's children, Jack and Ella, who came rushing out to greet the dog like a couple of selfie-seeking groupies.

Jack, fourteen, was a pupil at Rhyminster's ancient grammar school, Bishop Lunt's, and ten-year-old Ella was still at the Cathedral School.

"Come on, Barker. We're playing cricket," shouted Jack.

It would soon be dark, but there was just enough daylight left for a few overs; Barker had gained an excellent reputation for fielding in the deep, and was pretty nifty in the covers.

Tedesco joined them, bowling a couple of full tosses for Jack to thwack – which sent Barker trotting off into the undergrowth in eager pursuit of the tennis ball – before he handed bowling duties back to Ella.

Nicky was the tactile sibling, and so she greeted her brother with outstretched arms, before enveloping him in a lingering hug.

"Hello, old man, what can I do you for?" she said as she led him into the huge, tech-stuffed kitchen.

Tedesco declined alcohol, as he was driving, and settled down at one of the islands, sipping a fizzy elderflower something or other.

Nicky worked as a reporter on Searchlight, *the flagship evening magazine programme for the Plymouth-based outpost of the BBC, which covered a vast chunk of the south-west.*

She had worked her patch for over twenty years, having joined the Beeb from the Plymouth Herald, *where she had started straight after her A-levels, selling advertising space, before gradually moving into reporting.*

It was during her spell on the Herald *that she had met her future husband, Jeremy 'Chag' Wills. He was from Chagford, hence the nickname.*

Wills was just setting out in business, seeking to grow his empire of upmarket used car outlets – in those pre-digital days, a full-page spread in the Friday edition of the Herald *was a must for the budding West Country entrepreneur.*

While Tedesco still had to watch his weight, Nicky's husband remained annoyingly thin, as wiry as a whippet – he still looked like a marathon runner or a naval PTI, despite half a lifetime spent successfully draining the contents of several local breweries.

These days, Tedesco's visits to Crane House were carefully choreographed to avoid 'the Chagster', a task which had become progressively easier over time: Wills would invariably be absent at a sales conference, wining and dining his VIP customers, or out on the lash with his equally voluble mates, the local branch of the red trouser brigade.

He returned to his sister's opening gambit by explaining about the missing Oliver Canford.

"Why on earth are you asking me?" she said.

He reminded her that Bishop Robert had been a not infrequent interviewee on *Searchlight* and that, as press liaison was within the remit of the Bishop's lay assistant, maybe she had had dealings with him.

Nicky hadn't come across Canford herself but suggested a call to Victoria Thomas.

Vicki Thomas had been the studio-based anchor on Searchlight *for as long as Tedesco could remember.*

He knew that Vicki had a long-standing gig acting as MC for the annual Radio Devon and Cornwall Carol Service at the Cathedral, and that she had interviewed Bishop Bob several times, once in his back garden.

Canford must have had to arrange at least one of these slots. And he had arrived in post before the latest carol service.

"I'll try her now," Nicky said. "She finishes at the studio at seven-ish, and so she should be back home in Fowey by now, enjoying a glass of wine with her view of the river.

"Vicki! Hi! Sorry to disturb your Friday wind-down. Good programme tonight – isn't that new MP for Falmouth a prize tosser? Yeah, maintaining BBC impartiality is never easy. Look, I need to pick your brains about the Bishop of Rhyminster."

"Ah," said Victoria Thomas, "the lovely Bishop Bob, about the only cleric I have time for. Pick away."

"Well," Nicky replied, "when we deal with the Bishop, is Oliver Canford our contact point?"

"Yeah, that's right, the Bishop's assistant."

Tedesco sipped his elderflower and fiddled with his glasses, trying to tune into what seemed to him to have developed into a girly chat.

When the call finally ended, his sister told him that Victoria Thomas most certainly knew Canford.

The Bishop's assistant had quite shamelessly chatted her up after the Cathedral Carol Concert, even suggesting that they swap numbers.

Brave man, thought Tedesco.

Nicky added that the local TV legend had firmly informed Canford that he was punching way above his weight, that toy boys weren't really her thing, and – in best pronunciation unit diction – she told him to go and do one, just as the Bishop's wife was heading over for a chat...

There had been other rumours circulating in the studio about Canford, from getting overfamiliar with a female camera person to the now – familiar stuff about his fan club in the Close.

Nicky wondered aloud whether Canford was holed up with one of his admirers.

"I don't think so," her brother responded.

"While he is relatively young and single, he isn't completely free. He may not be ordained, but he occupies a quasi-clerical role, and he wouldn't risk anything that might cast doubt on his continued suitability for the role – he loves his job by all accounts."

"Only because it gives him carte blanche to ponce around the Close," Nicky retorted.

"Look, John, I'm going to dish up now. It's your favourite old – school lasagne, so could you round up the kids and see if Barker needs a drink?"

Tedesco appreciated any chance to spend time with Jack and Ella. Straining to avoid any more 'Boomer' references, he spent a pleasant evening discussing favourite episodes of *Family Guy* with Jack, and the Cathedral School with Ella. She told him how much she liked one of her new teachers – Mrs Tantum.

He was somewhat less pleased to see that Nicky was making short work of the bottle of red – he worried about his sister.

Having already decided to be gone by 10.15pm – partly to avoid Chag and partly to get back for *Newsnight* – he made his excuses.

Barker, by contrast, seemed more than happy to stay and bask in the love.

"Sorry, Barker, time to go, I'm afraid."

"Woof," replied the border terrier, a touch grumpily.

As his precious Lancia crossed the river, Tedesco caught up with Nick Drake, while Barker fell fast asleep.

SIX

Lynne Davey was up early the following morning.

Her Saturday routine involved a brisk walk from her little terrace in Water Lane to Smithers, the newsagents where she picked up the *Guardian,* then, after a quick skim of the weekend section over an espresso, she took an idyllic cycle ride through the water meadows to King George Field, home of the weekly Park Run.

Sally, inevitably, was one of the team of marshals. Dressed today in an ill-fitting tiger onesie, she was selling pink ribbons in support of Breast Cancer Awareness.

Lynne felt a twinge of guilt as she successfully managed to swerve her.

People like her can be a pain, but society depends on the likes of Sally Munks, she reflected to herself as she fell in with a group of familiar faces, joining in with their pre-run discussions about the conditions, personal bests and the coolest water bottles.

But however much she enjoyed meeting people, for Lynne the run was very much the thing.

She appreciated the way that the 5km circuit had been designed to offer the best views of the Cathedral and the small city surrounding it, and she loved the sheer buzz she got from fitness.

After clocking an above-average time, she remembered that she was on a mission, and sought out a suitable companion to go with her to Starbucks – as she had finished just behind the Dean's wife, it seemed only natural to approach her and suggest a brief detour for coffee.

It wasn't easy to miss Jo Luxmoore, with her garish green running gear, and her 'Crystal Tipps' frizzy hair.

She and her husband, Dean Dan, had found making the transition from a trendy parish in Clifton to the rarefied air of a cathedral environment somewhat challenging.

Jo was a yoga teacher, with a sideline in mindfulness – not quite what the guides and the sidesmen had in mind when they thought of a typical dean's wife.

Jo accepted Lynne's offer of coffee with alacrity – it seemed that she was in urgent need of soulmates.

They quickly bonded over their post-run lattes, Lynne agreeing to join Jo's yoga group which met at the Deanery on Wednesday evenings.

Lynne asked her if anyone else from the Cathedral came to Park Run.

"I think I saw that young chaplain the other week," she prompted.

"Oh, you mean the lay assistant, Oliver," Jo replied.

"He's one of our regulars, but I didn't see him today, or his normal running buddy Ginny Tantum. She must be an ANGEL for putting up with Charles."

Lynne let slip that she was a member of Tantum's choir, and when she referenced Tantum's tantrums, this set Jo off on one.

The Dean's wife explained that as the Deanery was next to The Pelistry, the residence of the Master of Musick, she had to suffer Tantum practising his scales at full volume, his shouting at Ginny, and yelling at his children.

The Tantums had two boys, Aldhelm and Osmund, "named after two Wessex saints, poor things – Aldo and Ozzie they call them."

As Jo had to excuse herself – she had pre-arranged to meet Dean Dan at Waitrose after coffee – Lynne decided to make a house call on Tedesco and Barker. As St Budeaux Place was on her route home, she cycled over and banged on the iron door knocker.

This immediately summoned Barker, closely followed by his master, pint-sized mug of tea in hand that bore the slogan *Plymouth Argyle – the Mighty Pilgrims*.

Tedesco looked surprised to see her – but not unpleasantly so – and led the way into the tiny kitchen.

Lynne declined further refreshment, giving Barker a gentle stroke while Tedesco asked her how the run went and if she had picked up anything of interest.

"I've got a new bezzie friend," said Lynne. "Jo Luxmoore, the Dean's wife."

"And how is Crystal Tipps?" asked Tedesco, provoking first a grimace, then a pointed riposte.

"I can only just about remember Crystal Tipps and Alistair. I expect that you were already qualified when it finished."

"Fair point, Lynne, if a little cutting. Another middle-aged reference, I suppose. Anyway, isn't she a bit ditsy? Barker thinks she is."

"Very funny. Look, I found her really friendly, open and

going to join her yoga group – and she gave

– guess who Canford runs with?"

One of the glamorous Ladies of the Close?"

d for the big reveal.

inny Tantum."

a while to take this in. He couldn't imagine

Ginny on a 1k walk, let alone a 5k run.

kr vs how she puts up with Charles, as

Tantums to one side for a second, I

ith Roy Baird yesterday."

r whatever, looks like Bilbo

e that Canford spends most

of h. nd seems to have centred

his socia.

"So?" said L, nint of insolence.

"Okay – boring church stuff alert – although the Cathedral is the seat of the Bishop, his responsibility is to the hundreds of parishes in the Diocese. Dean Dan looks after the Cathedral.

"So, by rights, a Bishop's assistant should be devoted to assisting His Grace in his diocesan role, and shouldn't have spare time to spend hovering around in the Cathedral and the Close."

He removed his glasses, put them on again, then continued.

"Anyway, it gets better. Canford normally likes to hang back after the evening service, making a beeline for the chorister mums. However, after Wednesday's service, he was having a long heart-to-heart with none other than Mrs Tantum – to the extent that Roy had to ask them if they had homes to go to. That was the last known sighting of young Ollie."

"Perhaps I could do with that cup of tea after all," said Lynne.

Tedesco popped two bags of Dorset Tea into his ancient teapot, reboiled the kettle and gave Lynne a mug bearing the inscription, *Let's kill all the lawyers.*

He opened his case book, freshly updated in his immaculate handwriting, and started to read out the latest updates.

Lynne butted in when he referred to his visit to Nicky.

"Hang on. Did you just say that Canford tried it on with Victoria Thomas? *Searchlight* Victoria Thomas? He's got more balls than I'd have given him credit for!"

"I agree, I think," Tedesco replied, a bit sheepishly.

"Tell me, Lynne, what do you make of Canford? From a female perspective. Why do the dowagers of Rhyminster fling themselves at his feet, or come down with an attack of the vapours?"

Lynne took a sip of her tea – could have done with a tad more milk.

"From what I've seen of him, he certainly isn't my type.

"He is quite good-looking, but in a blond, 'Tomorrow Belongs to Me' sort of way – which doesn't work for me on any level – and he has a weak chin.

"What he does have is supreme confidence mixed with an oily charm, which is probably catnip for a neglected wife like Ginny Tantum."

"Or an attractive widow like Liz Gerrey," Tedesco added.

"So what do we know about his background?" she asked.

Tedesco went back over his notes, summarising his conversation with Bishop Bob.

"Not that much to go on, is there?" was Lynne's instant opinion.

She said that she would cycle back to Water Lane, have a quick lunch, chill out with the *Guardian* then get down to work on Canford's digital footprint.

"He must be on Facebook, at least."

"Or Minstergram?" said Tedesco.

Lynne groaned, cuddled Barker under the chin and then cycled home through the Close.

SEVEN

Tedesco's Saturday routine habitually involved a Jenks pasty for lunch, gobbled down while watching *Football Focus*, then a long woof with Barker, followed by an anxious wait for Argyle's result.

Once *Football Focus* was over – *should be called Premier League Focus the way it ignores teams like mine*, thought the detective – he texted Bishop Bob to see if he might be free that evening.

Within a couple of minutes, the familiar sound of John Sousa's *Semper Fidelis* march rang out from his phone.

This was Plymouth Argyle's theme tune and they had run out to it since before he was born.

Barker hated his master's ringtone, and scurried off. It was even worse than the sound of the hoover.

"John? It's Bob. I'm barely enduring a meeting of the south-west bishops up in Weymouth. Got to go back inside soon for a workshop on 'enabling rural ministry.'"

"I know how much you love workshops, Your Grace. Anyway, still no sighting of Ollie but I may have an idea or two."

The Bishop allowed himself a subversive smile.

"I should be back in Rhyme by about six. Fancy popping

over for a pre-supper drink? I could do with one after all this. About 6.30? Barker is equally welcome, of course."

"We will see you then. I think I might put in an appearance at Evensong on the way over."

"Come on, Barker," said Tedesco. "Time for our weekly workout."

Tedesco really looked forward to his Saturday afternoons with his best mate.

While he loved his life in this beautiful little place, it did sometimes feel as if he were living within the pages of Anthony Trollope – or put another way, life within the Liberty of the Close could be bloody claustrophobic.

A hazy sun greeted him as he let Barker into the Lancia. He drove over the cobbles until he was safely outside the Liberty, and then he joined the ring road.

As per usual, most of the traffic was heading in the opposite direction, towards the Trago Mills Retail Park, and Tedesco felt a familiar sense of smugness as he followed signs for the moors, alternating his in-car entertainment between the Radio Devon and Cornwall football preview and Carole King – *Rhymes & Reasons* – from his CD collection. He loved his singer songwriters.

"Over the grids now, Barker!" he exclaimed as they entered the national park.

He had never lost that feeling of entering a forgotten world – his love of Dartmoor was one of the few things he had inherited from his dad.

After a couple of miles, and with a somewhat uncharacteristic flamboyance, Tedesco brought the car to a screeching halt, just managing to avoid overshooting the little gravel car park.

"Not many up here today, so more space for us, old friend," he said as he attached the terrier to his lead.

The pair of them headed out across the moor in companionable silence, their usual plan being to walk up to one of the smaller of the granite tors, then back via a circular route which allowed Barker some time to extend his workout off the lead, and the opportunity for an ice-cold dip in one of the streams or ponds that prevailed in this area of the moor.

Once they had found an appropriate spot, Tedesco double-checked to make sure there were no animals in the vicinity, and then he let Barker loose while he had a think about Canford – his appointment had been most unBoblike.

Sarah Dillon had been exceptional – a serious academic who retained a reassuring humanity – but Bob must surely have hoped for a more suitable replacement than the Adonis of the Close.

He recalled an earlier conversation with His Grace – before his fateful encounter in Venice – when Bob had admitted that the conventional applicants for Sarah's role had been hopeless.

"The spirit of the late Derek Nimmo is still alive and kicking in what remains of our theological colleges," he had said, with a note of palpable sadness.

Canford must have employed his seductive magic – although clearly not on Hilary. A deadly combination of the urgency of the situation and the Bishop being caught off guard amidst the splendour of La Serenissima had somehow worked in the young man's favour.

Despite this, Bob must have done some research on Canford when he got back from Italy – or at least asked for a CV and references. These were questions for this evening.

Back in the natural world, Barker, fresh from his swim, was shaking himself dry.

If I'd wanted to jump into a mass of ice-cold water on the moor, I'd have joined the terrier equivalent of the SAS, he seemed to be thinking.

The crystalline silence was broken by a beep from Tedesco's mobile phone.

He frowned. Should have switched the bloody thing off. It was a long message from his sister.

Hi, Bro! Sorry to interrupt your bonding session with Barker.

I think you should know that when my lovely husband staggered in at silly past midnight last night he asked me about our evening.

I mentioned Ollie – not that he was missing, mind, and incredibly – wait for this – Chag knows him!

He found – or 'sourced' – that red sports car he goes around in, and here's the thing – Ollie told him that 'The Merry Widow' couldn't wait to go for a spin in it. What do you reckon?

Anyway, love to Barker, and hope Argyle win!

Tedesco pulled a face – he'd check the half-time score when they got back to the car, but he didn't have a good feeling about it.

'The Merry Widow' – could be Liz – but there were several candidates for that description in or around the Close. He'd ask Lynne what she thought.

A dried-off Barker hopped into the back of the Lancia just as Tedesco checked in with Radio D and C.

One-nil down at half time. Away to Oldham Athletic, bloody northerners!

41

"Oh well, at least there's the second half," he muttered to himself.

Heard that one before, thought Barker.

*

There is a one-way system in force for the Cathedral Close.

This meant that in order to return to St Budeaux Place, Tedesco was forced to drive right around it, taking care to avoid the loafing tourists who seemed incapable of grasping that the Close was an actual road rather than a designated area for dripping around while taking selfies or munching burgers.

Berating himself for becoming a miserable old git – "I'll be applying to join the guides or the sidesmen next" – he hoped that at least some of the road blockers might be tempted into the Cathedral for Choral Evensong.

The marketing people had branded it as 'the Best Free Concert in the South-West', and just this once they were on the money.

Safely back in the den at St Budeaux Place, Tedesco reached for the remote, the screen appearing just as Mike West announced: *Oldham Athletic, One* – pregnant pause – *Plymouth Argyle, Two.*

Tedesco punched the air. "Res-ult! That will send us shooting up the table, Barker!"

His canine companion lay at his feet fast asleep.

EIGHT

Tedesco, buoyed up by Argyle's win, was floating on air as he walked through the South Gate on his way to Evensong.

Argyle's recent away form had been lavatorial, but perhaps a corner had been turned, and his lifelong dream of seeing the Pilgrims in the Premier League would come true.

Reaching the South Porch, he noted that there were three sidesmen on duty.

Must be expecting a big gate, maybe some away fans, he thought, his mind still on the football.

The sidesmen wore yellow sashes, to distinguish them from the crimson ones worn by the guides, and they tended to view their rival group of elderly volunteers in the same way that the Home Guard viewed the ARP wardens in Dad's Army.

As the Quire was rapidly filling up, Tedesco practically ran through the centre aisle, squeezing into one of the last vacant stalls.

In football terms, Tedesco was a creature of the Stand, rather than the Terrace – in cathedral terms, this manifested itself in his preference for the Quire over the Nave.

The regular Evensong crowd had already drifted in – shades of Billy Joel's *Piano Man*, he mused – and he was pleased to see that they had been joined by an encouraging contingent of visitors, as well as some random locals on their way back from the shops.

The chorister mums were out in force, upsetting the tutting regulars by sitting in 'their' seats, and by greeting each other loudly, as if they were bumping into friends at Glyndebourne.

Tedesco saw them as the Millwall supporters of the Cathedral community – "No one likes us, we don't care."

Dean Dan interrupted these ironic musings by suddenly appearing at a microphone stand at the Tower Crossing.

After announcing that the service would begin in a few minutes, he offered special greetings to 'any of you guys' who were first-time worshippers at the Cathedral, before inviting the congregation to 'just take a moment' before the first hymn.

The ghosts of canons, deans and bishops past joined together across the centuries in a collective cringe...

Tedesco rather liked Dean Dan. It couldn't be easy for him, being so much younger than those he managed, and being of an entirely different generation from most of the congregation and volunteers.

Dan was a keen advocate of 'fresh expressions' of ministry, but was up against a mentality that visibly hated such 'new-fangled, woke' ideas as the handshake of peace, which had featured in communion services since the 1970s.

The Church wouldn't survive without new blood, and although Tedesco wasn't exactly a fan of modern worship, he accepted that it wasn't aimed at him.

And Dan, for all his earnest evangelising, did at least have a sense of humour.

As the procession moved at its usual funereal speed from the vestry towards the Quire, John Tedesco was pleased to see that the girls' choir was singing tonight.

Rhyminster had been one of the last of the ancient cathedrals to introduce female choristers.

Salisbury had formed the first girls' choir back in 1991, and Rhyminster eventually decided that the game was up in 2016, despite entirely predictable opposition from the Master of Musick.

"What am I going to do with a load of dopey girls!" he had thundered.

"They'll sound like a bloody HEN PARTY!"

Dean Dan's predecessor had been sorely tempted by Tantum's repeated resignation threats, but a good old Anglican compromise had been reached whereby Tantum would concentrate on the boys' section and the Precentor, the saintly Wilfred Drake, would direct the girls.

The angelic voices of the girls added to Tedesco's joyful mood. Seeing Lynne at home, a great walk with Barker, Argyle winning…

His reverie was interrupted by the announcement of the first lesson.

Liz Gerrey, elegant as ever in a dark red trouser suit, commenced the reading, her modulated Morningside vowels ringing off the ancient carved stalls.

Tedesco, to his shame, failed to concentrate on the verses from Job as he noticed, not for the first time, just how strikingly attractive the reader was, and he could only imagine what an appealing prospect she would be for an ambitious lay assistant.

Once Liz had concluded her reading, he spent the rest of

the service in something of a trance, coming to just in time for the final hymn.

As he scanned the departing congregation for familiar faces, he spotted Ginny Tantum clustered with a group of chorister parents, who were waiting impatiently to be reunited with their offspring.

Charles, of course, boycotted any service involving the 'shrieking harpies' – the man really was a prize berk – but Ginny's role at the Cathedral School ensured her regular attendance.

He established fleeting eye contact with Liz and waved in recognition, shyly deciding to leave her for another day, and once he'd been through the ritual 'vicars' double handshake' and small talk with the Dean and the Precentor, he headed towards the vestry, hoping to catch a word with Ginny.

Finding her busy forming her charges into a crocodile in readiness for their short walk back to the boarding house, he took the opportunity to pop his head around the vestry door.

Roy Baird was open to visitors in his candlelit lair, and he quickly confirmed that there had been no further word of Canford.

Having explained to the Head Verger that he was hoping to see Ginny, Baird sent out his deputy, Colin Scopes, to supervise the crocodile in her stead.

Scopes had worked at the Cathedral forever, or so it seemed. Tedesco thought of him as Rhyminster's version of Quasimodo but without the physical disfigurement. Scopes was always polite but seemed terrified of anyone in authority.

While Tedesco was left to twiddle his thumbs, Baird went in search of Mrs Tantum.

Once Roy had found her, Tedesco joined them in the main room of the vestry, where they arranged themselves around the large circular table.

Ginny, visibly shaking, said that she had wanted to see Tedesco herself, as she was extremely worried about Canford.

"Charles thinks I'm neurotic, but Oliver has disappeared, and no one seems to care or be in the least bit bothered about him.

"I know that you look into disappeared people, Mr Tedesco, so I was hoping you might be able to help. No one else is doing anything!"

Tedesco considered the woman before him, in many ways the opposite of Liz Gerrey. She seemed to have no confidence at all and was clearly exhausted; far too exhausted to be overly concerned about her appearance.

She was small rather than tiny, and her expression had become progressively pinched. *This is what being married to a pig like Tantum does*, he thought, remembering the young, vibrant, pretty Ginny who had moved down to Rhyme all those years ago with her husband.

Ginny was wearing a shapeless hessian-type coat, and her greying hair could do with a wash, he thought, with an atypical lack of gallantry.

His heart went out to her.

"Ginny – please don't worry. I do undertake some delicate investigations for the Bishop, and I can fully assure you that he is worried about Oliver.

"In fact, I have been looking into his disappearance since yesterday and that's why I wanted a quiet word with you. Please can you promise not to discuss this with anyone else for now?"

Yeah, like your husband, for example, Roy Baird thought to himself.

Ginny, gradually soothed by Tedesco's well-honed bedside manner, began to open up about her nascent friendship with Canford.

"I saw him last Wednesday, after Evensong.

"It had been an awful week. Charles returned from his choir practice foaming at the mouth, taking it out on Ozzie and Aldo. The Cathedral School OFSTED inspection was still stressing us all out, and so poor, dear Ollie was right in the firing line when I needed to offload on someone.

"Roy – you remember – we were keeping you from your supper."

Baird nodded, and Ginny continued.

"Oliver is so kind to us all, and several of us are encouraging him to pursue his vocation. He would be a wonderful priest – if only the Bishop agreed!"

Tedesco mentally filed that comment away, ready to be inscribed in his counsel's notebook.

"Ginny," he asked, "could you tell me what happened after you both left via the Dean's door?"

"Oh, I would have taken my usual shortcut home over the Green – you can ignore the *Keep Off the Grass* signs by then. We live at The Pelistry."

"Yes, I know," Tedesco replied, "next to the Deanery."

"I needed to get cracking with cooking supper for Charles and the boys."

"I assume he wasn't singing at Evensong that night?"

"No," replied Ginny, gaining confidence, "he's still maintaining his idiotic boycott of the girls' choir.

"Anyway," she continued, "Oliver gave me a lovely hug,

48

and then he walked away in the opposite direction, towards his flat in the Bishop's Palace."

"Ginny, have you tried to contact Oliver since then?"

She blushed a little, and then responded with previously unseen venom.

"No, I haven't. He offered me his contact details, but my husband doesn't like me calling people without his permission – his 'express consent', he calls it. Charles only lets me have my own phone on condition that I use it for emergencies, and he knows the password."

She looked down at the floor.

"Mr Tedesco – how long will you wait before the police are involved?"

"Well," he replied, "if you think about it, Oliver has only been missing for a matter of a day or two. He could turn up at any minute. I half expected to see him at the service this evening.

"My business partner, Lynne, used to work for the police, and she will liaise with her contact there once this needs to be made official, but for the moment we don't want to waste their valuable time. I will let you know if the situation changes. Until then, I suggest we all stay calm."

Ginny nodded, seemingly close to tears.

Having wished her a good evening – unlikely to be a quiet night in with Tantum on the premises – Tedesco retraced Canford's footsteps from Wednesday.

As he was leaving the Cathedral around the same time as Canford had, he would get a good idea as to whether many people were out in the Close at that hour – if tonight was a guide, then the place would have been deserted.

The Bishop's Palace, the North Canonry, was situated to the left of a bend in the main Close road.

If you didn't turn off for the Palace, you exited via Broad Street Gate into the pedestrianised shopping zone. If you carried on further, you reached the railway station.

Could Ginny have been wrong in her assumption that Canford was going home on Wednesday evening?

Bishop Bob, Jo Luxmoore and others had referred to his frequent visits up to town and to his refined choir, the Tuneful Company of Minstrels, so could he have been on his way to Rhyminster Station that night?

NINE

As he approached the Bishop's Palace, he noticed a welcoming light going on in the porch, where he was greeted by Hilary.

"No Barker tonight?" she said, clearly disappointed.

"He sends his apologies. He rather overdid the exercise today, so I've left him at home to chill."

"I blame you for that, John. Make sure you bring him soon."

She led him into the private quarters, a modest first-floor apartment, where he found His Grace the Bishop with his feet up watching *Pointless Celebrities*.

Tedesco gratefully accepted the offer of one of Hilary's legendary vodka martinis, while the Bishop pressed the pause button so he could catch up with Alexander and Richard and their whimsical banter later – then the three of them enjoyed a few minutes of social chat before Hilary left to prep supper.

"So, John, what have you got for me?" said Bob, back to business mode.

Tedesco cleared his throat. "We haven't found him, of course – but we have unearthed some interesting stuff."

"Do tell," replied the Bishop.

"Well, Bob, there may be an angle. To kick off, the last sighting of Canford, at least in Rhyminster, was after Evensong.

"He left the Cathedral with Ginny Tantum, who walked with him part of the way over the Green. She assumes that he headed back here."

"If he did, he was noticeably quiet about it. And he clearly didn't spend the night here."

"Anyway," Tedesco continued, "I went to Evensong on my way here tonight and managed to detain Ginny after the service.

"It turns out that she was waiting to ask me to look into the disappearance – don't worry, I've given her the client confidentiality spiel.

"Also, Lynne went to Park Run this morning, and chummed up with Jo Luxmoore, who provided the interesting news that Canford's regular running partner is none other than Mrs Tantum."

The Bishop rolled his eyes.

"Anyway, I spoke to my sister and she produced some titillating stuff about Oliver trying it on with her colleague Victoria Thomas after the local radio carol service."

"Bloody hell," spluttered Bob as Tedesco resumed.

"Nicky gave me another useful snippet – Canford bought his sports car from my brother-in-law. And he in turn remembers Oliver commenting that the 'Merry Widow' was looking forward to a spin in it.

"I was thinking – Liz Gerrey?"

The Bishop paused to consider what he had just heard.

"I find that hard to believe, frankly. Sounds like wishful thinking on Canford's side. You remember that Hilary worked with Roddy Gerrey on the cardiac unit?

"She and Liz became very close after he died. Our Mrs Gerrey strikes me as a woman of some quality and the last person to get involved with a young fool like Oliver.

"Anyway, it seems that when he's not comforting poor Mrs Tantum, he's showing off to the yummy mummies of the Cathedral School. I don't know where he finds the time or the energy for that, let alone chancing his arm with Liz."

Tedesco let this sink in then continued.

"Bob, could you fill in a few blanks for me? Remind me how you recruited him, what checks were made, background, CV, safeguarding, and so on?"

The Bishop patiently reprised how his anniversary trip to Venice had fallen during an especially tough period, reminding Tedesco how desperate he had been for someone to take over from Sarah Dillon, how the normal recruitment channels had produced a 'smorgasbord of wet idiots', and how he had experienced a eureka moment, which with hindsight looked more like a moment of madness, when he met Canford.

The young tour guide had contacted him soon after his return from the Veneto and an impromptu interview was set up, with Dean Dan and Amanda Leonard completing the panel.

Bob remembered that Dan had seemed enthusiastic but that Amanda, the hyper-efficient Diocesan Secretary, shared Hilary's concerns. Nevertheless, and after much prayerful consideration, the Bishop offered Canford the job as his lay assistant.

"Just what was it about him that convinced you, Bob? Was it just a case of first impressions, gut instinct?"

"Mainly, but not entirely."

"Canford's CV checked out. He read Theology at Cambridge, got a decent upper second, and I know one of his tutors, Gerald Freeborn, who gave him a generally good reference.

"Gerry confirmed that Canford had been serious about exploring a vocation but he let slip that he had a weakness for the social side of things.

"Oliver was a member of a notorious college club that was inspired by an Order of Carthusians who were famed for their love of wine, women and song."

"Sounds delightful, "said Tedesco, barely able to conceal a sneer.

"Gerry thought it was probably a passing phase – we were all young once. Anyway, I questioned Canford about it, and he said that the 'Merrie Monks of Mirth' was really a touring cricket club, with a strong social side to keep them busy in the winter."

Tedesco kept his chippy grammar – school thoughts to himself, as Bishop Bob went on to explain that Canford's line manager at Bel Paese had also been incredibly positive about him – he was a real star, apparently, and they would do all they could to keep him in the travel industry.

"Oliver's late father had been an archdeacon in Guildford, so he had the C of E in his DNA, which would save me a lot of training time explaining the difference between a diocesan secretary and the Chancellor of the Diocese, and so on."

The Bishop paused to sip his martini.

"It may seem crazy now, John, but Oliver came over as bright, intellectually stimulating and engaging. I was really excited by his appointment. As Hilary put it, I had a shiny young brain to play with."

Bishop Robert Dwyer seemed to sink slowly into his sofa.

"What I got, in reality, was an opportunistic social climber. After all, what is the 'Tuneful Company of Minstrels' other than a grown-up version of the 'Merrie Monks', both presumably organisations with all the right connections?

"Canford would rather slink around the salons of the Close than visit parishes in the depths of Devon and Cornwall, let alone our deprived urban areas. And his total lack of organisational skills is piling more pressure on the sainted Barbara."

"Perhaps you should have promoted her to become your lay assistant," Tedesco cheekily suggested.

At this, the Bishop rose to his feet.

"I meant to ask you, John. How did Argyle get on...?"

Tedesco correctly took this as his cue to leave.

He wandered back to St Budeaux Place, stopping only to gaze back at the floodlit Cathedral tower before letting himself in.

Noting that Barker was still asleep, he opted to spend an hour updating his counsel's notebook before a suddenly wide-awake terrier came in search of supper.

Barker's hunger having been duly sated by a bowl of Essential Waitrose dog biscuits, Tedesco went to fix himself a plate of pasta with a stir-in carbonara sauce before settling down to *Match of the Day*.

He and his faithful friend both dozed off as soon as Alan Shearer started to analyse a goalless draw at West Brom.

TEN

Tedesco, finding himself awake pointlessly early for a Sunday, couldn't get back to sleep, so crept downstairs to avoid disturbing Barker.

He boiled a kettle, poured himself some tea in his jumbo-sized Plymouth Argyle mug and took it back to bed, rising again at seven.

"Come on, Barker, woof time!"

They turned right out of St Budeaux Place, away from the Close and over the pretty river bridge to the little general stores where Tedesco picked up the Sunday papers.

Once Barker had neatly performed his ablutions conveniently close to a dog poo bin, they headed home again; Sunday was the day for 'proper' coffee, and so Tedesco brewed himself a cafetière and made some toast and Marmite.

As it was warm enough to sit in his walled garden, he reviewed the Sunday papers outside while enjoying his breakfast with Barker sat at his feet, both of them happily soaking up the last rays of the Indian summer.

After a delightful hour or so, he had a brainwave – he could do with updating Lynne on progress before work tomorrow, and he fancied a trip out, so he called her on the off chance and, to his great surprise, found her at home.

"I thought you'd be training for a triathlon, or at least halfway through an assault course by now – anyway, as it's such a beautiful day, how do you fancy a trip out to the coast for lunch?"

"This is a first," she said.

"Do I need to tart myself up? I assume Barker will act as chaperone."

"I'll take that as a yes then – I'll swing by around eleven if that's okay – and don't worry, Barker will be there."

He managed to book the last table at a trendy beach café near Modbury, then he revealed his plan to Barker.

The border terrier seemed favourable to the suggestion, as long as his master remembered to pack his favourite yellow tennis ball and that he had checked that the restaurant welcomed dogs.

So, on the dot of eleven, Tedesco pulled up across the road from Water Lane; as the narrow, terraced houses fronted onto a small channel of the River Rhyme, there was no direct vehicular access.

Lynne dashed across the road and squeezed into the front passenger seat before turning round to greet Barker, who seemed perplexed.

I see this person during the working week, and now she's appeared twice this weekend. What's going on here? he seemed to be thinking.

Tedesco gave Lynne the good news – he'd secured a table at the Seafood Shack, but as it wasn't available till 1.30, they could enjoy a walk on the beach before lunch.

"Sounds like a plan to me – what do you think, Barker?"

*

On a good day, you could reach the South Hams coast in under twenty minutes. However, on a warm Sunday at the end of the season, with pelotons of Lycra-clad cyclists with anger management issues clogging the narrow roads, it would be more like an hour.

Once they reached the café, the trio found that the beach car park was already rammed, so Tedesco drove on to the modern vicarage where he had a standing invitation to park – one of the perks of his Registrar days.

The Team Rector, Paul Notte, would be hard at work commuting between his seven churches, so there was plenty of room on his drive for the Lancia.

Tedesco, Lynne and Barker strolled down the lane to the little beach. The tide was out and they were greeted by the familiar buzz of excited small children and barking dogs.

Barker was eager to join them, and so, lead removed, he charged into the sea, quickly exiting once he'd tested the temperature.

Tedesco and Lynne then took it in turns to throw the tennis ball for their furry colleague to chase and return while they enjoyed some stone skimming, Barker clearly less than impressed by their lack of prowess.

As their lunch reservation approached, Lynne dried off Barker with his special Argyle dog towel – which bore the slogan, *I'm a Midfield Terrier* – and then they all wandered across the road to the upmarket bistro.

Tedesco remembered the place from boyhood, when it had been a proper beach café, serving pasties on trays, dandelion and burdock-flavoured pop, and selling flags of the home nations to put on your sandcastle.

Now it had been extended and boasted a 'New England beach vibe', according to the website.

A wannabe surf dude with sun-bleached mullet-style hair guided them to their table, told them that he was called Jez, explained the menu and produced a branded dog bowl for Barker.

Tedesco and Lynne agreed to share a whole pan-fried sea bass, ordered two glasses of Muscadet de Sèvre et Maine Sur Lie for themselves and some water for Barker.

Just as Jez reappeared with some complimentary nibbles, Lynne, clearly distracted by something, gave Tedesco a playful shove.

An unlikely couple were leaving the café. It was the Merry Widow. And that rather peculiar Cathedral guide... Richard Swain.

Lynne was sure that Liz Gerrey had spotted them but Tedesco delayed any comment until they had driven off, Liz resplendent at the wheel of her Mercedes.

"Lynne," he half whispered, "I had suggested this place as I thought we would be far enough away from the Cathedral to allow us to discuss the case in peace. We'd better speak quietly in case the Society of Sidesmen turn up, or the provisional wing of the Mothers' Union."

He reminded his partner that he had seen Liz in animated conversation with the dull-looking guide on a previous occasion, so the sight of Liz and Swain out here was more than interesting.

The surf dude resurfaced with the fish, making a big deal of theatrically removing the backbone before commanding them to 'enjoy'.

"I know exactly what you are thinking," said Lynne.

"What do you mean?"

"I'll enjoy it if I want to. We aren't guys, we are ladies and gentlemen…"

"Okay, so I need to get with the programme," he responded with good grace.

She took a bite of the sea bass, pronouncing it excellent, and then asked Tedesco why he found it so interesting that Liz and Swain were at lunch together, and why he had avoided eye contact with them.

"Why should they care two hoots what anyone else might think?" she said. "If someone had seen us here together – Sally, for example – they might have assumed we were out on a date as well."

"Sally certainly would! No, it's just that Swain and Liz seem very unlikely luncheon companions, even if that is all they are.

"He comes over as utterly charmless. If the 'Merry Widow' were out for some excitement, wouldn't she choose Canford? The other Cathedral women would be green with envy."

Tedesco may have been right about the Ladies of the Close, but Lynne felt he'd betrayed a typically male mindset in assuming that Liz would prefer the company of Canford over Swain.

"You say that this Richard chap is a guide at the Cathedral and has just moved to Rhyminster. That gives them two things in common. She's only been here for, what, two years?

"And," she added, "they're about the same age, give or take five years perhaps. And they may just be lonely. I think it's rather nice."

Noting her colleague's unconvinced expression, she tried another tack.

"Look, Canford is way more charming, and easier on the eye – but she wouldn't really be interested. He's much younger. What would they find to talk about?"

"Point taken, but I still find her friendship with Swain troubling. I think it's time to take a look at Tricky Dicky.

"Anyway, Lynne, after your chat with your new mate Crystal Tipps," he began, before recoiling in exaggerated pain as he was kicked from under the table.

"Sorry. I meant to say Jo Luxmoore. So, after what you told me, I went in search of Ginny after Evensong last night.

"It turns out that she had been waiting to talk to me. She was worried about Oliver, as no one else seemed to be remotely concerned about him. I explained that we were already on the case, which seemed to reassure her, and she promised to keep our involvement to herself. Ginny admitted that she had left the Cathedral with him on Wednesday evening and that she saw him heading back in the direction of the North Canonry."

He stopped to enjoy a final sip of the wine then carried on.

"As you know, he didn't spend the night there, so he either popped out later or he might have continued round the Close."

"To the station perhaps," Lynne interjected, then added – "I started my checks on Canford yesterday, beginning with Doctor Google. This led me to his LinkedIn profile. The photo looked like a professional job. Anyway, the profile gives you a person's educational background, job history, and so on."

"I do know what 'LinkedIn' is, you know," Tedesco muttered.

"Okay, so you will know that you can post all sorts of stuff, articles, points of interest, and so on. This is how I learned about his choir, the Tuneful Company of Minstrels."

Tedesco butted in. "I gather from Bob that Charles Tantum has his own special name for them."

"I can well imagine," sighed Lynne, struggling to maintain her train of thought.

"Anyway – moving on, I had a look at the choir's web page and they are everywhere on social media, Facebook, Twitter, the usual suspects.

"'Smug Company of Gits' was my initial reaction when I saw the singers' profiles – totally up themselves. The men are all chinless wonders and the women look like they run right-of-centre think tanks."

Tedesco chuckled. He liked that one.

"However, I discovered that despite their exclusive image, they were still keen to recruit new members – and that they rehearse on Wednesday evenings.

"So I took the plunge and emailed the membership secretary, who turned out to be a very pleasant lady called, no surprises there, Charlotte."

She successfully swatted away a persistent wasp, and then went on.

"I told her that as I often had to work in London during the week, I was looking for a choir in the capital. Charlotte asked me how I knew about the Minstrels, and so, having laid it on with a trowel – how everyone knew about their world-wide reputation, and so on – I dropped in that I was a friend of Oliver Canford.

"I mixed in some choral credibility by mentioning Rhyme in Rhythm, and I almost believed her when she said how much she admired them."

At this point, Jez the waiter dude resurfaced.

"Sorry to hassle you guys, but can I tempt you with the dessert board?"

He started to recite a list of puddings, but Lynne cut in.

"You had me at sticky toffee."

They agreed to share one helping, with clotted cream, and ordered coffee to follow, with the bill and some more water for Barker – who was evidently expecting a second helping of beach frolics.

"So," said Tedesco, "how did Charlotte react to the mention of Canford?"

"Okay," she replied, "are you ready for this? Canford was in London on Wednesday night. She saw him at the rehearsal. And she remembers that he had to leave just before the end to get the last train home."

Once the sticky toffee pudding arrived, Tedesco halved it meticulously.

"Okay," he ventured, "so we need to check if he was on that last train."

Lynne had a fairly free diary the next morning, so she offered to visit the station and show Canford's mug shot to the taxi drivers. They don't miss much.

She felt that the ticket office wouldn't be much help, as it closed before the last train crawled back from Paddington. She could call in some favours and ask about CCTV, but she doubted that it extended onto the forecourt.

When the bill eventually appeared, Tedesco decided that as the element of pleasure had outweighed that of work, he couldn't in all conscience claim the meal on expenses, so he paid on his personal credit card.

By now, they all fancied another spot of exercise, so Barker found a couple of fellow terriers to racket around the beach with, while Tedesco and Davey strolled along in easy company, discussing their latest reading: Tedesco was revisiting his beloved Hardy – *Two on a Tower* – while Lynne was struggling through her book club assignment, the latest Elena Ferrante.

After a pleasant half an hour or so, Tedesco called Barker to heel, attached his lead and then they retraced their steps to the vicarage, as he wanted to beat the homeward traffic.

Reverend Paul Notte, now back in residence, was admiring the Lancia.

"Great to see you again, John, and you, Barker." Barker wagged his tail obligingly as Lynne nudged Tedesco in the ribs.

"Paul, this is Lynne Davey, my business partner."

"Lynne. Glad to meet you at last. I've heard all about your discreet work for us from the Archdeacon – that dreadful business over at Ugborough!"

As they meandered back to Rhyminster in the late-afternoon sun, Tedesco asked Lynne to pick a CD at random from the glove compartment.

She struck gold. Catherine Howe: *What a Beautiful Place.*

ELEVEN

Tedesco was up by seven, got showered, into his suit, then it was coffee and toast to the accompaniment of Martha Kearney and Nick Robinson on Radio 4.

After a quick stroll around the perimeter of the Cathedral, he and Barker arrived outside 4A Minster Precincts at 7.45, just in time to spot Sally Munks arriving at the little courtyard.

Her morning ritual involved cycling in, leaving her bike at work, then wandering over to Costa or Starbucks for an overpriced coffee and some heavy-duty scrolling through social media.

Although he would never understand why his PA paid a fortune for her caffeine hit when he offered free instant at the office, her expensive habit did at least guarantee him a blissful hour of peace, the most productive part of his day.

He opened the case file, turned over the latest page and inscribed his latest thoughts.

Why did Canford disappear? He had found his dream job and there had been no suggestion of serious financial worries.

Or perhaps he had been disappeared.

Who would want him out of Rhyminster? Bishop Bob had intimated that Canford was next to useless, but he would painstakingly adhere to the capability process if he concluded that Canford wasn't up to it.

What about Charles Tantum? If Canford really was seriously involved with Ginny, which Tedesco still found hard to believe, then Charles might confront him; but he doubted if the Master of Musick would do much more than shout at the lay assistant, or throw a music stand at him.

Was there something going on between Canford and Liz? If so Swain might want to get shot of him.

Despite the evidence of the Seafood Shack, he wasn't buying this theory either. At least not yet.

His musing was interrupted by the sound of his PA crashing into the office.

He instantly regretted asking Sally about her weekend, as he was treated to detailed descriptions of, respectively, Saturday's Park Run, her successful tin rattling at the hospice fete on Sunday and David Attenborough's latest nature programme, which he politely agreed to watch on catchup.

He told Sally to hold any calls for Lynne – she would be late in, as she was calling in at the station on the way to work.

Then he took a call from an anxious former client of his law firm who held power of attorney for his elderly mother, who had been conned out of her savings by phone scammers.

Tedesco agreed to look into it, which meant a long call to his old friend Rob Stone at Trading Standards.

Sally produced his 11am tea just before Lynne came running up the stairs, waking Barker in the process.

Just another day in Hazzard County, he thought to himself as Lynne gestured towards the small meeting room. He followed her in, taking extra care not to spill his hot drink.

She started briskly: "No joy on CCTV. There's no one at the station who remembers me from CID days so we will have to involve Bloomfield if we want access to footage, but there was better news from the cabbies.

"One of the drivers had been on duty last Wednesday night, Dane from Towercabs, waiting to pick up some returning opera-goers.

"I showed him Oliver's photo and he was pretty convinced that he had seen him coming out of the station with another passenger. Then it gets interesting – he saw him get into this other guy's car."

"No description of this other chap, I suppose?"

"No. Dane saw Ollie first – his blond mane does make him distinctive. However, he remembers the car. A red hatchback, possibly a Suzuki or maybe a Seat. The logos are pretty similar. The driver took off at speed, almost clipping Dane's wing mirror."

"So," said Tedesco, "we should check if CCTV shows Canford boarding the train and arriving at Rhyminster, but until then we need to concentrate on this mystery man."

Lynne restrained herself from saying, "No shit, Sherlock," and instead confined her remarks to agreeing with her partner, adding that Dane the taxi driver was sure that Canford had simply accepted the lift – there was no suggestion that he had been bundled into the car against his will. Dane thought that Oliver and the driver seemed like old friends.

A knock on the door from Sally interrupted their discussion.

"Sorry to barge in but there's someone on the phone for you, Lynne. Sounded upset but very pushy. She wants to see you today."

"Okay, Sally," Lynne replied, a little testily. "Tell her I'll call back later. Did she give a name?"

"Mrs Gerrey."

Tedesco and Lynne shared a knowing look.

"Sally – on second thoughts, put her straight through."

On the stroke of one, Tedesco headed out to lunch with Barker.

Lunch may have been for wimps in Wall Street but twenty minutes strolling round town amounted to the best free marketing he knew.

Over the years, he'd got to know several professional contacts and clients this way, and Barker had played his part by looking suitably cute.

Tuna and mayo on granary was Tedesco's Monday-ish choice; Joan tried to upsell him a cheese straw.

Then, after picking up his newspaper, he noticed two familiar but forgettable faces having lunch outside Côte brasserie.

To his amazement, never having seen him outside the Cathedral, one of them was Colin Scopes, and his companion none other than Richard Swain.

They struck him as a most unlikely pairing – perhaps Rhyminster was hosting an international Charisma Bypass Convention.

TWELVE

Back at the office, he was struggling with one of the clues in his easy crossword: 'Victorian Pleasure Garden Marketeer'.

It began with 'B'.

Looking over the gabled roofs for inspiration, he turned once again to his faithful companion. "Of course – six letters – Barker!"

He looked up and saw that Sally was hovering with intent. With most staff, this either meant that they wanted a pay rise, a day off, or they were handing in their notice.

Not Sally. Rhyminster General was organising a midnight 'Walk for Wards' in December and she felt that as Lynne had already signed up, it would be nice if all the office took part.

After a ritual but futile grumble, Tedesco waved the white flag of surrender, adding his signature to her form, while Barker stamped his pawprint.

"How long is this thing, Sally? I should have checked before I signed up!"

Sally advised that it was 'only' five kilometres, and so Tedesco confirmed that he would be there on one condition – no fancy dress.

Lynne's lunchtime routine was somewhat more strenuous, involving a run or cycle around the Close and the water meadows – but her daily lunch was somewhat spartan in contrast to that of her colleague, appearing to Tedesco like a random mixture of unappetising green leaves in a Tupperware container.

For a special treat, she sometimes picked up a bento box from the new Japanese place in St Thomas' Street.

On the stroke of two, the former DS Davey ran up the stairs, signalling to Tedesco that she wanted a word in private, and so he meekly followed her into the interview room, where they sat at opposite ends of the table, divided by Tedesco's counsel's notebook and her laptop.

She told him that she had spoken to Liz Gerrey and that the Merry Widow was due in the office within the hour.

Liz wanted to see Lynne on her own – he tried to hide his disappointment.

"That seems odd, Lynne. Assuming this is Canford-related, she knows that I am asking around, and she saw me at Evensong on Saturday. Perhaps she wants to tell you what she was doing with Swain yesterday."

"Who knows? If it is to do with Oliver, can I see her?"

"I assume you're worried about a possible conflict of interest with the Bishop."

She nodded. Tedesco mulled things over for a moment.

"I suggest that you let her ask you what she wants from us. If it is to do with Canford, then tread carefully, explain that we might be conflicted."

"Of course. Looks like a fun afternoon!"

Tedesco returned to the main office, where he was loudly busying himself with paperwork when Liz Gerrey arrived, box-fresh in a houndstooth jacket worn over her usual silk blouse and pearls combination, matched with a pencil skirt and her trademark patent leather heels. Tedesco felt himself start to blush like a lovesick teenager.

Lynne greeted the Merry Widow with a firm handshake. Her offer of refreshments was politely declined, and so she led her potential client into the recently vacated meeting room.

The former DS Davey, direct as ever, started by asking Mrs Gerrey why she needed to see her so urgently.

Liz took a deep breath. "This is very delicate. I lost my husband, as I think you know. I have avoided any meaningful relationships since Roddy passed. It just never felt right."

Lynne had moderated her interview technique since leaving the CID.

"It's not the same, I know," she replied, "but that's how I have felt since my divorce."

"I knew you'd understand. Perhaps you can see why I wanted to see another woman, although I'm sure John is a good listener.

"Look," she went on, "before we go any further, you saw me at the Seafood Shack yesterday and so I wanted to ask you not to mention who I was with."

Lynne, momentarily nonplussed, confirmed that the conversation was confidential.

"Who were you with? John thought it was one of the guides."

"Yes, it was. Richard Swain. John had seen us together before, in the cloisters.

"Look, there's nothing serious going on, never will be as far as I am concerned. We're both on our own – it does get lonely – and so companionship has become important. I just don't want to be the centre of gossip."

"You don't have to tell me how small this place is, nor how

small-minded people can be," Lynne remarked. "However, Mrs Gerrey, I'm not sure how I can help, other than by not mentioning that we saw you yesterday. Relationship advice isn't what we do."

"Call me Liz, please. That's all I want you to do. The other reason I needed to see you – the main one – was about Oliver Canford. I know that John is making discreet enquiries for the Bishop, but as several of us in the Cathedral community are really worried about him, I've been asked to act as their spokesperson.

"Anyway, we don't suppose the Bishop has deep pockets, and so I have been sent here to put forward a suggestion. Our group can pay you and John, whatever it takes, if this means you can devote more time to Oliver."

Wow, thought Lynne. *Wasn't expecting that.*

She carefully calibrated her response.

"Liz, I will have to discuss this with John, and he will advise the Bishop. Do I understand that your little group is effectively agreeing to underwrite the work we are doing for him? I mean, we can't run two separate investigations."

"Oh, of course. I totally understand. But we all feel that there needs to be more urgency!"

"Liz – why are your friends so keen to help out here? Is Oliver that important to you all?"

"Lynne. To be frank, I'm a little cooler about him than the others. I had doubts about him at the start. But I've seen how he is with people, and now he's counselling poor little Ginny Tantum.

"She can't cope without him. And the congregation simply cannot fathom why he isn't being supported for ordination! There! I hope you understand now."

Lynne looked directly at the glamorous guide. One tough cookie. But she rather admired her.

"Liz. Let me talk to John, as I said."

Before Lynne could show her out, Liz wanted to know when she could expect to hear, and emphasised that her group was ready to make a substantial payment on account.

Once Sally had safely guided Liz down the precipitous staircase and out into the comparative safety of the Close, Tedesco poked his head around the meeting – room door.

"Safe to talk?"

Lynne summarised the main points of the interview. Tedesco, predictably, wanted to ask Bishop Bob how he felt about the surprise offer of funding. If it was agreed, then Liz and her crew would need to be tied down to some detailed terms of business, and accept that Tedesco and Davey would only take instruction from Bob.

"Why do you suppose that the Ladies of the Close are so desperate to throw money at us?"

"It does seem pretty weird. I wonder if they're anxious to keep the police away from it."

"Maybe. Perhaps they think that if they incentivise us to hurl the kitchen sink at it, no expense spared, then we can quietly find him before Bloomfield gets his mitts on the investigation. The ladies wouldn't want a scandal, would they?"

"No, but this doesn't fully explain it. Are any of them involved in the disappearance, do you think? Or do they know something?"

"It's intriguing, certainly," Tedesco answered. "Oh, and, Lynne, how much did you say she offered up front?"

"I didn't. She used the word 'substantial'."

Tedesco whistled. "They are in a hurry."

"Oh, some good news for you, John – there's nothing going on with her and Swain, or Canford."

Although he was secretly rather pleased, he affected to ignore this and changed the subject, telling her about his surprise sighting of Swain and Scopes at lunch together.

"As a lawyer, I always followed the evidence. As an investigator, I am learning to follow my gut instinct. Something has been niggling away since I first met Swain. And now he keeps cropping up in strange places. The Seafood Shack with Liz, having lunch with Scopes, of all people."

"The Merry Widow speaks highly of him – as a companion," said Lynne.

Tedesco, overlooking the last comment, said that he would give Barbara Battershill a ring to see if Bob was going to be around after morning prayers one day this week.

"Okay, good idea. I'm going to Jo Luxmoore's yoga class on Wednesday to see if I can pick up some more tittle-tattle about Canford and Ginny.

"And," she added, "I have the unadulterated joy of choir practice with R in R tonight."

"Try not to wind up the conductor," said Tedesco.

THIRTEEN

"I'm going to be leaving you with Sally today," Tedesco explained to Barker. "I will make sure she takes you for a good woof around and remembers to feed you."

Barker accepted the news with equanimity.

Since retiring from legal practice, Tedesco continued to keep up with developments in the law.

Two or three times a year, he would take the train to Bristol, where he would spend the day in an air-conditioned room in a soulless conference hotel, to be updated on divorce law, injunctions, or any other aspect of his former profession that crossed over into his new life.

Today's thrill-a-minute topic was 'Wills and Lasting Powers of Attorney'.

He hoped that this would help him with his former client who held a power of attorney for his elderly mother, and with a potential new case involving a contested will.

Lynne, meanwhile, was back in Somerset taking further statements from alleged victims of the predatory lawyer.

So, despite the generous funding offer from Liz Gerrey and her coven, the firm of Tedesco and Davey would be taking a day's holiday from Oliver Canford.

As his train pulled away, Tedesco glanced back at the tower as it disappeared from view – he always felt a twinge of melancholia at these moments, but was comforted by the thought of the Cathedral still being there to welcome him on his return. He loved that building and would never get bored by it.

It seemed to him as if it had grown there, rather than having been meticulously crafted and maintained over nine centuries.

Reaching inside his suit pocket, he retrieved his phone and got straight through to Barbara at the North Canonry. It always paid to call early.

"He's in London till Wednesday afternoon, John. House of Lords. You could catch him at the Cathedral first thing on Thursday."

"Morning prayers? That's great, Barbara. Barker and I will see His Grace in the Lady Chapel – still no sight of Oliver, I suppose?"

"No," she replied, "and he isn't answering his phone either."

The express, bang on time for once, glided through river valleys and lush meadows until modern life reimposed itself in all its grottiness as the train crawled through the anonymous outskirts of Bristol.

A taxi took him from Temple Meads to the corporate hotel, where he had time for a coffee and a pastry and the chance to size up his fellow delegates.

Since his early days as a lawyer, the profession had become progressively feminised, to the extent that the majority of solicitors were women.

He felt at home in this world and looked back with horror at the days when masonic connections were often a route to the top, and at the seedy 'gentlemen's evenings' that he had always managed to swerve.

The course was more stimulating than the venue. The lecturer was Gill Withers, well known as an expert in her field and, unlike many, as good a communicator as she was a lawyer.

The morning session left him feeling relieved at how much he still knew, while his mind was still active enough to pick up on latest developments and insights, but when Gill announced a lunch break, he decided to escape the confines of the air-conditioned hotel for a stroll around the reclaimed docks, scanning the skyline in vain for a view of St Mary Redcliffe.

Sadly, the branch network of Jenks bakery didn't extend to Bristol, so he had to resort to a disappointing Tesco Express sandwich – egg and cress.

Once he had located a vacant riverside bench, he checked in with the office. All well, according to Sally. She would be taking Barker for a walk by the water meadows to give him a change from Tedesco's rigid regime.

Meanwhile, Lynne had stopped in a lay-by and was picking at her salad – having taken more statements, she was due to meet her client for another briefing before heading back to Rhyminster.

As they had agreed to catch up with each other at about half past one, it came as no surprise to Tedesco when the familiar blast of Sousa emanated from his mobile, attracting a disapproving glare from a tattoo-festooned bloke wearing a replica Bristol Rovers shirt.

"How's your Wills and Probate course, John? 'Dead' boring, I expect?"

"Very droll. Actually, it's been really good so far. How was your morning?"

She gave him a brief summary of her interviews and then suggested that he might be more interested in how she had spent the previous evening.

"Of course," Tedesco said. "How was the choir? Any Vesuvian eruptions from Charles?"

"That's the weird thing," Lynne went on. "I've never known him so calm. Not exactly zen, but we are talking about Tantum here.

"No hurling his score to the floor, no tears from the sopranos – he even managed to compliment us, and thanked us all for coming. It was so strange that I almost missed the old Charles."

"What if his positive vibes were down to the disappearance of a certain young man?" Tedesco asked.

"My thoughts exactly," Lynne said, adding that she needed to go, running late for her client.

Tedesco struggled to stay awake during the afternoon session – he'd always been a morning person, and this trait had become more pronounced with age – but he perked up considerably during the mid-afternoon tea break when Gill Withers came over to join him.

"Did I see you nodding off, Mr Registrar?" she asked.

"Sorry, Gill. Post-lunch dip. How's Steve?"

Her husband was another private client lawyer, and for several years had somehow managed to combine his legal work with being an effective leader of the local council.

"Not missing the political game, that's for certain," she said. "Like you, he keeps interested, keeps his hand in. Helps me run the training agency."

Tedesco made a mental note to get in touch with her about his contested will case. She could be a real help.

Gill, sensitive to the delegates' need to avoid rush-hour traffic, or get to the station, allowed them to leave a few minutes before the scheduled end time, and as Tedesco found that he had forty minutes before the next Plymouth-bound train, he decided to walk back to Temple Meads, taking advantage of the autumn sun.

He even managed to find a window seat on the crowded express and had just dropped off to sleep as the train pulled out of Exeter St David's when Sousa rang out again.

It was his sister. "Hi, Bro!" she yelled above the hubbub of the carriage.

"Why have you been ignoring my texts!"

"For the very good reason that I have been on a course and we have to switch off our phones," he drily replied.

She explained that she was doing a short piece for *Searchlight* about the girls' choir, and so she would be filming in Rhyminster early on Thursday.

Nicky asked him if he could help her with some background.

"How about meeting me tonight? Sally has got Barker. She is going to bring him over to St Budeaux Place at nine. I could meet you on my walk home from the station."

They agreed to rendezvous at the Kingfisher, a riverside gastropub with enviable Cathedral views.

The train, seemingly exhausted by its long journey, appeared to wheeze its way into Rhyminster. As he got up to leave the carriage, Tedesco glanced out of the window – good news, the Cathedral was still standing.

Glad to be home, and buoyed by the unexpected pleasure

of seeing Nicky, he almost skipped through the ticket barrier, leaving the station by the side entrance, which gave him access to the path through the water meadows; although he loved his wine, there were times when he could murder a pint, and this was one of them.

As he strolled through the meadows, Tedesco knew that he should be thinking of Keats, especially at this time of year, but it was Clifford T Ward's *Home Thoughts from Abroad* that he was hearing on his subconscious playlist.

He soon caught sight of Nicola Tedesco, local TV celebrity but troubled wife, as she approached the pub from the opposite direction, and as it was still just about warm enough to sit outside, they took a table in the garden, overlooking the river.

Nicky, conscious that she would be driving home, ordered a white wine spritzer. Tedesco, on foot, ordered a full-fat pint of Summer Rhyme.

It became clear to him that while his sister had carried out some perfunctory research into the girls' choir, she was in urgent need of a guiding hand, as she started by telling him that her interview was with Wilfred Drake, *The Placenta*.

Tedesco patiently explained to her the historic role of precentor in English cathedrals, as being responsible for leading choral worship, rather like the role of cantor in a synagogue.

"Our precentor, Wilf, is a lovely man. You won't have any problems there."

Then he set out the controversy that had raged over the introduction of the girls' choir, at which point Nicky visibly recoiled at the existence of such institutional sexism in the recent past.

"Are there any old dinosaurs who still don't accept them?" she said.

"Oh yes. They exist in both sexes, but their numbers have dwindled. Some have accepted the girls, even admitting that they can sing at least as well as the boys. Others boycotted the Cathedral in disgust, and quite a few have died. The leader of the rump of reactionaries is the Master of Musick."

"That's Mrs Tantum's husband, isn't it? She teaches Ella at the Cathedral School, don't forget."

"That's right – Charles Tantum. He still refuses to have anything to do with the girls' choir, but he is tolerated for his musicianship. He can't be far off retirement, praise be, but meanwhile, Wilf can manage the girls perfectly well on his own."

Nicky decided to change the subject.

"How are you and Lynne getting along?"

"Fine. We work well together, I think. We're quite different personalities, but you need that in a team, even a team of two."

"You know that's not what I meant," Nicky said, swirling her glass playfully, before adding, "You know you have feelings for her. And don't give me that 'married to the job' bollocks. That no longer washes. And Barker clearly approves."

"He told you that, did he?" said Tedesco, before swiftly asking after his sister's family.

"The kids are thriving, as you saw for yourself the other night. Jack is already talking about an engineering degree, and Ella is still young enough to be a delightful pre-teen."

"All that trouble to come, eh?" Tedesco commented, before waspishly adding, "And how is that husband of yours?"

"Let's not spoil a lovely evening," said Nicky.

Tedesco made it home with ten minutes to spare. Sally Munks declined the offer of coffee, as she was en route to her 'other book club'.

Barker looked as if he'd been walked off his paws and, as Tedesco was tired after his day in the big city, they silently agreed on a quick supper followed by an early night.

FOURTEEN

"How was the rest of your course?" Lynne asked, as they arrived at the office.

"Good, thanks. I've known Gill Withers, the lecturer, for years. She could be a real help with the contested will case. I was by far the oldest there, of course."

"That's the case where the widow cut out the kids and left it all to the GP, isn't it?"

Tedesco nodded.

Lynne reported that she had reached an impasse in Taunton. While she had found plenty of evidence against the solicitor, her client was having cold feet, worried about being dragged through courts, publicity, social media.

"Looks like 'Me Too' needs to come to Somerset," said Tedesco, "and I hope she does proceed, not just for herself but for the others. I don't envy her the decision.

"Lynne," he continued, "I'm still exercised about Swain. Could you get his photo off the Cathedral volunteers' website? – they have pictures of all the guides, a real gallery of the grotesque – and show it around to Dane and the other taxi drivers?

"I know it's a long shot," he went on, "but we need to focus on the mystery man who gave Canford a lift home."

"Don't be so rotten about the guides – the ones I've met are all lovely," said Lynne, "but we've had twenty-four hours away from Canford and still no real developments. We can't keep this from Bloomfield for much longer, surely?"

"I am seeing Bob Dwyer first thing tomorrow," said Tedesco, "and if our elusive charmer is still AWOL by then, I agree – we should get hold of Jimmy. Time to call in the cops."

DCI Jimmy Bloomfield had been Lynne's CID boss. Tall and thin, his granny glasses and waistcoat made him look more like an antique dealer than a senior detective. He even wore a bow tie.

"He's going to be pretty pissed off with us," said Lynne. "He will say that we've given Canford a head start, if he's on the run."

"I'm not sure," Tedesco replied. "Didn't you used to tell me that most MISPER calls were a serious waste of police time, with the alleged escapee turning up as soon as they started searching for them?"

Lynne ignored this and told him that she had contacted Bel Paese, as Canford had agreed to carry out locum work for them in his holidays. Perhaps he was in Italy.

However, from her chat with their HR department, it was clear that he had no plans to drag another bunch of prosperous oldies around Florence or Verona anytime soon. His next gig was a week next spring – 'Jewels of the Amalfi Coast'.

Barbara Battershill confirmed that Canford had booked the time off in the diary.

Tedesco still silently clung to the hope that Bishop Bob's lay assistant might suddenly turn up for Evensong one night, oblivious to all the worry and hassle he had caused.

After his ritual wander down to Jenks, he'd call in at the Cathedral, try and grab a word with Roy Baird, or he might even try and engage the preternaturally shy Colin in conversation.

FIFTEEN

There was a discernible mid-morning lull at the train station by the time Lynne and Barker arrived.

The hardy band of early commuters had long gone, and the usual crowds of incoming Bishop Lunt's grammar boys were safely corralled behind the school walls, so there would be little in the way of action until the arrival of the 11.30 from Paddington, which would disgorge a sizeable gaggle of foreign tourists, and curious retirees.

Rhyminster had just been chosen as 'the Best Place to live in the UK' by a national newspaper, and this had resulted in a corny marketing campaign built around the slogan 'It's Time for Rhyme'.

It was everywhere – on billboards, beer mats, tee-shirts, all over print and digital media.

Dean Dan had even blessed a digital billboard in Piccadilly Circus, encouraging the punters to 'Have the Best Time in Rhyme'.

Lynne was suddenly aware of a Towercab taxi drawing up. The driver lowered the window from which his huge face peered out, like a Halloween lantern made flesh.

"Oi! Sarge!" the lantern shouted.

Lynne turned round. It was Mickey Hunn, retired policeman, and mainstay of the bar at the rugby club.

"Where can I take you, DS Davey?"

Lynne told him that she was no longer with the force and didn't need a ride.

Mickey got out of the cab. "Shame that. It's dead here until the grockles arrive. Good to see you, Sarge!"

"It's Lynne now, Mickey. To come clean, I'm still in the detective business."

Mickey cut in. "I see – gone over to the dark side."

"Hardly. I set up an agency a couple of years ago. With John Tedesco?"

"I remember him! Old-school solicitor, had him in the back of the cab a few times. Good on you both," said Mickey.

Lynne explained that she was making enquiries for a client about a recent disappearance.

"Is it about that mush that Dane saw?"

Word had obviously spread through the Rank Mafia.

"Yes, Mickey. It is connected to that. Dane told me that he recognised the man we are looking for and that he was given a lift by the driver of a red hatchback. I need to find that driver."

"Okay. How can I help?" said Mickey.

Lynne produced the likeness of Canford that Barbara Battershill had forwarded to her.

"Yeah. I know him. I've taken him to the Bishop's gaff a few times, normally really late. He has to get out to open the gate."

The Broad Street gate to the Close was locked at 11pm.

"Okay, Mickey. The person you have identified is the one that Dane saw. That's really helpful. Let me show you this."

Barker looked on as she produced a second photo, the one she had downloaded from the Cathedral website before she set off for the station.

Mickey screwed up his huge face, shook his head a few times, and then pronounced his verdict.

"Looks a bit familiar. Trouble is, it's one of them faces – you know, no personality."

You aren't so daft, are you? she thought.

Mickey offered to show the photo to the other guys and would get back to her.

He walked slowly back to the cab then turned around abruptly.

"Sarge! That first bloke – the blond mush. Probably nothing, but I saw him the other day. He was waiting over there, in a red Stag. Real bird-pulling motor back in the day."

Lynne ignored the casual sexism. She also remembered that Mickey was a well-known petrolhead, and would start talking torque if she didn't move the conversation on.

"What was he doing? I assume he was waiting for someone?"

"Yeah! That's right. He met a lady off the London train, took her luggage, put it in the boot and drove her away."

"Do you remember what she looked like?"

Lynne was treated to an encore of facial contortions and head-scratching before Mickey pronounced that she was a "posh-looking lady, put me in mind of Maggie Thatcher, if you know what I mean."

Could be Liz Gerrey? Got to be, Lynne thought.

She left him her card, and Mickey cheerfully confirmed that either he or Dane would give her a bell.

"Cute dog you've got there!" he called after her. Barker looked suitably bashful.

SIXTEEN

Over at Minster Precincts, Tedesco was carrying out his own background checks on Swain. All he really had to go on was that Liz Gerrey had told him that Richard had retired from the Civil Service.

Tedesco had assumed, from his appearance and general demeanour, that Swain would have been high-ranking. He doubted if he had spent his career processing driving licences in Swansea.

Barbara Battershill drew a blank – she reminded him, as he should have been well aware, that the Diocese was not responsible for Cathedral volunteers. She would have a word with Wilf Drake; in addition to his role as 'Placenta', Drake was the Canon responsible for the oversight of the 500-strong volunteer community.

He logged on to his PC – although Lynne was far more skilled at carrying out background checks, Tedesco had mastered the basics, and a quick search revealed that Swain's name matched his forgettable features; there was a plethora of 'Richard Swains' out there, but none of them seemed to be our man, unless he had a sideline running a mobile disco in Paignton, or had played Rugby League for Widnes in the 1980s.

After another fruitless hour or so, Sousa alerted him to another call. It was Wilf, to say that Barbara had been in touch with him.

The Precentor added that he was in residence this afternoon – which meant that he was on call in the Cathedral, ready to talk to anyone who needed spiritual help, or to placate any disrupters, axe grinders, or oddballs. He could see Tedesco in the vestry at three.

Tedesco accepted the offer, which would allow ample time to stroll over to Jenks for lunch.

However, he found Broad Street thronged with tourists 'spending time in Rhyme', blocking the roads, entirely oblivious to traffic, and his progress was further hindered by Barker's impressive collection of fans, all enquiring as to the whereabouts of their canine hero.

Smoked salmon and cream cheese on brown was an appropriate choice for a Wednesday, he thought; a good compromise between end-of-the-week luxury and early-in-the-week basic.

"I should have put a fiver on that," said Joan.

As he left the shop, he couldn't believe his eyes – it was Swain and Scopes having lunch again. This time they were in Pret. What's going on? A bromance of bores?

After his lunch *al desko*, and a quick ten minutes with the easy crossword, he took up his fountain pen and finished updating the case file before wandering over to the Cathedral, a good twenty minutes before his scheduled meeting in the vestry.

SEVENTEEN

He noticed that Swain was on duty, explaining the scale model of the Cathedral to a group of bewildered Estonian tourists.

The guide was embellishing the prescribed tour notes with his own amusing anecdotes – mostly bullshit from what Tedesco was able to overhear – the lawyerly detective managing to avoid Swain's gaze by the simple act of standing behind a column.

Tedesco momentarily envisioned himself as David Essex playing the role of Che in *Evita*, as he too had observed the vagaries of life while hiding behind pillars – *Oh, What a Circus* indeed.

Deciding that he was now too old to indulge in musical fantasies, he went to seek out Colin Scopes on the pretext of looking for Wilf.

He soon spotted him lurking in the narrow vestibule that led to the vestry, clutching a clipboard as if his life depended on it, upon which there appeared to be some sort of seating plan.

The Cathedral was hosting a reception for a local accountancy firm that evening, and this would necessitate some nifty rearrangement of the deckchairs once the visitors had left.

"Colin, isn't it?" Tedesco asked. Scopes looked puzzled. "I'm John Tedesco."

"Oh, of course. Mr Tedesco. I didn't recognise you without the wig and gown."

This wasn't as bizarre as it might have sounded. Scopes would have come across Tedesco in his official capacity as Registrar of the Diocese, and his ceremonial appearances in the Cathedral on 'Law Sunday' and the like would have required him to robe.

Scopes clearly thought he had given offence, as at that precise moment he resembled a terrified water vole, so Tedesco did his best to put him at ease.

"It's okay, Colin, it really is. Perhaps you can help me. I'm looking for the Precentor."

"Of course, sir," said Scopes. "He's down in the vestry with the Head Verger."

Although Tedesco knew the way, he deliberately allowed Scopes to lead him.

"Did I see you having lunch at Pret a Manger today, Colin?" he asked.

"Oh," Scopes replied defensively. "Yes, I was there. With Richard. Do you know him?"

Tedesco considered his response. "He's one of the guides, I gather."

"Yes. He knows much more about the Cathedral than most of them do, even though he hasn't been here very long. That's why we get on so well."

"That sounds great, Colin. It's always good to find someone who shares your passions," said Tedesco, a touch wistfully.

Scopes halted just outside Roy Baird's little alcove.

"Here we are, sir. I will leave you with the Precentor. I need to get on. I've got a long night ahead of me."

Interesting, thought Tedesco, mentally filing the verger's remark as Wilf Drake greeted him.

"I've turfed Roy out of his cubby hole, so we can be private here."

"Seems a bit harsh," Tedesco said.

Drake explained that he really didn't feel too bad about it, as all the vergers needed to be on the floor of the Cathedral to prepare for the 'god awful' corporate event.

Wilf's untidy hair and 'Jesus boot' sandals may have conjured up a meek vicar from Central Casting, but as Tedesco had come to realise, the Precentor was a force. Not many people could take on Charles Tantum and emerge unscathed.

After the usual polite exchanges about families and a quick chat about the upcoming *Searchlight* feature, Wilf produced a manila folder.

"We don't keep MI5 dossiers on our volunteers – although I suppose there could always be a Mati Hari lurking among the Holy Dusters – but they all need safeguarding checks and updates these days."

Tedesco nodded sympathetically and let Drake continue.

"All volunteers have to sign up to our Core Values, and we keep a record of their employment history and medical records. The majority are long in years, so we have to keep a loving eye on them all."

Tedesco kept his thoughts to himself. One of his bugbears with the legal profession had been its adoption of corporate speak. And now it was infecting religion.

Surely, the New Testament represented the 'Core Values' of the Church?

Wilf knew exactly what the former Registrar was thinking, so he threw him a bone.

"And we have to keep the HR department happy," he concluded, giving Tedesco a conspiratorial wink.

"Anything of interest about our man?" asked Tedesco.

Drake slid Swain's personnel file across the desk.

"Have a look. It's somewhat thin, as he's a new recruit, but one thing stands out."

Tedesco turned a page. Previous employment. Swain had worked for the Ministry of Defence, most recently at the Chemical Weapon Research facility in Wiltshire.

"That's near Salisbury, isn't it? But there nothing in his history to indicate that he volunteered at the Cathedral. Isn't that a bit odd? He was clearly a busy boy up there – National Trust, school governor, and so on."

"It does seem strange," Drake said, "particularly bearing in mind his obsession with cathedrals. Salisbury isn't a patch on us, of course, nowhere is, but it's hardly League Two."

Drake hoped that Tedesco would appreciate the footballing metaphor.

"I will get on to my former counterpart up in Wiltshire. See if she's heard anything. Thanks, Wilf. None of this will go any further."

The Precentor stood up.

"I'm looking forward to being grilled by your sister tomorrow," he said, as they walked back up the north aisle together.

"I've told her to go easy," said Tedesco.

*

Lynne changed into her exercise kit then popped on a fleece before cycling over to the Deanery.

Jo Luxmoore had already texted her to explain that there were no changing facilities, and so participants turned up 'ready to rock and roll'. She signed off her message with a row of smiling face emojis.

Lynne arrived in the Close with a few minutes to spare. Not wanting to be first to arrive, she chained her bike to the dwarf wall separating the residences from Cathedral Green and enjoyed a brief stroll around until she saw signs of life at the Deanery, then she wandered over, briefly pausing to gaze at the outside of the building.

The Dean's residence was a beautifully proportioned Georgian villa, one of the 'new' houses built for clergy when the Close was re-ordered in the late eighteenth century.

Finding that the door was open, she wandered in and made a beeline for Jo, who greeted her with a hug, and with what Lynne now realised was her natural exuberance.

Her frizzy hair was held in place by a huge pink hairband, which clashed with her bright yellow leotard and orange eighties-style leg warmers, leaving Lynne feeling somewhat underdressed in her running vest and old trainers.

"My studio is in the extension at the back. Dan's predecessor used it for Christian healing, so it's got a chilled vibe. In the summer, we get the mats out on the lawn.

"I was hoping to introduce you to Dan," Jo went on, "but he's stuck at a ghastly corporate do in the Cathedral."

Lynne sighed. "I suppose even cathedrals have to hire themselves out to Mammon these days."

Jo gave her an approving smile and then led her through

to the studio, which was larger than Lynne had expected, and wonderfully light and airy – a chilled vibe, indeed.

The other participants – yogees? – were a reassuringly mixed bunch.

The chorister mums were out in force, all gym-honed bodies and designer water bottles, but they were balanced out by some older ladies drawn from the ranks of the Cathedral volunteers.

The yummy mummies all seemed to be called Sophie or Emma, and clearly knew each other, so Lynne introduced herself to Myrtle, who revealed that she was over seventy, and one of the team of holy dusters responsible for cleaning the choir stalls and the memorials.

After a quick warm-up, Lynne started to enjoy herself. She hadn't been to a class in years but was pleasantly surprised to find that she was as supple as most of the others, and felt that the session ended all too quickly.

Jo was really good. Underneath the hippy-dippy exterior, there was a professional teacher, encouraging the slower learners with a mixture of clear instruction and empathy.

After class, Jo took Lynne to one side and asked if she wanted to come to future sessions. Tonight's had been a free 'taster'.

Lynne was tempted but didn't want to commit to anything regular until the Canford situation had been resolved.

"By the way," Lynne said, having almost forgotten that she was on a spying mission, "I was anticipating noises off from next door. I assume that Charles is at the fundraiser."

Jo looked horrified. "There is absolutely no way that Dan would let that man loose on any potential donors. One of our American benefactors nearly threw himself off the tower after a few minutes' exposure to Charles.

"To be fair," she added, "he has been much quieter of late, almost suspiciously so."

Lynne replied that the new, improved version of Tantum, with the volume dialled right down, had been unveiled at choir practice on Monday.

"You don't think that this outbreak of bonhomie is linked to the disappearance of Ginny's little ally, do you?" Jo asked.

"John and I have been having the same thoughts," Lynne replied, adding that it was now a week since Canford had gone missing.

"Is it time to involve the police?" ventured Jo.

Lynne looked around for potential eavesdroppers.

"Yes. But please keep this to yourself for now."

EIGHTEEN

The residents of 17 St Budeaux Place were up bright and early. Tedesco demolished a quick slice of toast, while Barker made equally short work of a bowl of dog biscuits, then they walked over to the Cathedral together for morning prayer.

This daily ritual took place in the Lady Chapel, situated in the oldest part of the building, and Tedesco wasn't alone in sensing that it had an especially spiritual aura at this time of the day.

On the way over, Tedesco clocked the BBC outside broadcast van parked near the visitor entrance, so Nicky wouldn't be far behind.

Wilf Drake was going to be interviewed by her once the morning prayer had finished, so he had drawn the short straw and would be taking the service.

There was an audible sound of creaking joints as the congregation rose at the sight of the Precentor entering the chapel on the stroke of 7.30, preceded by Colin Scopes.

Colin was wielding the verge, or ceremonial silver stick used in cathedral processions; a custom which dated from when the cathedral clergy needed to be protected from the mob rather than from tabloid journalists or social media trolls.

Scopes was looking especially anxious this morning, Tedesco reflected as he sat down again, signalling to Barker, who lay down silently in front of him; here was one dog who knew how to behave in church.

His master surveyed the congregation – the usual ten or so.

Bishop Bob slipped in quietly at the last moment, raising the average attendance by several percentage points.

Who needs expensive mindfulness courses when you can come here, completely free? Tedesco mused, as the Precentor went through the introductory prayer.

The service only lasted half an hour, so before he knew it Tedesco was listening to Wilf bless the little group before sending them out to do God's work.

As the congregation slipped quietly away, some of them to silent, lonely homes, Tedesco fell into step with the Bishop; he would raise the question of the funding offer once they were safely outside.

Then Barker suddenly, and completely out of character, began to tug hard on his lead.

"Barker! Stop it!" Tedesco commanded. "Bad dog!" He never had to speak to his friend like this – what was going on?

The border terrier pulled with increased determination. This was completely unprecedented. Something was really upsetting him.

Barker dragged his bewildered master in the direction of the Rhyme Chantry, a forbidding iron structure known to all in the Cathedral as 'the Cage'.

As far as Tedesco was aware, the Chantry was completely out of bounds, the only key being held by the current Earl of Rhyminster.

"Barker, old friend," said Tedesco, trying to sound reassuring, "I know that the Cage looks a bit sinister, but there really isn't anything to worry about."

Tedesco asked the Bishop to take Barker's lead while he went to the vestry in search of a verger.

He thought he might have overheard an anxious, whispered conversation coming from within, but when he got there, he found Roy Baird drinking tea and reading the *Church Times* as if a communion wafer wouldn't melt in his mouth.

"Roy," said Tedesco, "Barker seems to think that there's something of interest in the Rhyme Chantry. I don't know, a dead pigeon maybe. Anyway, is there a way of getting inside without disturbing the Earl?"

The Head Verger looked decidedly uncomfortable.

"You should know by now, Mr Registrar. The Chantry isn't ours. But we do have a spare key somewhere. I've never used it. We only keep it in case the original goes missing, and the chances of that are pretty much nil."

Roy summoned a petrified-looking Colin, who loudly rummaged in the large safe, eventually producing the spare key. It was a massive instrument, like something out of *The Count of Monte Cristo*.

Baird snatched the key and headed to the Cage.

It took the Head Verger a few wiggles and jiggles and then the appliance of just the right level of force to open the gaol-like entrance to the Chantry, thus displaying a familiarity with the mechanism which Tedesco felt cast doubt on Baird's claim that he had never used the key before.

As soon as the door was forced open, Barker rushed straight inside, dragging Bishop Bob in with him, closely followed by Tedesco.

Despite its sinister aspect, the reality of the Cage proved something of a disappointment to the former Registrar of the Diocese.

Apart from the famed motifs decorating the roof, the space was taken up with disused photocopiers, rolls of old carpet and worn-out kneelers. This cast further doubt on the accuracy of Baird's comment that the spare key had not been in use – someone must have put these items there, and it wasn't the Earl.

Barker remained agitated. He was focusing his attention on a particular roll of lino and was barking at it, looking up at Tedesco as if to say, *How many more clues do you need? You are the detective here!*

Baird tried to move the lino and discovered that it was surprisingly heavy, so he called Colin for assistance. The two of them then began to haul the lino out of the Chantry together, with great difficulty and accompanying moans and groans, putting Tedesco in mind of the Chuckle Brothers.

"There must be something large rolled up in it," he said, as the vergers got down on their hands and knees.

"Time to roll away the stone, I think," said Bishop Bob.

As the vergers began to untangle the lino, Scopes started to convulse, and then Baird shook his head.

"Someone needs to call an ambulance. It's a body."

Bishop Bob and Tedesco didn't need to look. They somehow knew that it would be Canford.

Tedesco called 999 and requested urgent police assistance. It was too late for an ambulance.

And, he suddenly realised, his sister was just about to land the biggest story of her life…

*

His next call was to Water Lane, where Lynne had just got in from her jog. She would come straight over once she'd called Jimmy Bloomfield.

Then a familiar voice echoed down the north aisle. "Hi, Bro!"

He took Nicky to one side. The girls' choir would just have to wait for another day. She would have a massively bigger fish to fry.

NINETEEN

Swain found himself barred from the Cathedral when he arrived for duty.

"Let me in! I've got a party of ten booked on a tower tour at 9.30!"

This remark was aimed at the younger of the two police officers who were blocking his way.

His more experienced colleague politely explained that the Cathedral was closed, and there were no exceptions, even for guides.

"We'll see about that," replied Swain, his colour rising to match that of his crimson sash, before he stomped off into the cloisters, reaching for his phone.

Down in the main body of the Cathedral, the vergers had been busy roping off the aisles, while Lynne Davey was to be found in the north transept, deep in conversation with her former mentor.

DCI Bloomfield, normally a model of calm and master of the carefully considered response, was seething.

"Bloody hell, Lynne. I know you are a civilian now, but why the hell didn't you tell me about this earlier?"

Lynne took him to one side, indicating one of the stone benches that girdled the nave. As Swain would have delighted in telling them, these were used by the old and infirm when congregations used to stand for Mass, hence the expression, 'the weak go to the wall'.

As they sat on the cold surface of the bench, Lynne quickly got Bloomfield up to speed, explaining who Canford was, and how at first sight his absence had just looked like a classic case of someone absentmindedly going off without thinking of telling anyone.

She added that Canford's cavalier tendencies supported this assumption and, whether Bloomfield chose to believe her or not, she and Tedesco had already agreed that the police would need to be informed if he still hadn't shown up by this morning.

"Who found him?" asked the DCI.

"Technically, it was Barker," Lynne replied.

"Oh, well done, Barker. Give that dog a bone," was Bloomfield's sarcastic response, to which he added – "I always knew that he was the brains of your little outfit."

Pointedly choosing to ignore this, Lynne offered to make their case file available to the police.

"One of Tedesco's medieval manuscripts, I suppose."

"Look, Jimmy. We have some good ideas on who might have been glad to see the back of Canford. But we never imagined murder."

Bloomfield peered over the rim of his wire-framed glasses, looking disconcertingly like John Lennon during the Yoko era – if he had a sideline as an antique dealer, obviously.

"I'll come over to Minster Precincts once I've finished up here. Show me what you've got."

Lynne nodded in silent agreement, while over at

Cathedral Green, Nicky was finishing her hastily assembled piece to camera.

"In conclusion, what we have is a mystery body discovered in the very heart of iconic Rhyminster Cathedral, and a sleepy tourist city in a state of shock. This is Nicola Tedesco, for BBC Searchlight."

A blue Volvo estate drew up outside the Great West Door, from which an extremely large middle-aged man wearing a donkey jacket emerged somewhat clumsily, clutching a battered leather bag.

He could be politely described as being burly in appearance; impolitely, as a big old unit. It was Dr Nigel Brimacombe, the police pathologist.

The two policemen guarding the visitor entrance let him through, as he stumbled, rather than dashed, into the Cathedral, where he was enthusiastically greeted by Tedesco.

"Good result for Argyle on Saturday, Nige?"

Brimacombe was just about the only other person in Rhyminster who shared Tedesco's passionate love affair with the 'Pilgrims'.

"Yeah. About bloody time, though. Just about saved the manager's skin. This looks like fun, doesn't it?"

As the two of them walked down the North Aisle, Bloomfield emerged out of the gloom like a spindly poltergeist, gesturing to them to come through to where the body lay.

Brimacombe knelt down – clearly not a pain-free manoeuvre – while Tedesco looked on as the medic dictated his notes into an old-fashioned Dictaphone, looking up only to ask if anyone had touched the corpse.

"Roy Baird and Colin Scopes moved the roll of lino that contained the body, but I don't think they touched the contents," Tedesco commented, before leaving Brimacombe to his examination.

The dreadful news soon reached Dean Dan – he and the Bishop held emergency talks, which resulted in the swift offer of the Chapter House.

This building was located off the cloisters, its original purpose being for daily meetings of the Cathedral clergy.

Nowadays, it housed the treasures of the Cathedral, principally the twelfth-century Rhyminster Bible, *a Romanesque illustrated manuscript specifically created for the Minster.*

The Chapter House held the great advantage that it could be sealed off from the rest of the site, as it boasted its own entrance and landline, was connected to the Cathedral's Wi-Fi and even had a panic button.

Bloomfield could see straightaway how this might work as a makeshift incident room-cum-media liaison hub.

He'd already clocked the BBC van. Others would be on their way, many less deferential to authority than Auntie.

"Lynne," said Bloomfield, addressing her as if she remained under his command, "we will need statements from everyone who was in the building when the body was found. Do you have a list?"

"Here's one I made earlier," she said, giving him a swiftly drawn-up list which contained the names and contact details of Tedesco, Bishop Bob, Colin Scopes and Roy Baird. The rest of the congregation had dispersed before Barker made his gruesome discovery.

"I will start with the Bishop."

"Remember to address him as 'my lord'. Or 'Your Grace'," Lynne reminded him, as she went in search of the 78th Bishop of Rhyminster.

Lynne found him sitting quietly in the tiny side chapel dedicated to St Nonna. She hesitated before interrupting what might have been a prayerful moment, but Bishop Bob gave her a lovely smile and gestured for her to join him.

While he was happy to see Bloomfield immediately, he told Lynne that he would have to get Barbara to reschedule his weekly two-hour session with Amanda Leonard, the formidable Diocesan Secretary.

In a secular organisation, the Diocesan Secretary would be referred to as the Chief Executive.

In Amanda's case, she was more often labelled as 'Bob's Assassin' or the 'Real Power'.

Barbara told her boss that Amanda was already waiting for him. "Don't worry – I'll explain to her that it is an emergency – but you owe me, Your Grace."

As the Bishop guided Bloomfield across Cathedral Green towards the North Canonry, ignoring the *Keep Off the Grass* signs, he spotted an agitated–looking Amanda Leonard tottering in her vertiginous heels towards Church House, the Diocesan offices situated just outside the Close.

The Bishop and the Inspector entered by the main door of the Bishop's Palace, where Barbara was awaiting them in the study with a cafetière of coffee.

"Thanks, Barbara – I hope you've made this extra strong."

Bishop Bob gestured towards the window seats.

"DCI Bloomfield. It's been a while since we worked together. I'd normally add that it is good to see you."

"You can drop the 'DCI', Your Grace. Please call me Jimmy."

"Very well, Jimmy. As long as you drop 'Your Grace' and call me Bob."

Bloomfield didn't mess about. He raised the awkward matter of why Bob had conspired with Davey and Tedesco to keep him in the dark about Canford for almost a week since his disappearance.

The Bishop corroborated Lynne's explanation, namely that it was entirely in character for Canford to 'wander off on a frolic of his own', and in the light of this pattern of behaviour, neither of them had wanted to waste valuable police time.

"Okay, Bob, I hear you, but we may need to revisit this, and I expect I might need to ask you more about Canford's role, and so on. Now, I gather that John and Lynne were looking into the disappearance at your instigation. Can I assume that you are happy for them to share their findings with me?"

"Of course, if it helps. And I presume that if I declined, you could get a warrant or whatever."

"Thanks, Bob. I've already spoken to Lynne, and I will see them both later. Just wanted to check with you first – belt and braces."

Then he took the Bishop through the events of the morning, leading to the dramatic discovery of the body in the Cage.

He wasn't going to get much further with Bishop Bob today, and he had a team to put together, so he ended the interview, being courteously ushered out by Barbara.

Bloomfield had decided to call up DS Julia Tagg. Jools

was the safest of safe pairs of hands, had been under Lynne Davey's wing, and would go far, if he had anything to do with it. She would be the ideal officer to interview the vergers. He correctly assumed that they would be gentle souls, who would need sensitive handling.

His own immediate plan was to return to the Cathedral, see how Nigel was getting on, then decamp to the Ops Room in the Chapter House. As well as Jools, he could do with another trusted aide – DC Matt Lovell.

As soon as he had heard the dreadful news that morning, he'd called Area Commander Jacqueline Hinton at Truro HQ.

"Jimmy. This is going to be a massive story. Leave me to sweat about the budget," she said.

Meanwhile, Richard Swain had also been busy on his phone.

He had to make a cringeworthy call to the organiser of that morning's tour to explain that the group from Tallinn would have to find something else to occupy them today – they certainly wouldn't be enjoying a once-in-a–lifetime climb up the tower.

His first call, however, had been to Colin Scopes…

TWENTY

"How is it looking, Nige?"

Dr Brimacombe's preliminary findings were that a single blow to the head with a blunt instrument had done for the Bishop's assistant.

However, subject to the lab report, it seemed that while the blow had been administered a few days ago, Canford had been unconscious for several hours beforehand.

Crudely stated, it looked as if Canford had been drugged, plonked in the Chantry, left there to marinate for a while, then despatched later.

The SOCOs had already dusted for prints, and as the Chantry was practically out of bounds, there shouldn't be a problem with site contamination.

The incident room was fitted out at record speed. Lovell and Tagg had arrived and were manning the Chapter House, while the civilian media relations guy, Luke Barnard, was on his way up from HQ.

It was time for the DCI to visit Tedesco and Davey. Bloomfield gave them ten minutes' notice, ample time for him to wander over to Minster Precincts.

"Sally," Lynne called out to the PA, "DCI Bloomfield is a stickler for good coffee, so none of the usual instant. And we'll need some lunch. Take a twenty from petty cash and get a selection from Jenks. You're a star."

Tedesco would never have been this direct, she thought. *He's too nice for management.*

As the tall CID man edged carefully up the steep stairway, Sally, duly primed, welcomed him with the offer of coffee, which he politely accepted – despite having already received a more-than-adequate caffeine hit with the Bishop – and then he made a point of congratulating her on the excellent marshalling of the Rhyminster 10k last month, before seeking out Barker, who was lounging on his day bed.

"How's the hero of the hour?" he asked, giving him a gentle stroke. Barker returned him his best *Gee, Officer, it was nothing* expression.

As Sally was taking the DCI's sandwich order, the two private investigators emerged from the meeting room, Bloomfield noting at once that Tedesco was clutching one of his famed handwritten casebooks.

Once they had settled around the small table, Lynne decided to open the batting with the last known sightings of the victim, as Canford had tragically become.

"Dane Keetch, a driver with Towercabs, saw him at the railway station in the early hours of Thursday morning. He was met off the last train from Paddington and was driven away in a red hatchback, possibly a Suzuki.

"One of Dane's cabbie mates," she went on, "had remembered picking up Canford at other times, always off the late train.

"This driver, Mickey Hunn—"

Bloomfield interrupted her, asking if this was the same

Mickey Hunn who was renowned as the Monster of the Police Social Club Bar.

She replied that it was the very same, but that his legendary status had transferred its allegiance to the bar of the Rugby Club.

"Mickey also remembered seeing Canford collect a woman from the station, driving her away in his sports car. We think she might have been Mrs Elizabeth Gerrey, a prominent Cathedral volunteer."

"And let's not forget, a wealthy, rather attractive widow..." added Tedesco.

"Prior to that," Lynne continued, resuming her thread, "there had been a certain amount of gossip around the Close about the victim's friendship with Virginia Tantum, the Master of Musick's wife. Apart from Dane Keetch and the mystery man in the red car, she was the last person in Rhyminster to see him alive, as far as we know."

"Okay," Bloomfield said, "back to basics. What exactly was Canford's role? I don't suppose the Bishop paid him to chase after eligible widows. What about family? Interests?"

Lynne left it to Tedesco to outline the role of Bishop's lay assistant, which he explained as being a modern take on the age-old position of Bishop's chaplain.

Bloomfield looked nonplussed.

"Okay, so, in layman's terms, he was a gofer for His Grace then."

It was Tedesco's turn to pull a face.

Lynne took over, explaining that Canford had no living relatives, as far as they could gather, but that he must have been left quite well off if his lifestyle was any guide – the statement car, the regular trips to Chelsea.

She also referenced his previous job as a travel guide, and his involvement with the exclusive London choir.

"Anyone with a grudge against him?"

Tedesco and Davey looked at each other. Before they could respond, Sally Munks entered with the sandwiches.

Tedesco turned his nose up at the cheese and pickle she'd selected for him – too boring even for a Monday – then he waited until Sally had closed the door behind her before carrying on.

"Okay. Grudges. As Lynne has intimated, Canford and Mrs Tantum have been the talk of the washhouse for some time. They make an unlikely couple. Ginny Tantum is quiet and gentle, dominated by her husband, who is notorious for his mood swings and incredibly loud voice. The Noise Abatement Society have him on speed dial.

"Canford is probably the most glamorous figure in Ginny's life, and she seems to be besotted with him."

"The husband," Bloomfield interjected, "is he the jealous type?"

"Without a doubt," Lynne replied. "I sing in one of his choirs, and I have witnessed his bullying at first hand. No one knows how Ginny puts up with him, quite frankly.

"That said," she continued, "Charles – the husband – seemed much quieter when I saw him at choir this week, and the Dean's wife, Jo, told me that he seemed to be a changed man. She lives next door to the Tantums and reports that all has been calm since Canford disappeared, which is interesting."

Bloomfield removed his glasses, extracted his silk pocket square and used it to give them a quick polish.

"Seems like Charles Tantum may be the early bookies' favourite," he said. "Tell me about the widow, Mrs Gerrey."

Tedesco replayed the dreadful tale of how Roddy Gerrey had died shortly after a major career move from Edinburgh, and how Bob's wife and Roddy's former colleague, Hilary Dwyer, had supported her, which eventually led to Liz becoming a mainstay of life in the Close.

Lynne added that Canford had referred to Liz as the Merry Widow, and that she had been seen out and about with him in his sports car.

"I don't suppose that Mrs Tantum is a fan of hers, then," said Bloomfield.

"I doubt if she is. And Liz threw a curveball the other day. She made an appointment to see me at short notice, very agitated at Canford's disappearance and the seeming lack of any urgency in sending out a search party. She claimed to be the spokesperson for a group of Cathedral ladies who were worried about 'Poor Oliver', who were offering to underwrite our investigation."

Tedesco butted in. "As you know, Bishop Bob is our client in cases like this, so I was due to ask him about this funding proposal this very morning.

"Jimmy," he continued, "I'm not someone who trusts gut instincts, hunches, and so on, but Liz Gerrey is friendly with one of the other volunteers. A chap called Swain. I've never seen such cold eyes outside of the slab at the fish counter."

"We saw Liz with this chap at lunch the other day, over in the South Hams," added Lynne. "And we have discovered that he's formed an unlikely alliance with one of the vergers."

"What a tangled web," said Bloomfield.

What a terrible cliché, thought Tedesco.

"What are you thinking, John? That this Swain bloke saw Canford as a rival for Liz's affections?

"Looks like young Oliver liked to live dangerously. Any other jealous guys I should know about, apart from Tantum and Swain?"

Tedesco shrugged. "Who knows?"

Bloomfield peered over his granny glasses, looking down at his notes.

"What about Canford's work in Italy? Anything there? Did he get on the wrong side of the Mafia? And what about the poncey London choir?"

"I was coming to that," said Lynne. "He has sung with them for several years. They do have a starry reputation in the choral world, and I know that Canford loved to wind Tantum up by making unfavourable comparisons between his London group and Tantum's own choir here in Rhyminster."

"And," said Tedesco, "we think that Canford was up in town with his refined choral group on the night he disappeared."

"Yes," said Lynne, jumping in. "The membership secretary confirmed that he had been present at their last rehearsal."

"You'd better give me the details. What's the choir called?"

"The Tuneful Company of Minstrels," Tedesco and Davey replied in unison.

"Sally will give you a bound copy of the up-to-date case file on the way out. I hope you can read my hieroglyphics," said Tedesco.

While the three of them were in conference, Canford's body was being taken away to the morgue, where Nigel Brimacombe's superior, Peter Gill, would be conducting the post-mortem.

The Cathedral remained closed to visitors for the first time since the Great Rhyminster Plague.

TWENTY-ONE

Meanwhile, another meeting was taking place just outside the city at Rhyminster Down, a nature reserve that was looked after by the County Council.

Richard Swain, his best guiding suit covered by a green Berghaus fleece, scrambled up Prysten Hill, visibly impatient with his dilatory companion.

"Get a move on, you stupid moron!"

Scopes, who was wearing a brown knitted cardigan – a Christmas present from the Mothers' Union – wheezed up the gentle incline.

"I haven't dragged you up here for the view," barked Swain.

That said, if they had bothered to look, the vista extended to three counties on a clear day.

Scopes shivered as Swain continued to harangue him.

"Now. Remember. When the police talk to you, all you know is that you were called over by Roy Baird when that wretched hound started yelping, and then you helped old Bilbo to yank the lino out of the Chantry.

"All you need to do is confirm these facts. It should be a piece of cake. So please don't screw up. You got that?"

Scopes whimpered, the woodland creature exposed to the sunlight.

"I have never lied in my life, Richard."

Swain grabbed him around the neck.

"What did I tell you? All you need to do is give them the facts. You helped Bilbo Baggins move the lino. End of story."

He gradually released his grip.

"Anyway, Colin, neither of us has the first clue as to how Canford died, do we?"

*

At the end of a uniquely long day, Tedesco was only too glad to make it home and shut out the world.

He opened a cheap bottle of wine, 'Essential Waitrose claret'.

"Claret is essential, Barker, especially after a day like this."

Having drained his first glass, he tried his sister on the landline, which was picked up by his nephew, Jack.

Jack was a lovely lad. It wasn't his fault that his father was a bore.

"Mum's down in Plymouth, Uncle John. Did you see her on the news? She's recording a piece about the murder for *Newsnight*."

He spent a further twenty minutes chatting to Jack, who promised to let Nicky know he had called.

Feeling himself beginning to nod off, Tedesco got up and poured himself a second glass. He needed it, and an appropriate song to end this day.

He chose familiar comfort – James Taylor: *You Can Close Your Eyes.*

TWENTY-TWO

Tedesco was up and about by six, champing at the bit to see how the media were going to cover the biggest news story to hit Rhyminster since about twenty years ago, when there had been a rumoured sighting of Dr Ian Paisley wandering around the crypt.

BBC *Breakfast* had made Canford their lead story, and his heart overflowed with pride when the Salford-based presenters handed over to Nicky in Plymouth, standing rather incongruously below Smeaton's Tower.

She must have stayed at the Premier Inn last night, or with one of her many friends and colleagues down there in their home city.

His sister played it with a straight bat.

"The police await the results of a post-mortem."

"It's far too early to speculate on the cause of death."

"The Cathedral community is still in shock."

The next section of the programme was devoted to a review of the day's newspaper headlines and online news platforms; *Assistant to Gay Marriage Bishop found in Cathedral Tomb* being a typical banner.

Tedesco could feel his blood pressure rising at the sickeningly crude tabloid tactics.

"How dare they make snide insinuations against Bob. Why do they always demonise the decent and fawn over the mediocre?"

He angrily zapped the remote. "Come on, Barker. Let's see what's going on outside."

They were unable to enjoy an uninterrupted walk, as Cathedral Green was already awash with satellite dishes, pop-up TV studios and miles of cabling. A whole village had suddenly appeared.

Tedesco hoped that the Cathedral had been consulted about this, and that they were being generously compensated for the desecration.

Barker wasn't much happier – it was all too noisy for him.

Once they got back to the sanctuary of St Budeaux Place, Tedesco decided to spend the first part of his morning working from home, as he couldn't face the media scrum again, and he could do with some peace and quiet to assist with the meticulous inscription of his casebook.

It was after nine before he tried to call Sally, but as the landline to the office was constantly engaged, he texted Lynne, asking her to hold the fort while he put his thoughts down on paper.

Am I looking at this from the wrong angle?

As Bloomfield has already decided, Tantum is the obvious suspect. He has motive and anger issues. The sudden change of character from Tantum the Terrible to Cheerful Charlie once Canford disappeared. But a killer? Jimmy seems convinced that this is an open and shut case...

Or are choirs the common factor in some strange way?

Tantum has links to two of them, the Cathedral boys' choir, and Rhyme in Rhythm.

Ginny is linked to both Cathedral choirs, by dint of her work at the Cathedral School.

Oliver Canford himself was tangentially attached to all the local choirs, but was also a member of the 'Tuneful Company'.

This choral connection is intriguing, but where does Swain fit in?

He had animus against Canford – the young man was far too friendly with Liz – but why is he suddenly bezzie mates with Scopes of all people?

And what did Colin mean by his comment about 'being in for a long night' when he spoke to him on Wednesday?

A quarter of a mile away, at Minster Precincts, Lynne Davey was feeling less than gruntled at being left to deal with a tsunami of calls and emails.

"It's all very well for John to need time to think, but this isn't on," she told herself.

The grapevine was operating with its usual efficiency, like the hidden hand of the market, and it soon became clear that everyone and his uncle knew that Tedesco had been present when the body was found. Sally had even taken a call from a Canadian cable company requesting an exclusive interview with Barker.

So it came as a relief to her, and to Sally, when the familiar foot and pawsteps of Tedesco and Barker were heard on the stairs, followed by John Sousa and his rousing march blasting out from Tedesco's mobile as soon as he entered the office.

The caller was Nigel Brimacombe. Tedesco put him on loudspeaker so Lynne could hear.

The tubby medic had seen the preliminary findings from Peter Gill, and as he had predicted, Canford had been swiftly dispatched by a single massive blow to the back of his head, but he had been rendered unconscious several hours beforehand.

It looked like some kind of anaesthetic, possibly chloroform, had been used to subdue him.

How could Tantum get hold of that? wondered Tedesco.

Why go to the trouble of putting Canford to sleep, leaving it for a few hours and then killing him? thought Lynne.

Brimacombe added that Bloomfield was holding a press conference in the Chapter House at eleven, and that Jimmy had asked him to extend an invitation to DS Davey.

"Why not me, Nige?"

"Lynne's still one of us, John. They call us the 'Fuzz' for a reason, you know."

Tedesco reminded himself – *Because you all stick together. Of course.*

While engaged in updating his casebook, he had spotted a note that prompted him to contact the Salisbury Diocesan Registrar; he wanted to check whether she had come across Richard Swain during his time in Wiltshire.

Having emailed her a request for a few minutes of her time, she replied by return, agreeing to call him at eleven, just as the press conference would be getting underway.

Before she wandered over to the Chapter House, Lynne updated him on the many calls she and Sally had dealt with, one of which might have a bearing on the investigation.

Dane Keetch from Towercabs had been in touch to say that he vaguely recognised the picture of Swain that she had asked Mickey Hunn to circulate – but he was clear that it wasn't the same person who had driven Canford away last week.

TWENTY-THREE

Lynne got the impression that the drivers were getting overexcited – or at least a bit giddy – about being part of a big story, so she warned Dane not to speak to journalists, adding that the police might want a statement.

"Shame it wasn't Richard who picked him up," Tedesco commented, going on to share his theory that there might be a choral link to Canford's disappearance and subsequent death.

"Could you bear to miss this week's yoga session with Crystal Tipps?"

Lynne visibly groaned at this.

"I assume you mean Jo. I can read your mind, Mr Tedesco. You want me to get in touch with the Tuneful Company and invite myself to their next rehearsal."

"Correct. It would be a re-enactment of sorts, following Oliver on his journey of last week."

Lynne – slightly reluctantly, he thought – agreed, on the proviso that the accuracy of the proposed reimagining wouldn't extend to accepting a lift home from a dodgy bloke in a red hatchback.

She left Minster Precincts by 10.45, having opted to allow herself extra time to take a look at what was happening on the Green before securing a decent seat in the Chapter House.

Lynne saw straightaway that Tedesco's sister had made it back from Plymouth, as she was busy conducting vox pop interviews in front of the West Door.

Sky and ITV vans dominated the area immediately opposite, but local print media was represented by the familiar face of Julie Stringer.

Her regular column in the local weekly paper – *It Makes Me Mad!* – had become something of a cult in the city, and it was no surprise to Lynne when Julie greeted her with a conspiratorial wink.

"Makes you mad, doesn't it?" said Lynne, indicating the media village.

"Very funny," replied a smiling Julie, adding, "Do I assume we're going to the same place?"

Back at Minster Precincts, Sally was fixing Tedesco a welcome cuppa in time for his scheduled call with Lorna Campbell, the Salisbury Registrar.

He noticed that Sally was wearing a new ribbon today, a garish green and purple ensemble.

Daisy Chains for Peace, I expect, Tedesco thought to himself, then immediately felt guilty for being so petty and unkind; *Sally is all right.*

Lorna Campbell had been appointed to the role of legal adviser to the Bishop of Salisbury approximately two years before Tedesco had officially retired from his own role with Bishop Bob.

Like most lawyers who took on this job, Lorna had no previous experience of canon law – her field was commercial property – and so Tedesco had agreed to act as a long-distance mentor, always available at the end of a phone or the click of a mouse.

He was put through to her by an old-fashioned receptionist, which met with his approval, having stubbornly resisted the direct line culture when he had been in full-time practice. Yet more interruptions!

After thanking 'Madame Registrar' for making the time, he asked after her family.

He had met Howard Campbell, a pompous land agent, on a couple of occasions, and he correctly assumed that their daughter Rowena was now of an age to be away at boarding school.

Having confirmed that her husband and daughter were in good health, Lorna asked Tedesco if he missed private practice – no – and then it was straight down to business.

"So, Mr Registrar. How can I help?" she asked, breezily.

"Lorna, have you come across a character called Richard Swain? He recently moved down here from your neck of the woods."

"I don't suppose for a single moment that this is linked to the big news today?"

"Of course it is. Let me explain. Richard is one of the volunteers at the Cathedral here.

"He's not a suspect, but our bishop has asked me to make some enquiries about Canford, and Swain's name has come up. My initial view of him is that he is a bit odd – the sort of chap who always seems to be lurking in the nettles."

Lorna Campbell hesitated before offering a response.

"Rings vague bells, I can't say that I remember meeting him. But if he volunteers at Rhyminster then I wouldn't be at all surprised if he had volunteered at the Cathedral here in Salisbury.

"Tell you what, I'll have a word with the Chapter Clerk, Giles Wheeler. And I will make some discreet enquiries around the patch."

Tedesco agreed with her that it would indeed be odd if Swain hadn't been involved in Salisbury – unless he had developed his fascination with cathedrals after leaving Wiltshire.

"A damascene conversion on the A303 perhaps?" Lorna joked, adding that, "Giles will get back to me quickly. He's a terrible gossip."

"No, really? That doesn't sound like the Church of England I know," said Tedesco sarcastically. "Thanks, Lorna. I owe you one."

*

Meanwhile, at the Chapter House, the invited media corps quietened down as the press conference was about to begin.

Bloomfield sat at the centre of a table mounted on a hastily assembled dais, flanked by Nigel Brimacombe and Luke Barnard, the Media Liaison Officer.

The DCI made some anodyne opening remarks, before handing over to Brimacombe, who duly confirmed the cause of death.

The press pack were straining at the leash, but Barnard brought matters to a premature close, promising a future opportunity to ask questions once the investigation was in full flow.

As the media representatives filed out, Nicky Tedesco made an obvious beeline for Lynne, insisting that she and John come over for supper once the excitement had died down.

As long as you keep Chag away, or on a long lead, was Lynne's instant reaction, but which somehow came out as, "That would be lovely."

Julie Stringer caught up with them in the cloister, clearly on a high at being at the epicentre of a major story, probably for the first and only time in her career.

"I have a brilliant question! Where was the Devon and Cornwall force when Canford went missing? Instead of a Border force, does DCI Bloomfield agree that a Border Terrier force would be more use, given the circumstances of this case?"

"Might be worth keeping that one up your sleeve, Julie," said Lynne, as Nicky stifled a giggle.

"Anyway," she went on, "good to see the Home Team out in force."

Once safely snuggled up in Minster Precincts, Lynne checked her messages.

Charlotte Newbiggin, membership secretary of the Tuneful Company of Minstrels, had sent her a long email.

She had been delighted to hear from Lynne. Her request had been well timed, as the Choir was holding one of its regular social events on Saturday. Would Lynne like to come?

It would be a 'super' opportunity to meet everyone; she included a link to the directions.

Lynne pondered for a moment. She had no plans for Saturday evening beyond *Strictly*, so she could get a train up to Paddington in the afternoon, which would still allow time for Park Run.

Why not? She hadn't been to a social event for ages, and it would be good to see some new faces, so she got back to Charlotte, adding that she couldn't wait to meet her and the other singers.

TWENTY-FOUR

"That was quick," Tedesco said, as Lorna Campbell was put through again.

"I didn't want to interrupt your lunchtime walk with Barker – I assume that hasn't changed."

"Hell would freeze over first," said Tedesco.

"An-y-way," Lorna responded, emphasising each syllable, "I made up an excuse to speak to Giles, then I casually asked him about your Mr Swain."

"I'm all ears, Lorna."

"So... It seems that Richard had been an extremely keen volunteer at Salisbury, leading tour groups, helping out with archiving in the library, and so on, researching medieval graffiti, usual Cathedral stuff.

"All was going swimmingly for him. And then Dean Jane arrived."

Jane Le Prevost, ordained in her native Jersey, had enjoyed a meteoric rise in the church hierarchy, catching, and expertly riding, the wave of senior appointments of female clergy.

A curious mix of a slightly high-church Anglicanism blended with a radical feminist agenda, her appointment at Salisbury had been considered 'brave'.

Despite the forebodings, she managed, in time, to win over most of the sceptics, was popular locally, and despite having dreaded her arrival, the Cathedral community were now fearful that they would lose their star attraction to York, or even Canterbury.

"Swain wasn't too keen on the new Dean," Lorna continued.

He had, by all accounts, loudly condemned the idea of women as bishops, refused to attend services if the Dean was presiding, and made a thorough nuisance of himself.

'Mr R.G. Swain' was a frequent correspondent to the *Salisbury Journal*, using its letters page to lay into Dean Jane, albeit in the most eloquent terms.

The final straw had been during a Remembrance service, when Swain had – quite wrongly and incredibly stupidly – taken some remarks in her sermon as being pro-CND.

He made a huge fuss over resigning from his voluntary roles, and then he attached himself to one of the village churches which had become a receptacle for the anti-women, anti-same sex marriage, anti-liberal forces in the Diocese.

However, the 'CND Sermon' had served as a convenient excuse – the real reason he threw his toys out of the pram was the non-publication of his painstakingly researched history of the Cathedral. He had inserted a final chapter, which his publishers had to refer to their lawyers, who swiftly advised against its inclusion as it amounted to a scurrilous attack on Dean Jane.

Swain refused to remove it, and as no other publisher would touch his masterpiece with a bishop's crook, he decided to go it alone and self-publish.

However, the cat was out of the bag – even his own lawyers advised him not to go ahead, as the Dean would be strongly advised to sue. So, the book remained as a saved document on Swain's computer.

Little was seen of Richard after all that, which is why Lorna hadn't been aware of him – the waters had passed over by the time she was appointed.

"We've got an anti-women place here as well – St Barnabas," said Tedesco.

"What century do these people live in, John?"

"Lorna, didn't Swain realise that Rhyminster Diocese is hardly a hotbed of reaction? Had he even read up on Bishop Bob?"

"At least he's a man, I suppose," said Lorna, "but I agree. Rhyminster doesn't seem a natural fit for a relic like Swain."

After thanking Lorna for her assistance, Tedesco reflected that her evidence backed up his gut instinct about Richard – that he was a deeply unappealing character – and that his falling-out with Salisbury Cathedral explained his reluctance to fully disclose his volunteer history when he applied for guide training at Rhyminster.

To pleasanter duties – "Come on, Barker! Time for lunch."

They were forced to queue outside Jenks Bakery by the influx of hungry media types covering the Canford murder, and the tourists, their numbers multiplied both by the advertising campaign and an unhealthy interest in the sensational events of the past twenty-four hours.

The resultant increased demand for Jenks' delicious sandwiches meant that Tedesco had to settle for a pastrami on rye and a plain flapjack. Joan apologised profusely and threw in a cinnamon whirl.

As he left the little bakery, Tedesco sensed a perceptible, lightly perfumed breeze.

Chanel, he realised, as Liz Gerrey drifted past him. She was heading in the general direction of the Cathedral.

Of course – Friday was her guiding slot, but surely she must have realised that the Cathedral was out of bounds?

Once he and Barker made it safely back to the office, he quickly polished off his unsatisfactory lunch while completing his crossword.

It wasn't long before Lynne returned, face aglow after her power walk.

"Bloody London media! Arrogant as hell. One of them asked me why there aren't any Michelin-starred restaurants in Rhyminster," she ranted.

"The obvious answer to such an idiotic question being that we are in the deep south-west, not the home counties, and so we want to deter pillocks from moving down here," responded her business partner. He surprised her sometimes.

Her stress levels were further raised by the appearance of Sally Munks, who had been set what Lynne had considered to be the simple task of booking her an overnight stay in London.

Sally claimed to have been on every hotel booking site under the sun: "Nothing was available at short notice – this isn't really part of my job description, you know."

Once she had stopped wittering, Sally concluded by revealing that she had eventually managed to secure a room for Lynne at the Travelodge near Waterloo Station, but that it was 'very dear', and she could never understand why anyone would want to go to London in the first place.

Sally would not have realised it, but the location was just fine. The Tuneful Company were meeting in a room over a gastropub in Pimlico, so no real distance at all.

TWENTY-FIVE

Across the Green at the Chapter House, the detritus of the press conference had been cleared away, and DS Julia Tagg was preparing to take statements from the vergers.

Partitions had been installed, creating makeshift work stations which could double as interview rooms. As she gestured across to her colleague Matt Lovell, DS Tagg reflected that this was a place that would have heard plenty of interesting confessions over the centuries.

Lovell, acting on Tagg's signal, left the Chapter House to locate Baird and Swain, whom he soon discovered sitting on one of the benches in the cloisters, looking for all the world like naughty schoolboys who had been caught scrumping apples.

The DC asked Baird to follow him to the pop-up interview room and then invited him to take a seat opposite DS Tagg.

Having made the introductions, she went through the preliminaries – asking the Head Verger about his job, how long he had been doing it, and so on, before focusing on the Rhyme Chantry.

She started by asking him how many keys there were.

Baird replied that the Earl held the master key, but that the Cathedral kept a spare in the vestry.

"What is this Chantry used for exactly, Mr Baird? Not chanting, I assume?"

Roy sighed, and laboriously explained the historical significance of the Woolford and St Budeaux families, and how the present Earl had succeeded to the ownership of this 'golden treasure of our Cathedral'.

Still unenlightened, Tagg tried the direct approach.

"Okay. Nowadays, in the modern world, what is it used for?"

Baird replied that it was used as the family pew for the Earls of Rhyminster, and they tended to exercise their right to sit in it once a year.

"Oh yeah," Lovell interjected. "They come for the carol service at Christmas."

Baird seemed to take this as a personal affront.

"That is not correct. The family graciously attend the advent service."

"Advent, Christmas – it's all much the same, isn't it?" muttered Tagg, before enquiring of Baird as to the use of the Chantry during the other 364 days of the year.

The Head Verger somewhat uncomfortably admitted that his colleagues had occasionally used it as a glorified dumping ground for old photocopiers, worn-out rolls of carpet, spare hymn books and the like.

"We always clear it out and give it a good going-over before His Lordship's visits," he added.

"Okay, Mr Baird. So let's get this straight. Nobody is allowed in the Chantry except the Earl and his family, and the vergers. Correct?"

Baird took an age to respond. He sighed again, before reluctantly admitting that he had allowed one of the Cathedral guides to have a peek inside the Chantry.

The guide went by the name of Richard Swain, and he was an expert on English cathedrals.

"He wanted to see every inch of the building, you see. He's writing the definitive history of the Cathedral. Richard has become good friends with Colin Scopes, who you are talking to later, and Colin agreed to let him in, as a personal favour."

Lovell took over. "Mr Baird. Are you sure that Mr Swain was the only other person allowed to see inside?"

"Yes. Oh, wait a minute. That's not entirely correct. The Master of Musick was in the vestry when we let Richard see the Chantry. He followed us in there."

"What is he called, this Master of Musick?"

"Tantum. Charles Tantum."

*

Tedesco, painfully aware that he had been neglecting his clients, spent two hours locked away with his 'dodgy will' case, his mood lifted by half an hour on the phone with Gill Withers, who had made good on her promise to help him with any technical points.

She, understandably, was keen to ask about the Canford case, and was not at all surprised to hear that he and Lynne were in the thick of it. He offered to treat Gill and her husband, Steve, to dinner as a thank-you for her advice, and genuinely looked forward to seeing them once the current shenanigans were over.

Lynne carried out some more research into the Tuneful Company of Minstrels. She needed to gen up before meeting them the following evening.

The Tuneful Company had been formed in the 1980s by a group of keen amateur musicians in the City, who soon developed a following among their ilk, as well as ready access to sponsorship.

Their reputation soon outgrew the Square Mile, and they had become well known in classical music circles.

The choir put on an annual summer festival, either at a stately home or in a continental spa town, and regularly performed in cathedrals.

Their main event was the annual Christmas Concert, held in a prestigious London venue, such as one of the Inns of Court.

This year's offering was JS Bach's Christmas Oratorio.

Lynne had sung this piece with Rhyme in Rhythm, so she could already demonstrate some credibility when she met the gang and, with any luck, she hoped, Bach might clash with Tantum's annual Wassail Parade.

If only in his mind, Tantum's celebration was the highlight of the Rhyminster Christmas calendar.

Each year, he would inveigle the members of Rhyme in Rhythm, the boys' choir and various local singers into joining his merry band of Christmas wassailers.

Tantum would lead them round the Close singing carols, banging on doors and shouting, "Wassail!", putting the fear of God into the elderly residents and any small children lining the route.

From Tantum's lips, the meaning behind the festive message felt more like *I'm going to kick your head in* than a cheery yuletide greeting.

Once this dreadful show was over, it was back to The Pelistry for some mulled perry infused with rum, which Tantum called 'Rumpy Pumpy', and was every bit as gut-wrenchingly disgusting as the combination of ingredients implied.

So, all in all, Lynne was looking forward to a Saturday night away from Rhyminster, and as Charlotte would no doubt have briefed the others about her Canford connection, she wouldn't be short of attention.

*

Tedesco decided to leave the office early for the weekend, and as he and Barker walked home, he was pleased to see that the media circus had largely dissipated – there wasn't quite a breathless hush in the Close, but life was slowly returning to normal.

As there was no sight of the BBC outside broadcast unit, it was the weekend and the weather was still gorgeous, he proposed another drive over to Woolford, assuming that Barker was up for some more fielding practice.

Approaching the Cathedral, Tedesco noticed a sidesman hovering by the visitor entrance, one of the new breed of cheerful types that had been encouraged by Dean Dan.

His name badge proclaimed, 'I'm Chris. Here to Help!'

"Is the Cathedral open then?" the detective enquired.

Chris replied that it was open for a 'said' Evensong, and that it was being held in the St Budeaux Chapel.

This small chapel was rarely brought into service, but as it was situated some way away from the crime scene, Tedesco could see the sense in using it.

"Any guided tours take place today?" he asked.

"No, sir," said the ever-helpful Chris. "We have only opened for worship. I doubt if the Dean and Chapter will allow tours for a while – it might seem a bit ghoulish."

As Tedesco turned towards home, he caught the now-familiar zephyr-like waft of expensive scent.

It was Liz Gerrey striding towards the little car park…

Just what is she up to? he thought to himself, but within two minutes he was back in his cosy refuge within the Ancient Liberty, mentally decoupling from the Close as he changed into his weekend uniform: beige chinos, a Crew Company rugby top and his ancient pair of Docksides.

Barker, sensing a change of scene, was already waiting for him outside the Lancia, his tail wagging with palpable impatience.

His master didn't call ahead – this was a spontaneous visit – and if Nicky and the kids were out, he could always drive on to Creber Lake, where he and Barker could enjoy a scenic walk before it got dark.

Having selected Bridget St John – *Songs for the Gentle Man* – as his musical accompaniment, he drove over the cobbles and joined the main road south.

The traffic was Friday busy, so it was half an hour before they crossed the river and approached Crane House.

Spotting Nicky's RAV4 hybrid parked in the drive, he briefly hesitated before switching off the ignition, realising that this would be the third time he'd seen his sister in a week – he might be coming across as needy.

But before he could turn back, Jack and Ella charged towards him. "Come on, Uncle John," shouted Ella, before bundling Barker out of the back seat for a spell of wicket keeping.

Nicky emerged from the bifold doors and was soon enveloping him in a close hug.

"How's my sister the media star? I expect Fiona Bruce is quaking in her designer heels!"

"It's been exciting, nerve-racking, but I'll be glad when it all settles down to normal again."

"What, more *Searchlight* scoops like *Cat Stranded up Tree in Helston*, or *Naturist Rampage in Sidmouth*?"

Nicky released him from her bear hug and elbowed him sharply in the ribs.

While her brother made a meal of his injury, she led him through to the kitchen, where they sat together at one of the two islands, Tedesco quick to note the half-empty bottle of chardonnay.

He declined the offer of 'just one', opting instead for a can of zero-alcohol lager.

This would do for now – he had some unfinished business with the Essential Waitrose claret to look forward to later.

"I assume this is one of your spur-of-the-moment, just-needed-to-get–away-from-the-horrors-of-life-in-the-Close-for-a-while visits?

"Anyway, we're always glad to see you," she went on, "and how is the canine hero of the hour? I expect he's got his own Twitter following by now."

"Don't even go there. Sally got a call from a foreign TV company angling for an exclusive with him."

He continued: "Apart from hearing about Barker's exploits, did you pick up anything else from the press pack?"

"Lynne was at the conference, so I asked her to supper once this is over, an invitation that will extend to you, of course."

"Sis," he sighed, "Lynne and I are just work colleagues, and that's the way it will stay. Change the record."

"Ooh, touchy!" Nicky said.

"Okay. They weren't giving anything away. They put up that wet media liaison guy, Luke Barnard. At least Julie Stringer was there to lighten the mood – she called me afterwards."

"What was 'Making her Mad' this time, I wonder?"

"Very droll. She was asking me, as a Cathedral School mum, if I had heard any rumours about Ellie's teacher, Mrs Tantum, and Ollie Canford.

"Oh, and Vicki Thomas is wondering if she should come forward about her encounter with Ollie after the carol service."

"Tell her to wait a day or two – but it might be good background – more evidence of Canford's inappropriate behaviour to women could underline how vulnerable he might have been to an angry husband, for example."

"Are you thinking of Ginny Tantum's husband? The yummy mummies at the school have been gossiping about her and Ollie for weeks. Some of them seem really jealous. They can't understand how mousy little Ginny has done it. Apparently, her old man is a total ogre and so she's been turning to Ollie for some good old southern comfort. Is it him, do you think, Charles Tantum?"

"In confidence – he's the number-one suspect, at least as far as DCI Bloomfield is concerned. But I have my doubts…"

Declining his sister's invitation to stay for supper, he gathered up a visibly exhausted border terrier then made the short journey home.

Chag Wills had been absent again, no doubt dining out on his wife's national media profile.

He returned home to the increasingly rare sound of his landline messaging service breaching the peace at 17 St Budeaux Place.

"All right, all right. Bloody thing," he moaned, struggling to remember how to play back the messages.

You. Have. One. Message. Bleep. Seven zero five pm. Bleep. Today. Bleep.

139

"Shut up, you stupid machine!" he shouted, Tedesco's equable temperament not extending to inanimate objects.

He managed to play back the message:

Oh, John. Sorry not to reach you. I think your mobile must be switched off.

"Correct, it's the weekend," Tedesco said to the answer machine, which continued:

It's Jimmy. I need to see you. I'll call round at nine tomorrow. Your place.

He attempted to return the call but had to leave a reciprocal message on Bloomfield's machine.

"That's fine, Jimmy. I will see you tomorrow. At 9.30."

He refilled Barker's dog bowl, microwaved his Waitrose curry and poured himself a glass of claret.

Just as he had settled down in front of *Have I Got News for You*, the phone rang.

"Sod it!" he exclaimed, as the ringing interrupted one of Paul Merton's flights of fancy.

It was Jimmy. "John. Got your message. I need all you have on the Master of Musick. And I'll split the difference with you: 9.15."

TWENTY-SIX

At least the 9.15 start gave Tedesco and Barker the chance to enjoy the first part of their weekend morning ritual.

As ever, Tedesco relished the walk over the bridge to the newsagents, which he saw as one of life's important little pleasures, irrespective of whether it was blowing a gale, snowing, there was a stifling heat wave, or if it was just another cool, grey Rhyminster day.

Wondering to himself how long printed newspapers would last, he lamented another treasured aspect of his cosy world that was about to fade away.

Bloomfield arrived at the stroke of 9.15, just as Tedesco was halfway through the *Weekend* section.

The lanky DCI welcomed the offer of tea, "Just as long as it's not in an Argyle mug.

"I'll bring my British Lions one next time," he said, accepting his drink in a vessel bearing the snappy slogan, *Ecclesiastical Law Society Conference Brighton 2006.*

Bloomfield offered Barker a playful stroke, referring to him as 'The Legend', which the terrier took in his stride, then it was down to business – Bloomfield had been through the photocopy of the counsel's notebook.

"I hate to admit it, but it was a pleasure to read. How did you learn to write like that? I suppose you spent years bent over one of those upright desks, scratching away with your quill."

Tedesco ignored the barbed compliment, allowing Bloomfield to carry on.

"So, John, you had identified Tantum as a possible suspect early doors. You know him better than I do. Is he capable of murder?"

The former Diocesan Registrar mulled for a moment.

Tantum was an arrogant snob, a selfish bully, an appalling husband and father, and far too fond of the sound of his foghorn-like voice. But was he a killer?

From what Tedesco had observed over the years, the Master of Musick loved the limelight, considered himself to be one of the main tourist attractions of the Close and would balk at doing anything to shatter this self-perpetuated illusion.

Charles Tantum would hate any adverse media attention and wouldn't risk a custodial sentence unless he was given his own suite of rooms complete with Michelin-starred chef, a butler and a temperature-controlled wine cellar.

Sensing that he wasn't going to get a quick answer, Bloomfield mentioned that there had been a significant development.

"Jools – DS Tagg – interviewed the vergers yesterday. The head guy looks like a Muppet—"

Tedesco cut him off.

"Roy Baird. I consider him to be a friend. And he resembles a hobbit, not a Muppet."

"Right you are. I stand corrected. Anyway, Mr Baird volunteered that when one of the guides was shown around the Chantry, Tantum came along for the ride."

Tedesco looked suitably enthralled.

"And here is the thing. Tantum, in a loud voice, announced that the Chantry would make an excellent place to dispose of a corpse. Apparently, if the body were to be discovered on All Souls' Day, this would be hilarious. What do you make of that?

"He'd come up with the idea of placing a body there – which seems a pretty bizarre notion – and now a corpse has been discovered."

"DCI Bloomfield, Charles Tantum always speaks in a loud voice. In fact, his attempts at whispering have been compared to an amplified recording of a nuclear explosion.

"His reference to All Souls' Day is interesting but may just be down to his childish attention-seeking."

Bloomfield made the 'It's gone over my head' gesture, so Tedesco patiently explained the significance of the festival in the Christian Calendar.

"All Souls' Day, Jimmy, is the Commemoration of All the Faithful Departed, and the Day of the Dead."

"Bloody hell!" was the DCI's considered response, before adding that he had another nugget to share with him: back in January, the police had been called to a disturbance in the Close.

"Guess where? At The Pelistry – the residence of the Master of Musick."

"I know where Tantum lives. Where are you going with this?"

"John – we have a motive. Young Canford – even if he wasn't knocking off Mrs Tantum, he was certainly paying her plenty of attention, and she seemed to be lapping it up."

Tedesco nodded, as if to say, 'So far so good'.

"Then we find that Charles Tantum is part of a select group who have been allowed inside the Cage, which he swiftly identified as the ideal hiding place for a body. Added to that, we've got the incident in January – evidence of his angry temper."

"What was that all about? I didn't hear anything about it at the time."

"It was a domestic. One of the neighbours thought they had heard Tantum threatening some people on the Green.

"The vergers were called, and they found some grammar-school boys engaged in a heated argument with Tantum near his house.

"When we arrived, he denied any wrongdoing, of course, and said that they'd just been enjoying a friendly discussion about chamber music, which is all teenage boys think about these days, obviously."

Bloomfield paused, very deliberately, before looking directly at Tedesco.

"John – is everyone in that cathedral a certifiable lunatic?"

"I would assess the oddball quotient at Rhyminster Cathedral as broadly similar to that of other established institutions. Such as the judiciary – or the police, for example."

"Touché," said Bloomfield, "but whatever you think, I reckon we've got our man."

TWENTY-SEVEN

Lynne, meanwhile, had already packed her overnight bag before setting off through the water meadows for Park Run.

She'd pick up a copy of the *Guardian* at the station later – give her something to read on the train.

As she arrived at King George Field, she spotted that Sally Munks was in charge of the registration desk.

Sally gave her an exaggerated wave and then wished her all the best in the Big City.

"It's only for the night, Sally," she replied, immediately regretting her brisk tone, and wondered when the loyal PA had last visited the capital – or indeed if she had ever been there.

Plenty of Lynne's old schoolmates had never ventured that far north: "We got tenpin bowling, night clubs and everything down 'ere – why go all the way up London?"

Actually, she reflected, Tedesco could be a little nativist at times – when had he last ventured outside the Diocese?

As Lynne regained her focus, Jo Luxmoore joined her for the warm-up and asked her if she would be coming to yoga on Wednesday, to which ex-DS Davey replied that she might have to be in London, but that otherwise she would love to – "I really enjoyed it the other night."

Then she scanned the crowd for signs of Ginny…

*

After DCI Bloomfield had safely exited St Budeaux Place, Tedesco busied himself with housework. He loathed mess, but he hated doing the cleaning as well. Perhaps Sally knew someone who might 'do' for him.

Barker couldn't bear the hoover, and barked at it until Tedesco had finished, then his master pottered about until it was time for lunch and *Football Focus*.

He had toyed with the idea of driving down to Plymouth to catch Argyle taking on the might of Shrewsbury, but he couldn't leave Barker, and wouldn't want to deprive them both of their weekly yomp, so once they'd eaten, and Dan Walker had yet again inexplicably failed to mention Argyle, they set off in silence, Tedesco eschewing both Radio D and C and his singer songwriters in favour of going over that morning's meeting with Bloomfield.

The DCI was still jumping to the 'bleeding obvious' conclusion, surely?

Tantum might be running about the place as if he had an arrow pointing at him marked 'Guilty', but Bloomfield seemed to be missing another explanation – that by suggesting the Chantry as a final resting place, Tantum could have inadvertently given the idea to someone else. The vergers had been there, of course – but then so had Richard Swain.

*

After Park Run – an improvement on last week's time – Lynne sought out Jo and asked her if she was going for coffee; having been non-committal about the yoga class, she didn't want her to think that she was cooling off their nascent friendship.

As it turned out, Jo seemed only too delighted to join her.

"I didn't see Ginny today, Jo."

"No," she responded, "I called on her this morning. As you know, she lives in The Pelistry – next door – and we sometimes share a car to the start, especially if it's raining, no point getting soaked before we start running. When I knocked on the door earlier, there was no response."

"Is that unusual?"

The Dean's wife looked around anxiously, as if the Rhyminster branch of Starbucks had been bugged by the KGB, or Ceausescu's secret police.

"Almost unheard-of during term time. My first thought was that Ginny had already set off on her bike – but then why was Tantum's Volvo missing? And where were Aldo and Ozzie?"

"Perhaps they play rugby on Saturday mornings," Lynne suggested.

"They do – but the Cathedral School grounds are just down the lane, so they wouldn't have needed a lift.

"Anyway, when I saw that there was no sign of life at The Pelistry, I began to wonder what was going on."

"What do you mean, Jo? Are you really suggesting that Tantum has done a runner with the family?

"Perhaps there's an innocent explanation – Aldo and Ozzie walked to rugby, and Charles and Ginny went to B & Q or whatever."

The concept of Tantum visiting a DIY store elicited a broad grin from the Dean's wife.

"He might have gone to his wine merchant, I suppose, or at a pinch, Waitrose. You are probably right, Lynne. I'm overthinking things – but this awful business with Ollie is making us all paranoid.

"Putting to one side the rumours about Ginny, Charles took against Ollie from day one, you know."

Jo added that the Cathedral was fully reopening for services today, and so Charles would be expected at Evensong: it was the turn of the boys' choir.

They swapped contact details, Jo promising to text Lynne if Tantum turned up.

This investigation always comes back to choirs, thought Lynne, as she cycled back through the water meadows.

TWENTY-EIGHT

At the last possible moment, Tedesco decided to turn off the road to the Tors and Moors, uncharacteristically opting for a change in routine.

They hadn't been up to the nature reserve at Rhyminster Down for ages, and there would be good views today – maybe some bird watching.

He pulled into the car park, which was surprisingly empty on such a lovely afternoon – well, if the masses want to be stuck in a retail shed off the ring road rather than enjoying the benefits of nature, more fool them, he thought, as he extracted his old binoculars from the boot, together with his ancient copy of the *Observer Book of Bird*s, which he had been given as the 'Progress Prize' at primary school.

Tedesco wasn't a serious twitcher but took an interest in everything around him – like any good detective.

Once he'd changed into his hiking boots, he let out Barker, put him on a long lead, locked the car then stretched for a minute and looked out over the reserve.

"We should come here more often, don't you think?" he asked Barker, who signalled agreement by dragging Tedesco off to the nearest path.

Seeing that there were no grazing animals today, Barker

could be liberated to retrieve sticks of varying shapes and sizes, while his master took in deep breaths of the sparkling air and cleared his head.

As they climbed up Prysten Hill, Tedesco pointed out that the three counties were visible today; this made very little impression on his companion.

Suddenly remembering that he had his binoculars, Tedesco reached into his barn jacket, pulled them out, dusted off the lens and surveyed the landscape – the deep south-west was displaying its rich autumnal colours, and the contrast between the rugged moorland and the lush river valley below never failed to move him.

He could just about make out a couple of ramblers, one walking ahead of the other, his agitated stride conveying a distinct lack of patience with his dawdling colleague.

Something about this couple piqued his interest, so he focused the binoculars on the lead walker.

"If it isn't our old friend Mr Swain," he muttered to himself, as he turned the bins towards the dawdler.

And what do we have here? The lesser spotted Colin Scopes, if I'm not mistaken.

How very interesting…

It was soon time to round up Barker, who had exhausted his limited reserves of enthusiasm for the stick game.

"What does he think I am – a puppy?"

Tedesco led his beloved friend back down the hill towards the car park and turned on the car radio.

Argyle were heading for a nil-nil draw at Home Park.

Feeling a sense of disappointment – albeit mixed with relief at not having to drive back from Plymouth after such a poor match – he started the car and headed back to Rhyminster.

TWENTY-NINE

Just as Tedesco was heading for home, Lynne was checking in at the Travelodge, which had been converted from a Victorian hospital for foundlings, so displayed rather more character than the average budget hotel.

She had factored in ample time for a hot shower, followed by a snooze, before she had to think of changing. Having originally wondered about her favourite leather skirt, she decided to leave it behind in Water Lane, as on reflection it might be a little much for her first encounter with the choir.

Instead, she had opted for a pair of designer jeans from TK Maxx – no one would know – and her favourite red silk shirt, with matching heels.

As it was a balmy evening, she decided to walk across Westminster Bridge, briefly stopping to look down at the lights of the capital, calm before the oncoming Saturday night storm, then she flagged down a cab and was soon arriving at the Gallery in Lupus Street, the venue for her social event of the year.

A barman pointed the way to the upstairs function room, where she was relieved to find that it was already filling up.

A tall, studious-looking blonde spotted her and came over to greet her on arrival – it was Charlotte, the helpful membership secretary.

Displaying all the well-honed skills of the professional host, she guided Lynne towards a small group who were taking up one of the quieter corners of the room, effected introductions, and then glided off in search of other first-timers.

"So! You must be the new recruit from Rhyminster. Are you going to tell us what really happened to Oliver?"

"Ignore him," said a pleasant-sounding woman in an expensive-looking velvet jacket.

"I'm Ros, and this is my partner, Alasdair."

They chatted for a few minutes – Lynne was not at all surprised to learn that Alasdair was in investment management, nor that Ros was in TV production – before Ros took her off to meet Hugh.

Hugh Aglionby was the concert secretary.

Around Tedesco's vintage, she guessed, fifties or early sixties, blue blazer and chinos, expensive loafers, Tod's maybe.

Aglionby and Ros both interrogated her about Canford – obviously, the choir was reeling at the news – and they wanted to know about her choral experience and why she wanted to join the Tuneful Company.

Lynne had prepared her cover story well.

She worked in digital marketing, and as most of her accounts were in London, she was spending much of the week there.

Then she explained about Rhyme in Rhythm, how she was having to miss rehearsals due to being late back from town – adding, pretty convincingly she thought, that she needed to stretch herself musically.

This went down very well and allowed Aglionby the space to drone on about how superb his choir was, and how much they were looking forward to starting rehearsals for the *Christmas Oratorio*.

"I do wonder if I am up to your standards, Hugh, but Charlotte tells me that you are short of altos. And I have sung the *Oratorio* with my local choir, in the Cathedral."

"Don't worry – Oliver was always rude about the Rhyminster choir, but I know they have a growing reputation. Is it right that he fell out with your conductor?"

Before she could decide on how to answer Aglionby, whose fruity and condescending tones were starting to wind her up, the wonderful Charlotte scooped her up to meet some of the other singers.

The Minstrels and their guests proved to be charming, some genuinely so, and Lynne was starting to enjoy the feeling of being, for one night only, part of the 'metropolitan elite' that she had read so much about.

They might be a touch precious, but they made a refreshing change from the petty provincialism she often encountered back home. Perhaps there really was more to life than tenpin bowling.

Her enjoyment was cut short by the booming voice of a new arrival who was being led through the crowd by Charlotte like a prize bull in the parade ring.

"Lynne – look who's here!"

She wouldn't be getting a text from Jo Luxmoore after all – Charles Tantum was standing directly opposite her, stuffing his face with canapés, his disgusting mouth and jaw movements resembling the mechanical doors of a bin lorry opening wide to crush another helping of refuse.

It really was him, the great Charles Tantum – at the Gallery in Lupus Street, light years away from The Pelistry. What the hell was he doing here?

THIRTY

Upon his return to the Ancient Liberty, Tedesco checked up on the final score from Home Park – it had ended goalless.

Listening to his messages, he saw that Nigel Brimacombe had been in touch, and Bishop Bob had enquired as to whether he wanted to pop over later.

He called the North Canonry first.

Hilary answered, and having established that they had a Saturday-evening gap between Bob's bit of rubbish, *Pointless Celebrities,* and her equivalent, *Strictly,* he agreed to pop round at around the same time as the previous Saturday. Hilary made him promise to make sure that Barker joined him this time.

Then he called Brimacombe.

After sharing a ritual moan about the toothless Argyle strike force, the medic told him that the post-mortem results would be announced on Monday, but he would gladly offer Tedesco a heads-up now: as he had guessed, Canford had been sedated several hours before being struck on the back of his head.

"It looks like the anaesthetic was ammonia. And the weapon would have been extremely heavy in order to crush that part of the skull."

"I know it's not your area, Nige, but did they find any sign of the weapon in the Cathedral?"

Brimacombe replied that while there had been a painstaking search of the main building and the Close, no weapon had yet been found. The search had been hampered by objections from one of the residents on libertarian grounds.

"I wonder who that could have been, Nige."

His fellow Argyle fan added that although there were several artefacts in the Cathedral that were more than capable of doing serious damage, they were kept secure – it was like Fort Knox in the Treasury – and there had been no sign of any blood or prints on any of them.

THIRTY-ONE

Back in Pimlico, Lynne Davey, never knowingly overwhelmed, was nevertheless rendered speechless at the sudden appearance of Tantum's blob-like countenance.

The Master of Musick seemed equally perplexed, as evidenced by his quivering jowls.

Lynne composed herself. "Charles! What a pleasant surprise!"

Tantum roared back, "I could say the SAME!"

Alasdair, summoned by Tantum's stentorian tones, joined the group, and explained that Hugh Aglionby had been trying for some time to arrange for the Minstrels to perform at one of the Cathedral's musical fundraisers.

"When Oliver announced that he was moving to Rhyminster, Hugh thought he'd struck gold – Oliver should be able to ease the way, as it were."

Ros had followed her partner across the room and added that Canford had been surprisingly unreceptive, even hostile, to the idea of using his connections. "Perhaps he didn't want to come over as pushy."

Lynne bit her tongue.

Ros then explained that upon hearing of Oliver's tragic

death, Hugh had contacted the Dean to propose a memorial concert for their young friend.

Dean Dan was very receptive and put Aglionby in touch with the Master of Musick.

Alasdair leapt in: "It really was a no-brainer – Oliver had been a stalwart of the Minstrels and he had fallen in love with his new surroundings – so it would make perfect sense for us to come and honour his memory in your beautiful cathedral.

"The Dean felt that it would help the community to heal."

"What did you think, Charles?" asked Lynne, while reminding herself that the new surroundings weren't all that Canford had fallen for.

"Er, well, I thought it was a SPLENDID idea, of course," he spluttered, while choking on a vol-au-vent, "and I learnt that Hugh had been to my Cambridge college. A fellow King's man!"

"We invited Charles up to town so that we could start the ball rolling – always helps to meet socially, oils the wheels," said Tony, a way-too-smooth partner with one of the 'Magic Circle' law firms.

As the conversation started to wane, people drifted off to mingle with other groups, and so Lynne, perhaps inevitably, found herself alone with Tantum.

"Okay, Charles. Let's cut the crap, shall we? You should have been in the Cathedral this evening. What are you really doing up here? And what have you done with Ginny and the boys?"

"I could ask you the same question, Mrs Davey. What the hell are you doing here? Why aren't you back in Rhyminster, eking out your lonely TV dinner?"

Ignoring his customary boorishness, she pressed him for an answer.

"Come on, Charles. This doesn't look good. Remind me

again – what do you call our hosts?"

"'The Woeful Company of Wankers'. But that was just to annoy Canford. As you will have seen, he was always droning on about them, used to drive me insane."

"So now you've seen the light. But where is Ginny? What about the boys?"

"Sorry to blow your latest conspiracy theory, but they are in Wandsworth, staying with my sister. Great excuse for a treat. Aldo and Ozzie went on the London Eye earlier."

"Okay – so what about Evensong?"

"It was a said service tonight – no choir, due to the disappearance of that ghastly cretin Canford."

"I think you will find that he was murdered, Charles. By the way, I saw Jo earlier – she seemed pretty convinced that the choir were singing Evensong. I can easily check."

"Are you still in the CID? I don't think so. And so what if they are singing? The Precentor will step in, and to be really, really boring, you still haven't explained what you are doing here. Have you even ventured this far north before tonight?"

Lynne looked him straight in the eye.

"Charles. I was invited by Charlotte. And I am genuinely interested in joining the Minstrels – I need to move on from Rhyme in Rhythm. Bloody stupid name. And they are conducted by an egotistical martinet."

"I'll sue you for slander!"

"Charles. You don't frighten me – sorry to disappoint. I think it would be wise to accept my explanation at face value, don't you? Especially if you expect me to reciprocate. Are you with me?"

Tantum harrumphed, before going in search of more beige food to soak up the booze.

THIRTY-TWO

Tedesco, accompanied by his faithful friend, strolled round to the North Canonry, his shoes crunching on the gravel drive like a noisy eater with a bowl of cornflakes.

This alerted Hilary, who was waiting for them when they reached the main door.

She made a huge fuss of Barker – "You can come and help me in the kitchen while your master discusses some deadly boring stuff with my husband."

Barker trotted off with his customary eagerness, leaving Tedesco to find his own way to the private quarters.

"John – this is becoming a regular fixture," said Bishop Bob, by way of greeting.

"Jos Elsted dropped off a bottle of St Emilion the other day. I'm sure he'd value your opinion," he continued, pouring Tedesco a generous glass.

Jos was a small-scale wine merchant who had moved into the Close a few months ago, following the death of his partner, James.

Tedesco had only met him once but had marked him down as a good bloke.

"Anyway," Bob said, "before you pronounce on the wonder of God's vinicultural bounty, where exactly are we with Canford?"

Tedesco summarised the position – basically that while Bloomfield was convinced that Tantum was the obvious culprit, he still harboured serious doubts.

"So, John, apart from the gossip about Ginny Tantum and Oliver, what is Bloomfield basing his case on?"

"A previous pattern of behaviour – don't forget that the police were called to The Pelistry as recently as January."

The Bishop interrupted. "Do you – or indeed Jimmy Bloomfield – actually know why the police were called?"

"Some sort of arcane argument with a few Bishop Lunt's boys, that's what I heard."

"That must be the sanitised version. The real reason that the officers were called in was due to an argument that Tantum was having over the use of drones in the Close."

"'Drones in the Close'– sounds like a typical *Searchlight* item, or one of Julie's 'It Makes Me Mad' pieces in the local rag," Tedesco commented, smiling to himself.

"I agree, it does sound far-fetched – but it is the Master of Musick we're talking about. Bear with me, it's priceless.

"Early that morning, two chaps were about to launch a drone from the Green, directly opposite The Pelistry, but before they could release it, they were confronted by the gruesome sight of Tantum in his dressing gown and slippers advancing towards them with menaces."

At this point, Tedesco requested a top-up of the excellent claret – it sounded like he might need it.

The Bishop went on: "Tantum was flapping his arms about, telling the poor chaps that what they were about to do was 'against the law of the land', repeating the point ever louder as he advanced closer to them.

"As he continued to berate the pair, some Bishop Lunt's

160

boys were wandering through the Close on their way to school.

"Once they had spotted Tantum in his nightwear, they started pointing at him, shouting stuff like, 'We know what you've been doing,' 'You dirty old perv.' I'm sure you get the picture."

The Bishop waited for Tedesco to stop giggling, then recommenced.

"Of course, Tantum immediately turned on the lads. He asked them if they were accusing him of playing with himself, and then proceeded to inform them that onanism was not against the law of the land, unlike the flying of drones in the vicinity of a listed building."

"Well – he may have had a point," Tedesco said.

"Things looked like turning nasty, not least because Tantum's dressing gown was in imminent danger of flying open, and so someone summoned the vergers. They quickly decided that this was beyond their pay grade and called the police.

"A couple of young officers managed to calm the situation. It transpired that the drone operatives were within their rights, as they had been hired by the Cathedral to take aerial pictures of the tower as part of the repair process.

"Of course, Tantum was characteristically ungracious and moaned about lack of respect for the law of the land for weeks afterwards – and I think he wrote a nasty letter to the headmaster, threatening to sue Bishop Lunt's for allowing its pupils to defame him."

"Okay," said Tedesco, once he'd stopped sniggering, "so I think we can discount the January incident as evidence of murderous intent on Charles' part.

"But Bloomfield has a much stronger point. The real problem for Tantum is that he is one of the select few to have gained access to the Rhyme Chantry."

"How come? I don't imagine that he moves in the same circles as the Earl."

Tedesco explained that – according to the gospel account of Roy Baird – one of the tour guides was writing a detailed history of the Cathedral, and that said guide had expressed a keen interest in seeing inside the 'Cage' as part of his research.

Tantum just so happened to have been in the vestry on the day when the Chantry was opened up, and so he tagged along.

"Roy told the police that Tantum had stood in the Chantry, spread his arms wide and announced that this would make an excellent spot to leave a body, preferably on All Souls' Day."

The Bishop took a sip of Jos Elsted's velvety claret.

"Would Tantum really be stupid enough to suggest this in public if he intended to do away with Canford in this way?"

"Difficult to know with him – but my initial thought was that someone might have overheard him and decided to act on it, having the perfect alibi that Tantum had been heard making his macabre suggestion by several witnesses."

"The whole county could have overheard him, John."

"I was thinking about the tour guide – Richard Swain.

"However, there's been another development that might lead Bloomfield to conclude that Tantum did it – Lynne advises me that his entire family has gone AWOL, no sign of them at The Pelistry or anywhere."

"That is odd. Come to think of it, I saw Dean Dan in the Close earlier – Charles hadn't turned up for Evensong. This isn't looking great for him, is it?"

"I agree," added Tedesco, "but I just can't visualise Tantum as a cold-blooded killer – can you?"

"Hmm. There may be many mansions in God's kingdom, but I do struggle sometimes to imagine where Tantum might be housed... he is a nightmare – but no, probably not a killer."

The Bishop glanced at the clock on the mantelpiece. Supper was half an hour away.

"Tell me about your Swain theory."

Tedesco swirled his wine glass appreciatively, put it down again, and laid out his initial case against the Cathedral guide.

"Simply put, his name keeps cropping up. I have never been one for gut feelings, but there was something about him that bothered me from the first time I saw him, when Liz Gerrey introduced us in the cloisters.

"Since then, Lynne and I have spotted them together at the Beach Shack near Modbury."

The Bishop raised an episcopal eyebrow at this.

Tedesco noticed, and then carried on.

"And I have seen him having lunch with one of the vergers on a couple of occasions. I saw them again this afternoon, walking on Rhyminster Down."

"Why shouldn't Swain be friendly with a verger?"

"Because it's Colin Scopes. Nobody has ever befriended poor old Colin, and unless Swain is a genuinely good Samaritan, I can't see why he would choose to spend so much time with him. Especially if it could be spent with someone like Mrs Gerrey."

"Okay, John. What else can you tell me about Swain, apart from his interest in history?"

"Liz Gerrey introduced him to me as a retired civil servant, but I have since discovered that this was underplaying it somewhat.

"He was quite senior and ended up at the Chemical Weapons Research station at Porton Down.

"More interestingly, the Salisbury Registrar tells me that he was a thorn in the side of Jane Le Prevost."

"In what way?"

"He is resolutely opposed to women bishops, stopped volunteering at the Cathedral up there when Jane was appointed as Dean, used to write nasty letters to the local press, joined a hard-line anti-women church, the usual stuff.

"The final straw was when he completed the first draft of his history of the Cathedral – the last chapter was just a vitriolic, libellous attack on Dean Jane.

"No publisher would touch it. The Registrar and the Chancellor, armed with strong counsel's opinion, threatened an injunction if he tried to self-publish it without removing the offending words."

"So the book was never published. I see, but none of this links him to Canford, does it? Unless he was jealous of him because of Liz? You must have heard the rumours?"

"Of course, although I have never given them any credence. I guess that she may have enjoyed Oliver's attentions – and might even have enjoyed getting up the elegant noses of the Ladies of the Close – but I couldn't imagine anything serious between them."

"Nor me. As you know, Hilary and Liz are good friends, and from what I have observed, Liz is still grieving for Roddy. That said, I'm surprised that she would be seen dead with a misogynist like Swain – assuming she knows of his antediluvian opinions."

"But don't forget – what does link Swain to Canford is the Chantry," said Tedesco, looking serious, as if to emphasise that this was tonight's key message.

Hilary Dwyer entered at this point, followed by Barker, who had evidently been a great help with the supper preparation.

Correctly taking it as his cue to end the meeting, Tedesco got up, and Hilary and Bob came down the staircase with him.

As they reached the front door, Hilary gave the helpful terrier a gentle stroke and suggested that as the Cathedral had a College of Canons, perhaps they should start a College of Canines, of which Barker would be the founder member.

Choosing to ignore this, Bob – who didn't really do whimsy – commiserated with Tedesco over Argyle's dismal 0-0 draw, Hilary adding that Tedesco must come to supper soon, and that he should bring Lynne with him.

As the door of the Bishop's palace creaked shut behind them, Barker found a familiar tree to pee against, before completing the short walk home with his human companion.

"Well, Barker," said his master, "it's bad enough my sister trying to matchmake – now it's the Bishop's wife as well."

Once over the threshold of number 17, Tedesco heated up some chilli for himself and gave Barker his supper.

He made a note in the little book he kept by the phone: *Let Jos know the claret was superb,* then settled down to watch *Strictly*. His moment of peace didn't last long, as John Sousa blared out.

It was Lynne. "Am I interrupting anything? Is that Bruno Tonioli I can hear?"

"Guilty pleasure. How's the Smoke?"

"Smokin'. Listen, you will never guess who I saw tonight – Tantum!"

"What? With the Tuneful Company? I thought he despised them."

"I'll explain later. I need to go back in but thought you'd want to know. I've texted Jimmy as well."

"Good move. Lynne, please be careful. It looks like I might have underestimated Tantum. Let me know when you're on the train tomorrow, and I'll pick you up from the station."

Tedesco decided to give *Match of the Day* a miss, as Shearer was on again, and he could use the extra sleep, as long as he could stop worrying about Lynne…

*

Having checked out of the budget hotel early the next morning, still buzzing after her rare foray into the world of the urban elite, Lynne went for a walk along the deserted South Bank, stopping for an espresso at a pop-up kiosk, relishing the quiet of the hungover city.

She took the tube at Embankment, changed at Oxford Circus for Paddington – making it just in time to buy the *Observer* and a croissant before catching the 8.15 to Penzance – then once safely on board, she messaged Tedesco, let him know she was okay and, all being well, should be arriving in Rhyminster three hours later.

Three hours of premium me-time, she thought, leafing through the *Review* section as the train glided through the home counties.

She was largely successful in tuning out of work worries, but as the welcoming tower of Rhyminster Cathedral came into view she felt herself switch back on again, remembering to call Tedesco to let him know that her train was on time and wondering again to herself what Tantum had really been doing in Pimlico.

THIRTY-THREE

While Lynne was admiring the early-morning views across the Thames, Tedesco was out with Barker on their ritual walk, interrupting it to call Bloomfield, as it occurred to him that although Lynne had already texted the DCI about Tantum, Jimmy really ought to know about Swain's latest meeting with Scopes.

Bloomfield was already up and about, as he was due to take his son to play rugby just over the border with Cornwall – but he was happy to call round and see Tedesco for a late breakfast, as long as his lad Gavin could tag along.

"That's fine, Jimmy. I'm sure Barker will keep him entertained – and Lynne will be joining us."

Tedesco spent the first part of the morning meticulously updating the counsel's notebook, before breaking off to send a positive wine review to Jos Elsted then, seeing the time, he left Barker to chill in the garden while he went to collect Lynne in the Lancia.

In accordance with his punctual nature, Tedesco had allowed an extra few minutes to find a parking space at the station, but this being a Sunday, he needn't have worried, so he was able to snatch a blissful ten minutes of *Desert Island*

Discs before wandering over to the forecourt to meet Lynne off the train.

Tedesco's gentle eyes watched her as she eased through the ticket barrier, then he offered to take her bag as she came through.

He left it until they had exited the car park before offering her a late breakfast at St Budeaux Place.

"Do I have a choice?" she said.

He replied that it was more of a working brunch, and that Bloomfield and son were joining them – so that would mean a quick detour to Rhyminster's new branch of Waitrose to get some fresh bread and cold cuts.

Tedesco took the opportunity to share another Tantum story. The Master of Musick had been overheard during the usual Fairtrade coffee get-together after the main Sunday service justifying why he chose to pay more to shop at Waitrose: "I'm more than happy to pay TSAT – Tattooed Scum Avoidance Tax!"

Lynne said that entitled snobbery was no laughing matter and that there was no need for overpriced staples today – she had plenty of salad in the fridge and always kept a loaf in the freezer. And anyway, how did Tedesco know that she didn't have a tattoo?

Her friend and colleague chose to ignore that one but was unable to conceal his reflex blush.

So they briefly stopped off at Water Lane, arriving at St Budeaux Place as the Cathedral clock struck twelve, to be greeted by an impatient DCI Bloomfield and his mud-splattered son, who were kicking their heels on the cobbles.

Gavin was a tall lad but stockier than his father.

His face dissolved into a broad grin at the sight of Barker, and he was more than happy to stay in the little walled garden and throw tennis balls for his new friend to retrieve while his dad did police stuff.

"Thanks a bunch, John – he's been pestering us about getting a dog for months," said the DCI, with feeling.

Tedesco disappeared off into the kitchen to heat up the bread and brew yet another pot of coffee.

Bloomfield wouldn't need much to eat, as he was having a roast dinner later – and Gavin could certainly wait till then.

As her partner busied himself in the kitchen, Lynne took her former colleague through the events of the previous evening.

Bloomfield listened intently, jumping to the conclusion that Tantum's sudden appearance at the Gallery couldn't have been a coincidence.

"Funny how he didn't tell anyone at the Cathedral that he was going away – and we would never have found him if you hadn't been up there at the same time," he said, somewhat accusingly.

"Actually – just what were you doing yesterday evening?" he asked her.

As Tedesco came through with the coffee, she looked over at him for reassurance, before responding.

"We think there might be a choral link here. Tantum is Master of Musick and runs a local choir. Canford belonged to a rather smart singing group in London, which is where he was on the night he disappeared."

Tedesco took over. "So Lynne managed to charm her way into an invitation to one of the London choir's social gatherings, which took place last night."

Bloomfield took a gulp of his coffee. "Holy shit, that's

strong. Look, I think I get why you were there, Lynne, but it still doesn't explain Tantum's presence. Did he know that you were going to be at this cocktail party or whatever? How did he manage to infiltrate what I take to be an exclusive gathering?"

While Lynne considered her response, Tedesco reflected that while he had initially written off Tantum as the prime suspect – way too obvious – he had to admit that the sudden evacuation of the Tantum brood from The Pelistry, followed by the shock appearance in Pimlico, had given him pause for thought.

He may act the buffoon, but was Tantum cleverer, and more dangerous, than he had first assumed?

"Jimmy," said Lynne, "you want to know what Tantum was doing up there. One of the singers told me that they had invited Tantum to discuss the staging of a memorial concert for Oliver at the Cathedral.

"It was explained to me, plausibly, I think, that as Canford had links to both organisations, the Tuneful Company had decided to approach Dean Dan with the idea, which he had referred on to Charles."

She paused to take a sip of coffee.

"It's not that strong, DCI Bloomfield. Anyway, Tantum thought the musical tribute was a good idea. He contacted the concert secretary, who, naturally enough, had been at the same Cambridge college.

"And, lo and behold, Tantum was invited to Pimlico to meet the choir and get things moving."

"Hold on," Tedesco said, "Tantum is always incredibly rude about the Tuneful Company of What-Nots. Has something happened to change his mind, do you think?"

"Apart from hitting it off with Hugh Aglionby, his fellow college man, you mean?"

She waited for a reaction and, seeing none, carried on.

"Tantum – totally pissed by then – told me that it wasn't the London choir he despised, but the fact that Canford kept harping on about them. To be fair, I've been present when Canford has waxed lyrical about 'the Minstrels' while simultaneously doing down our own little group – it used to wind us all up."

"All sounds a bit too glib, too convenient to me," said Bloomfield.

Tedesco, nodding in agreement, asked Lynne if Tantum had told her where he was staying the previous evening.

"In Wandsworth, with his sister. I did think it odd that Ginny wasn't with him at the party, but I expect they both relished a night off from each other."

"Okay, we can check out the sister if he doesn't turn up here," noted Bloomfield.

"You might want to talk to the Cathedral School – the boys will be expected back tomorrow, as will Ginny – she teaches there, don't forget."

Tedesco decided to keep the meeting between Swain and Scopes on Rhyminster Down to himself for now.

Let's see how the Tantum saga pans out...

Although he still found Tantum an unlikely potential murderer, he had to agree with Bloomfield that the bombastic Master of Musick was doing himself no favours.

Bloomfield rounded up Gavin, much to his and Barker's chagrin. It would be even harder to put the lad off dogs now that he had met the legendary border terrier, and as father and son headed off together for their Sunday roast, Bloomfield promised to keep the private investigators in the loop about Tantum.

THIRTY-FOUR

Tedesco and Lynne took their barely touched salads out into the garden.

Neither of them fancied wine – she was starting to feel the effects of the night before, and he knew that even a single glass would write off the afternoon.

"How's it been down on the farm then?" she said, smiling.

"Get you, the urban sophisticate. Jimmy came round first thing yesterday – he was after some background on Tantum. Then Barker joined me on our weekly yomp."

"Dartmoor?"

Tedesco explained that he had felt a last-minute urge to vary the routine, and so they had driven to Rhyminster Down, taking the binoculars for some low-key bird watching.

"Any interesting sightings?"

"No protected species on view – unless you include Swain and Scopes."

Lynne leaned forward, eager to hear more.

"I saw them in the distance, heading back to the little gravel car park."

"Hmm. This bread is helping with the lingering hangover, but way too many calories – I'll get the bike out later.

"John – is it really beyond the realms of possibility that

Scopes and Swain are simply good mates? They're both single, into cathedrals and other weird stuff, and they are both – how can I put this nicely? – a wee bit sad."

"I'd agree with you about Colin, Lynne, but remember when we saw Swain with Liz Gerrey?

"I can't see her going out with a real saddo, can you, even if they are just friends?"

"I can't talk about poor taste in men," Lynne replied, with more than a touch of regret.

"John, I brushed off Jimmy's point about Ginny not being there last night. They might have wanted an evening away from each other, but from what Jo tells me, things have calmed down between them, so at first I was a bit surprised that he'd left Ginny with his sister, but if you'd seen Tantum last night, he was back to his usual brash self – he was out to get wasted."

Tedesco momentarily thought about protectively reaching across to hold her hand – as usual, his head trumped his heart.

"Lynne, if you are going out for a ride this afternoon could you take a break at the station?"

"You want me to chat up the cabbies again, I assume?"

"You've come back from that there London a right old cynic – but yes, that is what I had in mind. They have been shown pictures of Canford and Swain, but I don't know if Bloomfield has organised pictures of the others."

"You mean the rest of the gang who saw the Chantry? Tantum, Scopes and the hobbit lookalike."

"Roy Baird, that's right. I've printed off photos of them from the 'Our People' section of the Cathedral website. I'd do my own dirty work, but as you know Mickey Hunn of old…"

174

"O-kay then," she replied, shoulders slumping in mock indignation, "I will see what I can do."

"And," she added, "I can simply download the photos onto my smartphone, you old technophobe. Wasting paper again!"

Tedesco dropped Lynne back home, leaving Barker behind – the terrier was comprehensively wiped out, exhausted from entertaining Gavin.

On his return journey from Water Lane, Tedesco took a gentle detour around the Close towards The Pelistry. There was a police car parked a discreet distance away, which suggested that the Tantums had failed to return.

Observing that Barker remained comatose, he took a deckchair outside and spent a pleasant hour with his Sunday paper.

He read a positive review of a Roy Lichtenstein retrospective that had just opened at Tate Modern. Now that Lynne had caught the metropolitan bug, perhaps they could have a day up there together once this case was done and dusted. He hadn't been in London for a good while.

His daydream was invaded by the Argyle theme. *It must be work*, he thought, so he was pleasantly surprised to hear his sister's familiar "Hi, Bro."

After conclusion of the ritual pleasantries, it transpired that the call was work-related after all.

His delightful brother-in-law, Chag Will, was 'not a happy bunny'.

Nicky reminded him that Chag had sold the Triumph Stag to the late Oliver Canford. Canford hadn't paid the full amount, and so Chag was furious, wondering how he'd get his money back.

"A man has been murdered, Nicola. Listen, I don't mean

to criticise your husband, but what is a few hundred pounds compared to a man's life?"

"It was rather more than a few quid, John. Christ, I'm actually trying to help you here!"

"Sorry, Nicky – it must have been hard for you to call me – but you're surely not suggesting that Chag had anything to do with Canford's disappearance, are you?"

"I don't know what to think anymore." She closed the call.

Tedesco put his head in his hands, as if in deep prayer, and then made a note in the casebook.

He refused to believe that his brother-in-law was involved in murder – but could he have been behind the disappearance?

It was just possible. Although as the world's biggest atheist, Chag Wills tended to avoid cathedrals...

*

There was a fresher feel to the air as Lynne reprised her familiar circuit through the water meadows. Any traces of the night before had vanished by the time she reached the cab rank at Rhyminster Station.

No sign of Mickey Hunn, but Dane Keetch was there, leaning on the bonnet of his car, clearly bored out of his wits on a slow travel day.

Only too happy to go through the images on Lynne's phone, he recognised Tantum straight away – "Everyone in Rhyme knows that knobhead" – but struggled at first with the pictures of the vergers.

However, something made him take a second peek at one of them, peering intently at the posed shot for the Cathedral website.

He tapped the phone then scratched his head.

"I am sure I have seen this geezer somewhere – yeah, I'm positive. It was him that picked up Canford that night."

"Are you sure, Dane? Final answer?"

"Yeah, final answer – no need to phone a friend."

Keetch was staring at the image of Colin Scopes.

"Dane, this could be significant. Will you confirm this to the police?"

"Do I have a choice?"

Lynne got back on her bike, cycled home to Water Lane and took a long hot shower before calling Tedesco and messaging Bloomfield.

THIRTY-FIVE

Bloomfield was driven straight down to the Close as soon as Lovell reported fresh signs of life at The Pelistry.

Ginny, even more flustered than normal, came running at the sound of Bloomfield's urgent banging at the centuries-old door knocker.

She led the officers through to the kitchen, a stuffy, airless expanse which looked as if it could do with a deep clean, where her husband was dominating the room, noisily pouring himself a large gin and tonic.

He slowly turned to face them, like an overloaded passenger ferry reversing out of a tight harbour.

"What in Heaven's name are you doing invading my privacy on a Sunday evening? This is against the law of the land."

Lovell, a keen cricketer, decided to open the batting cautiously, in an effort to fend off Tantum's hostile opening spell.

"We are terribly sorry to be disturbing you this evening, sir. You will be aware of the sad death of Oliver Canford, and we just need you to help us with a few enquiries. It won't take long."

Lovell was taken aback by the sheer force of the Master of Musick's response:

"WHY on GOD'S EARTH do you want to ask me about little Canford? Sad death, you say? Sad death? Nothing remotely sad about it. Horrid, sly little pustule of a man. I know absolutely nothing about this – or, to put it in language that blockheads like you can understand, I know NAFF ALL!"

Tantum looked around the room, as if expecting rapturous applause.

Bloomfield remained silent for what seemed like several minutes, before calmly explaining to the Master of Musick that he and Lovell were politely asking him to assist with enquiries, and that this was prompted by the fact that he had been one of the few people who had been admitted to the Rhyme Chantry, where Canford had been discovered.

Tantum was not being singled out – far from it – as the others who had been inside the Chantry had either been questioned, or were about to be.

Tantum sighed, then took a huge gulp of G and T and yawned loudly.

"I've heard more than enough of your nonsense. You are the guilty ones – guilty of wasting your own police time.

"So! As it doesn't say in Luke Chapter Five beginning at Verse One, Get orf moi land before I sets moi hounds on you!"

Ginny scurried into the kitchen like an anxious dormouse.

"Charles! What on earth do you think you are doing? I know you had nothing to do with poor Ollie – but why can't you be public-spirited for once and help the officers?"

And you can spare us the patronising West Country accent, you stuck-up dick, Bloomfield thought to himself before he waded in.

"You would be well advised to listen to your wife, sir. The sooner you co-operate with us, then the sooner we can leave you in peace."

Tantum glanced across at Ginny, then took a decisive step towards Lovell, invading his personal space.

"All right," he said with a sneer. "I will assist you with your pathetic enquiries. But I want my lawyer present when I do."

"Very well, sir. We will be in touch, as they say. Good evening to you both. DC Lovell and I will see ourselves out."

Lovell drove Bloomfield home in the squad car, the usual force issue Skoda Octavia.

"Wow, DC Lovell. Quite a performance, don't you think?"

"I'm not sure, sir. He did seem genuine to me."

"Fair point – it's sometimes difficult to tell with these artistic types – but he has made a huge rod for his own back, admitting that he couldn't stand Canford and that he was pleased to see the back of him."

"I'm no churchgoer, sir, but don't you think it strange that the Cathedral employs someone like Tantum? He doesn't seem very Christian, does he?"

"I know what you mean. John Tedesco has tried to explain to me about Tantum's status – apparently he's got a job for life. No one can get rid of him unless he is found guilty of gross moral turpitude, thanks to some ancient law dating from when the Cathedral was a monastery.

"Anyway," he continued, "there is one thing I've learnt since coming to Rhyminster. That magnificent edifice acts like a magnet to some of the strangest people imaginable."

Lovell dropped his boss off at his home in Derrington, an anonymous four-bedroom estate house in an anonymous suburb of Rhyminster.

They both agreed that the following day was going to be another tricky one.

Rachel Bloomfield greeted her husband with the news that "Your pretty ex-colleague wants a call back – she said it was important."

"I assume you mean Lynne Davey," said Bloomfield, somewhat tetchily.

He got straight through to Water Lane.

"Jimmy, I don't know if you've interviewed him yet, but one of the taxi drivers with Towercabs, Dane Keetch, recognised a photo of one of the vergers, Colin Scopes.

"He is convinced that it was Scopes who he saw picking up Canford from Rhyminster Station. I've told him to expect a call."

"Why did we ever let you go, DS Davey?"

"Ask my ex-husband. Anyway, I hope this is useful."

Lynne's ex, Doug, was still with the force.

"Okay, Lynne – quid pro quo – Tantum has just resurfaced – Matt and I have been to see him. He's admitted to loathing Canford, and that he wasn't upset at his death. Not looking good for him. Not good at all."

"I'll keep it under my hat, apart from John, of course. See you at the press conference tomorrow. Jools told me, so I've taken that as my invite."

She called Tedesco, just as he was about to run his Sunday evening bath, sharing with him the news of Tantum's return and the taxi driver's revelation about the identity of Canford's mystery chauffeur. It might prove hard to sleep tonight – so she returned to her trusted *Borgen* box set.

Meanwhile, barely a mile away, the centuries-old walls of The Pelistry shook to the sound of Charles Tantum on speakerphone to one of his best friends from university, Maxwell Patrick, QC, MP.

Ginny had disappeared upstairs to check on the boys – Aldhelm and Osmund had rooms on the far side of the vast residence, but as Max Patrick rivalled her husband in the Brian Blessed vocal stakes, she wanted to check that they had managed to get to sleep – it was still a school night, whatever else was going on in their parents' world.

Patrick was the Member of Parliament for a vast tract of Somerset, his majority as massive as his brief fees.

The eminent QC summed up his advice to his client as 'Shock and Awe'.

"Agree to see the local plod but get yourself the best lawyer you can. You should go overboard – I'll do it, or if I'm booked, then I'll send one of the eager young reptiles from my Bristol set.

"That should scare the shit out of the straw munchers – I will get Frank to call you in the morning. Don't do anything, and don't say anything, until then."

Frank was Clerk to Patrick's chambers. His father had been Clerk before him, and 'Young Frank' would weave his magic to make sure that Tantum got the 'overboard' representation that the Queen's Counsel had prescribed.

THIRTY-SIX

Barker was still feeling groggy as his master dragged him out for an exceptionally early woof around the deserted Close.

Tantum's car was back – abandoned rather than parked, as usual – and a light was on in the Deanery.

The only sign of outside activity was on Cathedral Green, where the media circus had started to reassemble for that morning's hastily announced press briefing.

A bleary-eyed young man wearing a fleece with 'Crew' emblazoned on the back was doing something complicated with gaffer tape, but there was no sign of Nicky or any of her *Searchlight* team. *Perhaps they'll send the great Vicki Thomas,* mused Tedesco.

He carefully led Barker down Rounsevell Lane, one of a myriad of mews and alleys discreetly sited off the main Close road, and thus invisible to the gawping hordes of selfie stick-wielding tourists.

The vergers' house was to be found there – a sixties monstrosity incongruously wedged between two listed properties, both of which had been ruinously sold to private owners in the 1980s by the Dean and Chapter at the time.

One of these elegant townhouses even boasted shiny new 'Sod Off' iron gates.

"How the hell did the Council grant permission for those?" Tedesco wondered aloud.

The lane was a cul-de-sac with a little parking area at the far end, home to an incongruous mix of vehicles, and while some of them might be considered brand and age-appropriate for vergers, there was no sign of a small red hatchback among the muddle of stationary cars.

"Barker – sit!" commanded Tedesco. "We need to lurk here for a while."

Tedesco and his terrier crouched behind a large SUV, presumably belonging to a guest visiting one of the listed houses.

"Patience, old friend, one of them will appear soon."

On the stroke of seven, the new verger, Izzie, the first female to have the role in the Cathedral's 900-year history – newly arrived in Rhyminster after a spell of verging at St Giles, Edinburgh – trotted down the front steps of the hostel, followed five minutes later by a preoccupied-looking Colin Scopes.

Tedesco and Barker bided their time, then wandered quietly across the dewy Green.

The southern entrance was open to admit the small group of worshippers for early-morning prayers, so Barker was able to squeeze through the door, followed by his master.

The Cathedral appeared to be deserted, but Tedesco, seeing that lights were on in the vestry, ignored the *No Entry* sign and strolled into what he always thought of as the engine room of the ancient building.

Roy Baird's little cave was empty, but as he overheard Colin and Izzie chatting in the main vestry, he made the most of his opportunity.

"Colin! I was just taking Barker for a walk around the Close before the media descend, and I saw that the lights were on."

"Oh, I see. We are just getting ready for morning prayer."

"How's it been, with all the cameras, and so on?"

Scopes replied that the Cathedral had seen worse – Cromwell, plagues, wars...

Tedesco stopped Colin in mid-flow in order to introduce himself to Izzie, who was entranced by the dog.

"Mum and Dad have got a wee border – Otto."

While Izzie got to know Barker, Tedesco took the opportunity to question her colleague.

"Colin – is it true that choral Evensong is back on the agenda now?"

"Oh yes – we started again on Saturday – the boys' choir. Mr Tantum wasn't there, so the Precentor took over."

"And I'm sure he made an exceptionally good job of it. Anyway, good to see you both."

As he turned to leave, he hesitated as if he'd forgotten something.

"Sorry – I meant to say – Barker and I wandered down Rounsevell Lane earlier. Very fancy car parked there. Not yours, I suppose?"

Scopes smiled, somewhat warily.

"Alas no, Mr Tedesco. I rely on my trusty old bicycle – no real need for a car in this job, not that I could afford one."

"So, Barker," he said as they wandered off towards Minster Precincts, "either the taxi driver got the identification wrong, or Colin is hiding something."

*

185

Throughout his working life, Tedesco had never seen the point of commuting.

However, one downside to living so near the office was that he was lumbered with setting the alarm, listening to the answering machine and opening the post.

He was always surprised at how much physical post still arrived – Rhyminster ran a few steps behind societal change, but it still seemed odd.

After gathering up the pile of letters that had accumulated over the weekend, he switched on the kettle, logging on to his PC while it boiled.

The early-morning peace of the office was comprehensively wrecked by the sound of Sally Munks blundering her way up the stairs with her customary but baffling collection of carrier bags, containing who knew what.

"Good morning, you two! Shall I make the coffee as the kettle's just boiled?

"I wanted a word with you, Mr T – you haven't started training for Walk for the Wards yet!"

"I'm afraid it had completely slipped my mind – but don't worry, Barker and I will make sure we get ourselves fit in plenty of time."

He accepted the coffee with due grace, then busied himself with emails. Jos Elsted had sent him an elegantly worded note of thanks for the positive wine review, inviting him to his pre-Christmas tasting.

Tedesco had no hesitation in accepting, praying that it might clash with Sally's aforementioned charity walk or, even better, Tantum's ridiculous wassail party.

Gill Withers had sent him a useful summary of a recent case on undue influence, which could be helpful in the disputed will investigation, serving to remind him that his other cases still required his attention, tempting as it was to focus on Canford.

That good intention lasted until he heard Lynne running up the stairs.

She had already cleared her weekend emails at home, and so they moved into the meeting room and got down to business on the *cause célèbre*.

Lynne immediately raised an eyebrow at Tedesco's latest revelation – that Scopes didn't have transport, despite having been identified as the driver of the hatchback by Dane Keetch.

"So, if Colin hasn't got a car, then either Keetch is wrong or lying, neither of which sounds plausible."

"Unless someone allowed Scopes to drive their car?"

"Why would anyone lend Colin a car, just to pick someone up from the station? It makes no sense."

"Lynne, nothing about this case makes sense at the moment. Roy Baird has got an ancient Renault, but it's the wrong colour."

"Could Scopes have hired a motor? But why?"

Tedesco got up, stretched, and surveyed the red rooftops of Rhyminster.

"Bit of lateral thinking. I know you think I'm obsessed with Swain, but he and Scopes are clearly enjoying some sort of bromance.

"I saw Liz Gerrey wafting through the Close on Friday – might it be worth a word with her, see if she can confirm what Swain drives?"

"A bit contrived, but I think a chat with the Merry Widow would be in order. I haven't spoken to her since her offer to fund our investigation, so I'll suggest coffee and a catch-up."

"Of course," said Tedesco, "this may all be a waste of energy if Bloomfield thinks they've already got enough on Tantum. He has as good as admitted to Jimmy that he had it in for Oliver, and let's not forget that he came up with the brilliant wheeze of leaving the body in the Chantry."

"Let's see what goes down at the press conference. My guess is that Bloomfield will want to give the media some red meat, so I expect an announcement that they have identified a strong suspect, or something along those lines."

"Even if it is Tantum – and I still think it's a big if – he couldn't have manoeuvred Canford into the Cage without some help. So I think we still need to understand how Oliver got from Rhyminster Station to his medieval Airbnb in the Cathedral."

"Exactly," Lynne said. "It must have been a two-man job."

While Lynne got ready to wander over to the Chapter House, Tedesco decided to follow another lead.

Returning to his desktop, he googled 'Chag Wills Aspirational Cars'.

As he clicked on the website, Tedesco found a highly professional showcase for his brother-in-law's business.

It was packed with references to 'quality marques', 'carefully chosen for the discerning motorist', complete with a cascade of glowing testimonials from Wills' 'high-net-worth' clients.

He knew that Canford enjoyed the high life, but how could he afford these prices? And how come Chag hadn't taken the full amount for the Stag?

There was nothing about the availability of finance deals on this website. The message was clear: if you need a car loan, we don't need you.

However, as he scrolled the usual drop-down menu, it transpired that if you looked hard enough, Aspirational Cars were just as happy to flog you a used Mondeo as a classic Morgan.

After clicking on the button marked 'Small hatchbacks', Tedesco found Golf Polos, Seat Leons and Fiat 500s.

He assumed that these were available as runarounds for the wives, or as first cars for the offspring of Chag's golf club cronies.

As Lynne made to leave, Tedesco asked her to see if Nicky was at the press conference and, if so, could she ask his sister to pop over to the office later?

THIRTY-SEVEN

As the sundry media representatives squeezed into the ancient meeting place, Julie Stringer rushed forward to nab herself a front-row seat, while Lynne, spotting Nicky on the other side of the room, made the 'Call me' sign, which she hoped she'd pick up on.

Bloomfield made his familiar opening statement, before introducing Nigel Brimacombe to the media.

The medic gravely confirmed that Oliver Canford had been killed with a single blow to the back of his head with a heavy instrument.

He paused to allow this to sink in, before adding that prior to the blow being struck, Canford had been rendered unconscious by the use of chloroform; the strong signs were that he had been in an unconscious state for several hours before he was attacked with the murder weapon.

Once Brimacombe had concluded his summary, Bloomfield handed over to Luke Barnard, who acted as MC for a brief question-and-answer session.

Bloomfield and Brimacombe dealt smoothly with the predictable points, confirming that despite a thorough search, there was still no sign of a murder weapon, and they had been unable to establish why Canford had been drugged and then left for several hours before being despatched.

Julie had been persistently waving her hand at Barnard, like the show-off kid who knew the right answer.

"Julie! Good to see you. What's making you mad this morning?" said Barnard.

Bad move, thought Lynne. *Never take the mick out of the home team.*

"Good to see you too, Luke," said Julie, with the faintest hint at flirtation.

"Listen, is there any truth in the rumour that you have already identified a prime suspect, and that it is a prominent member of the Cathedral community?"

There was a collective intake of breath, followed by an audible murmuring from the press pack.

"I'd better take this one," Bloomfield whispered to Barnard.

"Thank you for your question, Julie. You should know me well enough to realise that as soon as we have anything to share with you, we will of course do so. An individual is helping us with our enquiries, but that's as much as I can say for the moment."

Barnard used this as his excuse to bring proceedings to a close, and as the audience filed out, Bloomfield went in search of Julia Tagg, whom he found lurking at the exit with Matt Lovell.

"Jools – what's the latest on Tantum?"

"He's agreed to talk to us with his lawyer present. He reckons he has hired a shit-hot QC who will blow us out of the water. Anyway, he's due here at 2.30 this afternoon."

"You and I will see him, with or without Rumpole of the Bailey. Meet me here an hour before they land – by the way, hot news – Lynne tells me that Colin Scopes, that quiet little verger, might have been the one who gave Canford a lift from the station. One of the guys at the taxi rank identified him. Could you go and see Colin before we reconvene?"

Tagg readily agreed – "He won't be hard to find."

*

As Lynne meandered through Cathedral Green on the way back to the office, she spotted Julie deep in conversation with Liz Gerrey, so she went over and barged in.

"Sorry to interrupt, Julie, but can I have a word with Liz? In private."

Julie, never one to take umbrage, scuttled off in search of other potential sources of gossip.

"Liz – how are you? You must be devastated."

"First Roddy, then Oliver. I am beginning to think that it's something to do with this place," said Liz, gazing warily up at the tower.

"Fancy a break? I could do with one."

*

DS Julia Tagg was by now a familiar presence in the Cathedral, so Colin Scopes was unsurprised when she moved towards him as he was repositioning a lectern.

"Sorry to disturb you again, Colin. I just need to ask you a few questions about Oliver Canford. Could you come over to the Chapter House?"

Scopes had been expecting this – he had helped to unravel the body, after all. Nevertheless, he was sweating profusely as he explained that he would need to ask his colleague to cover for him – he dashed into the vestry, eventually emerging with Izzie, who had agreed to carry on with the scene shifting, or whatever he had been up to.

Julia's attempts at small talk were stubbornly resisted as they walked the short distance to the pop-up Operations Room.

Lovell was guarding the door when they arrived, so Tagg asked one of the ever-helpful sidesmen if he could man the door for a while; she needed Lovell to go with her.

The three of them entered one of the rapidly installed interview pods and then DS Tagg made the formal introductions, thanking Colin for his co-operation.

"Don't look so worried, Colin. We just need to understand where you were on the night that Oliver disappeared."

"Oh. Okay. I was here. In the Cathedral. There had been a function. We get a lot of them these days."

"I gather there are a number of corporate events hosted here."

Scopes grimaced – "Yes, there are. It means a lot of extra work for our small team. At this time of year, a lot of the schools have speech days, or prize–givings. It was the grammar school that night – Bishop Lunt's."

"I see," said Lovell, gently, "that was my old school – so what time did you leave?"

Tagg thought she detected the briefest hint of panic before Scopes answered: "It was late. Extremely late. The place was packed. Our MP, Sir Vere Alston, was there, the Mayor, hundreds of parents – you would not believe the mess they left, orders of service and hymn books all over the floor."

"I see, so could you place a time on when you were able to go home?"

"One of the old boys gave the main speech, which must have gone on for an hour, and the prize-giving itself takes an age, so the building didn't empty until after eleven.

"Then there was the clearing up – all the chairs have to be moved out of the way for the next day, so the tourists can wander around."

"So it would have been after midnight?" asked Lovell.

"Easily. I was the last one to leave. I checked the building and locked up."

"Gosh," Julia said disarmingly, "and I thought we worked long hours!"

She went on – "Tell me, Colin, do you have a car?"

"That's funny. Mr Tedesco asked me that this morning. No, I don't. I passed my test years ago – at the fourth attempt, I'm ashamed to say – but I haven't needed to drive in this job, not that I could afford to."

Julia leaned in. "Colin, would it surprise you to hear that someone matching your description was seen outside the railway station in the early hours of Thursday morning, not long after the prize-giving service?"

Lovell joined in. "Colin, this person was spotted meeting Oliver Canford off a late train from London, and then he offered him a lift. In a small red car."

Scopes looked as if he was going to pass out, so Tagg went to the refectory for a glass of water, which she handed to the traumatised verger.

"I am sorry. I genuinely can't handle this – I feel sick. Can I go now?"

Tagg looked across to Lovell. Scopes wasn't going to

escape. And they weren't going to risk an accusation of obtaining evidence under duress.

"Okay. But we do need answers to these questions. I am sure that you want to find out who killed Oliver as much as we do."

"Of course I do. I'm just not used to this. I have to take pills for my nerves!"

They let him go for now, having secured his solemn promise not to leave Rhyminster without telling them – "Of course, but I never leave here."

The verger found himself a quiet bench in the cloisters, then called Swain on the special phone he had been given by him.

The guide and amateur historian was nothing if not clear, barking out his orders with staccato urgency.

"Say nothing without a solicitor. Did they offer you the duty guy? If they do, don't accept it.

"Leave me to arrange representation. Now get back to work. Tagg won't let you alone for long. Meet me in the Rhyminster Arms after Evensong. And ditch the phone. Drop it in the river on your way to the pub."

*

Lynne Davey and Liz Gerrey decided that Kaye's Kitchen, just off Southgate Street, would be the ideal place for a discreet catch-up.

Over two floors, and in an architectural style best described as Beams 'R' Us, there were plenty of concealed nooks and crannies where you could avoid eavesdroppers and prying eyes.

Lynne ordered an espresso, while Liz opted for a black americano.

"One thing I miss – decent coffee," said Liz. "It's not too bad in this place, but we were spoilt in Morningside."

"You must have wondered what I was doing on the Green," she continued.

Lynne let her carry on.

"The truth is, I tend to spend a lot of my time in the Cathedral and the Close. It's partly a comfort thing – but I hoped that I might pick up something from the reporters this morning."

She went on – "He, Oliver, doesn't have any family, you know, so who is going to organise a funeral? And where? It wouldn't feel right, holding it here, where he died. What do you think?"

Lynne decided not to mention the plans for a memorial concert that she had heard about on Saturday, opting to switch the subject.

"I'll see if John knows anything about the funeral, but I doubt if much will happen while the investigation is ongoing. On a lighter note, I couldn't help noticing your car parked in the Close. I'm quite jealous!"

Liz smiled. "It was Roddy's pride and joy – and now it's mine, and every time I drive it, it brings him back in a small way. When we arrived here, Roddy was told about this wonderful firm, Aspirational Cars."

Lynne laughed. "John Tedesco's sister is married to the owner, small world!"

"No, really? They were very discreet, so professional. I remember Roddy saying that Mr Wills was the first honest car salesman he had met!"

Lynne took this in – she now had Liz Gerrey, Chag and Canford on the same Venn diagram, but where did they intersect?

"I'm so sorry, Liz, I didn't mean to drag you over here to talk about cars – what was I thinking of – but you don't happen to know what Richard drives? I just wondered, as I've only ever seen him in yours."

The Widow suddenly appeared less than Merry.

"Why on earth do you want to…? Oh well, no skin off my nose. Richard sold his car. He's been banned for totting up twelve points on his licence. For six months, but I think it ends soon."

THIRTY-EIGHT

Earlier that morning, Ginny Tantum answered the old-fashioned dial-up telephone which stood on an antique table in the entrance hall at The Pelistry.

"Mrs Tantum? Sorry to disturb you. I am Frank, Mr Patrick's clerk. Is your husband available?"

"I know what it's about – and he's expecting your call."

Before she could summon him, she became aware of a thundering sound like racehorses nearing the finishing line as her husband clattered down the stairs.

He rudely grabbed the receiver from her.

"Tantum! What news?"

"Mr Patrick needs to be within reach of the Old Bailey this morning, so I have arranged for one of his colleagues to represent you today. Mr Rajesh Purbani, who is based at our Chambers Annexe in Bristol."

"Does he know what he is doing? Does he know who I am?"

"I have taken the liberty of attaching Mr Purbani's profile to an email this morning, sir. I am sure that this will reassure you. Mr Patrick has fully briefed him, and he is well aware of the particular delicacies in this matter, bearing in mind your local prominence."

While this seemed to pacify the Master of Musick, any peace proved to be short-lived.

"Mr Purbani will be travelling by rail today, and he would be grateful if you could arrange for him to be collected from Rhyminster Station at 1.15 this afternoon."

"What does he think I am, a bespoke fucking taxi service!"

"No, sir, but time is short, and it might be advisable for you to have access to your representative at the earliest opportunity."

Tantum slammed the phone down and summoned Ginny to help him open the PDF file that Frank had attached.

"IT department! I need you! Now!"

Ginny easily opened the attachment before rushing out of the door, late for school.

*

Tedesco was on the phone to his sister when he heard the familiar sound of Lynne rushing up the stairs just as the Cathedral bells rang out to signal noon.

Nicky had called him in response to Lynne's manic gesticulation at the press conference, and agreed to join her brother and his dog on their daily walk, as long as they didn't object to this modification of their legendary routine.

Once her partner had ended his call, Lynne swiftly brought him up to date.

"Nige had already given us a heads-up on the post-mortem, so no surprises there. However, Julie Stringer managed to get Jimmy to admit that they had a suspect – and he didn't deny that it was someone linked to the Cathedral."

"So it must be Tantum."

"Jimmy messaged me – they're seeing him this afternoon."

"I know I'm sounding like a cracked record, but isn't it still a bit premature, Lynne? I know Jimmy will be under pressure from above, the media and who knows else, but unless they can link Tantum to Scopes and his taxi service, how did he get the body into the Cathedral?"

"I agree. Nige thinks you would need at least two men to move a corpse from the Close into the Chantry," said Lynne.

"And by the way, I've just had a coffee with Liz Gerrey. I brought up the subject of her beloved Merc – guess who sourced it."

"Not my esteemed brother-in-law by any chance?"

"How did you guess? And she told me about Swain's wheels. He hasn't got any – he's been banned for six months."

*

Tedesco and Barker met Nicky at their prearranged meeting place at the Butter Cross, conveniently situated opposite Jenks bakery.

As it was a Monday, he opted for a suitably routine cheese and tomato, while Nicky opted for a vegan salad box.

"So you cater for New Age cranks now, Joan?" said Tedesco, provoking a sisterly glare.

"Just ignore him, Joan – I do." Joan told Nicky how much she enjoyed *Searchlight*.

Rhyme was busy for a Monday, and benches in the Close were at a premium, so after completing a quick circuit, they headed back to Minster Precincts for an *al desko* lunch.

"Okay, master detective. What was so urgent?"

He put down his half-eaten sandwich.

"Apart from the pleasure of your company? Well – and this is strictly off the record – Lynne and I have it on good authority that Canford was picked up at the train station on the night he disappeared.

"He was driven off in a red hatchback, and we suspect that the driver might be on the Cathedral staff.

"But – and this is the strange thing – the staff member we are looking at doesn't even own a car."

"Hang on," Nicky interjected, "so what has this got to do with me?"

"I'm coming to that. You told us that Chag had arranged the Triumph Stag for Canford, and that Oliver still owed him on it. Liz Gerrey told us that her husband's Merc came from Aspirational Cars as well."

Nicky shrugged. "And your point is, exactly…"

Tedesco carried on: "Bit of a long shot, but Chag doesn't have a spare Red Suzuki hanging around the forecourt, does he?"

"Search me, guv. I don't pay close attention to my husband's nefarious dealings."

"Think, Nicola. I know that little runarounds might not be Chag's core business, but if you look closely on his website, you can find Minis and so forth."

"Yeah – he sometimes gets requests for a 'uni car' for one of his clients' entitled brats. Hang on a second, let me think. They do keep a couple of pool cars. They use them when they deliver to customers."

"What do you mean?"

"One of the salesmen, or Chag himself if the new owner is a celeb, delivers the prestige motor, while a minion follows at a safe distance. The minion gives the sales guy a lift back in the pool car."

"And…?"

"I'm pretty sure one of these cars is a small red hatchback."

"Nicky," said Tedesco, "I know that it's your husband's business we are talking about, and this is the longest of long shots, but is there any way you could find out the make of the pool car?"

"I'll have a go. But keep my name out of this. Promise?"

THIRTY-NINE

Spaces were at a premium at the station car park. Raj Purbani, looking as if he had been poured into his crisp Savile Row suit, was anxiously scanning the forecourt for any sign of his lift when a thunderous voice grabbed his urgent attention.

"Now you listen to me, you blithering idiot. I know that this space is reserved for the so-called disabled community, but as no one of that description appears to require it, then I am well within my rights!"

Purbani edged nervously towards the developing fracas.

"Excuse me, are you Mr Tantum?"

"Ah, Mr Purbani, I presume! Well met, sir! Just in time to settle this little dispute."

"Oh, I see, you mean about the parking space – we really don't have any time to waste. Can we drive off now?"

Tantum opened the passenger door with a theatrical flourish, before driving his passenger towards the Close at breakneck speed.

"I'm really sorry about that. Where do the Great Western Railway find these little counter jumpers?"

Horrified tourists scattered in all directions as Tantum hurtled into the Cathedral Precincts, bringing the Volvo to an abrupt halt outside The Pelistry.

"We can be private in here," he told his counsel, indicating his magnificent residence.

And I thought Max Patrick was a dinosaur, Purbani thought to himself as he followed Tantum into the Georgian splendour of the Master's house.

*

Nicky didn't hang around. One of the news reporters, Danny Trainor, who had joined Searchlight *for a six-month spell from BBC Ulster, was at a bit of a loose end.*

On the pretext that Searchlight *was going to run an investigation into the murky world of used car dealerships, Trainor was more than happy to pose as a car buyer.*

As instructed, he called Aspirational Cars and told them that he was a colleague of George Sutton. Sutton was the owner of Rhyme Valley Dairies, and a close friend of Chag's.

Trainor explained that he and his wife had just started a family and that they needed a little car to help with the nursery run.

He knew that Aspirational Cars dealt with the very top of the range, but Mr Sutton had suggested they may be able to help.

"Okay, sir," said Bob Pooley, Chag's trusted number two, before going on to ask the young broadcaster about his budget and which type of car he was thinking of.

Pooley, initially lukewarm, suddenly remembered something.

"We do have a car that might work for you – if you don't mind an ex–demonstrator. We have a Skoda Fabia, which we've used as one of our pool cars.

"It's in good condition, low mileage, and we will give it a full valet and service before delivery, as we do with all our Aspirational Cars.

"We've lent it to one of our best customers for a few days, but it will be available soon. It might be just what you need, Mr Trainor, so why don't I send you a photo of it?"

Trainor didn't have long to wait before his inbox pinged. He opened the attachment – the little car was bright red.

*

Over at The Pelistry, Tantum led Purbani into his vast, untidy study, the room dominated by what Purbani took to be an ancient harpsichord.

"It's a spinet, of course," said Tantum.

"I like your choice of tie – episcopal purple – selected for the occasion, I assume," he added.

The barrister, calling time on this flummery, pointedly asked Tantum why the police would think that he was involved in the disappearance and subsequent murder of Oliver Canford.

Tantum, unused to direct questions, resorted to bluster.

"I have no idea. No idea at all. There are a lot of small-minded, jealous, thick people down here."

"Let me assist you. You admit that you visited the probable scene of the murder. What were you doing there?"

Tantum looked as if he were about to self-combust.

"AS I TOLD MAX – I just happened to be in the vestry when one of the guides was about to be shown round the Chantry.

"I'd always assumed that entry was restricted to the Earl

and his family, so I took the opportunity to have a look inside. Why does this make me a criminal? Why?"

Purbani made a show of consulting his brief.

"Yes, I see that the Chantry is still the property of the Earls of Rhyminster – fascinating."

He turned to face his client.

"So – what exactly took place in the Chantry?"

"Oh, well, we just looked around. The guide who requested the visit is a bit strange. He's obsessed with history and kept talking about the exquisite motifs carved on the roof. Yawn!

"He's writing a history of the Cathedral. Should be a real page-turner."

"And did you comment on what you saw?"

"Only that the Chantry would make a marvellous place to leave a body."

*

Nicky forwarded copies of the photo of the Skoda to Tedesco and Bloomfield. The number plate was clear as day. Her brother would ask Lynne to show the image to Dane Keetch and his mates.

*

As Purbani walked across Cathedral Green with his client, he repeated his advice to be civil to the officers and reminded him that until he was charged with an offence, he was free to go at any time, underlining to Tantum that if he had doubts about answering any of the questions, he should request a moment to consult his counsel.

Privately, Purbani was cursing Maxwell Patrick, QC, MP. His esteemed Head of Chambers had sold him a hospital pass with this one.

Bloomfield and Tagg sat on one side of the table, Tantum and Purbani the other.

After the polite conclusion of the formalities, Bloomfield asked Tantum why he had visited the Chantry.

Purbani was mightily relieved to see that his client had listened to his advice, giving a clear and calm explanation, even managing a decent stab at fending off the incriminating comment about the suitability of the Cage as host to a dead body.

"I thought I was being frightfully amusing, but with hindsight I can now see that my comment might have been considered less than appropriate."

Things went downhill when Tagg took over the questioning – if Tantum was uncomfortable with direct questions, his pain was greatly enhanced if the questioner was female.

"You didn't like Mr Canford, did you?"

Before Purbani could object, Tantum detonated.

"That's an understatement. He was a pimple, who became a pustule, and then a boil!"

"And boils have to be lanced, don't they?" said Tagg.

Purbani glared at her, before addressing his client.

"You don't have to respond. That wasn't a question. It was asking you for your opinion."

He turned and stared at Tagg. "That calls for speculation, DS Tagg. I think my client has been more than co-operative, and so unless you have some new evidence, or, indeed, any evidence, I think we should leave."

Bloomfield adopted a conciliatory approach.

"Your counsel is quite right, Mr Tantum. You are free to go. But I think it would be helpful to all of us if you could just confirm where you were on the Wednesday night before Mr Canford disappeared."

"Well, if this eliminates me as a suspect, I can confirm that I was at home."

"You weren't in the Cathedral? I understand that the Grammar School Prize-Giving was taking place."

Tantum shrugged. "No, I was not there. It is one of the most boring events in Christendom unless your own child is up for a prize.

"And our dear leader, *Dean Dan the Preacher Man*" – Tantum practically spat out each syllable – "has made it crystal clear that he doesn't want me anywhere near the great and the good!"

Give that dean a medal, thought Purbani.

Just as they were getting up to leave, Tagg chanced her arm with a further question.

"Just what were you doing in London on Saturday evening, Mr Tantum?"

FORTY

The Rhyminster Arms is the oldest pub in town. The oak beams are rumoured to have come from early sailing vessels, and the masons who worked on the Cathedral were said to have lodged there.

Of course, the Tourist Board included it in their 'Haunted Rhyme' programme, and the pub offered 'Shiver Me Timbers' tee-shirts alongside its selection of real ales.

Scopes, entering the old inn at precisely 6.30, had no need of any branding to advertise the fact that he was shaking like a leaf.

Swain, who had arrived early in order to nab the 'Wedge', a tiny snug area for two where privacy was assured, stood up and frantically waved at the verger.

"Come here and sit down, Colin! And do stop shaking!" hissed Swain as Scopes joined him. "This will calm you down."

Swain had ordered two pints of Bishop's Brew, the strongest of the ales in the Rhyme Brewery range.

"I don't normally drink," the verger whimpered.

"What about all that communion wine?" responded Swain.

Then he explained how he had arranged for Colin to be represented by Paula Fordham, a solicitor from a large regional firm with an office in Exeter – sufficiently far removed from the gossip pit of the Cathedral and its environs – and that he would, of course, cover the cost.

"I don't know, Richard. You've been a real friend, but I just don't think I can handle any of this anymore."

"Oh yes, you can. And you will. Look, neither of us killed Canford – and we genuinely don't know who did – probably that puffball Tantum."

Scopes nervously sipped his beer. He didn't like it but tried to look as if he did.

"Look, Colin, the police are circling, but they haven't found a murder weapon yet. All they know about our little adventure is that a random taxi driver thinks he might have spotted you at the station, and then saw you drive off with Canford."

"So you want me to lie, tell them it was mistaken identity or else that it was too dark to see clearly?"

Swain was exasperated. "Listen to me. I am paying for a top lawyer – take her advice and you will be fine. Colin, you are giving me a migraine. Are you listening?"

Scopes took another reluctant sip. He may have been listening, but he looked more at sea than ever.

"What about the car?"

"What about it? We've been through this a million times. Listen to Paula – but your story is that, as Izzie has replaced Peter, you were worried that you might have to drive for your work.

"She hasn't got her licence, Christ knows why, and Roy will be retiring soon."

"I know. Roy takes the choir to their concerts when they are on tour, and so I will be expected to drive the minibus – and I have hardly driven since I passed my test, so you kindly offered to help me get used to traffic again, especially driving in the dark."

"Something like that, but again, listen to Paula."

"But what about the car? I really don't know who it belongs to – I know it isn't yours."

Swain grabbed him by the shoulders, bringing his face level with that of his companion.

"No, Colin, you don't know who owns the car. And don't speculate. Tell me again what I've told you to say about Wednesday night," he added.

"Well, you let me keep the car near the vergers' hostel that evening, and so I thought I would go for a late drive on my own, after clearing up after the prize-giving. I decided on the station because I wanted to check some train times."

"Colin. As I said, Paula will help you, but if it gets this far – unless they throw out the cabbie's evidence – you will be asked why you didn't check the train times online, or go back in the morning when the travel centre opens."

"That's easy. I had a torch and could read the times off the departure boards in the forecourt. And I don't really do online."

"Coming from anyone else, this would sound ridiculous. From you, Colin, it has the indisputable ring of truth."

Swain let him go, then ordered himself a scotch.

Whether the police believed Colin or not might not be crucial to him. There was nothing to link them to the events of that night, and now that his ban had expired, he could return the little runaround to Chag Wills. Aspirational Cars would thoroughly valet the Skoda, so there wouldn't be any traces of either of them.

He swilled down the remains of his pint. Everything would be fine – as long as Colin didn't break down.

FORTY-ONE

The early risers among the denizens of the Cathedral community were greeted by the somehow beautifully eerie sight of the tower shrouded in mist.

It was still drizzling when Tedesco and Barker went for their pre-breakfast inspection of the Close.

Tedesco rather enjoyed the bittersweet tone of this weather – it reminded him of those soft rainy days in south-west Cork during his early twenties, when he realised that he had fallen in love for the first and only time.

After tea, toast and the *Today* programme, he and Barker wandered over to Minster Precincts, where Sally lay in wait, clipboard in hand.

"Good morning, both! You still haven't signed up to the training programme yet – for the Walk, remember?"

Tedesco raised his hands in mock surrender and signed his name, then hearing the sound of Lynne rushing up the stairs, he waited for her on the landing.

"Meeting room again?" she said, reading his mind.

"So," Lynne started, "Dane thinks that the red car could have been the Fabia in the photo from Aspirational Cars. I spoke to Bloomfield last night to let him know, and he exchanged a few highlights from the interview with Charles Tantum – as expected, he'd hired a hot-shot barrister.

"A quick search confirmed that Mr Rajesh Purbani is a member of the Chambers of Maxwell Patrick."

Tedesco cut in: "Fat Pat has been MP for most of Somerset for as long as I can remember. I bet he's an old schoolmate of Tantum's."

"Old uni pals, actually. Same Cambridge college. Twitter reveals that Purbani is active in local politics, and there are persistent rumours that Patrick is lining him up as his successor."

"Isn't British democracy a wonder to behold, Lynne?"

"Anyway," she went on, slightly impatiently, "Tantum had been well muzzled by his brief but threw his toys out of the pram when he was asked to explain why he wasn't invited to the Bishop Lunt's prize-giving, and whether he liked Canford.

"Then he refused to answer Julia's classic last question, 'What were you doing in London on Saturday night?'"

"Does Jimmy still think it's him?"

"He's got motive, he admits that he loathed Canford and that he suggested the Chantry as a burial place. But they still have no murder weapon, and this business with Scopes and the late-night pick-up might be giving our favourite DCI second thoughts."

"Okay. I'm going to see Bishop Bob later this morning to keep him in the picture."

"There is something else," said Lynne. "I've been doing some background checks on the officers of the Tuneful Company of Minstrels. Hugh Aglionby, the urbane concert secretary, was indeed a civil servant, as he told me on Saturday. Extremely high-ranking – and he spent some time in Porton Down in his earlier days."

"So he might have known our friend Swain? Good work, Mrs Davey."

"Didn't have you down as a patronising git – anyway, I'm in two minds whether to go back to London on Wednesday and try out for the *Christmas Oratorio*, or to give Jo's yoga class another go."

"Mmm. I'd avoid London if I were you. If Aglionby is an old university friend of Tantum's, then he will know Max Patrick – quite the old establishment network. If he doesn't already suspect your motives surrounding the choir, then a second visit will surely put him on his guard. Perhaps we can find a way of mentioning his name within earshot of Swain."

Leaving his partner to ponder her choir/yoga dilemma, he asked a delighted Sally if she could take Barker for his walk today.

*

Arriving a touch early for his meeting with the Bishop, Tedesco had to kick his heels for a further twenty minutes while Bob's meeting with the Diocesan Secretary moved well into added time.

There were worse places to hang around, Tedesco thought, as he accepted Barbara Battershill's welcome offer of refreshments.

"No Barker today?" said the Bishop's impeccably groomed PA. "You really must bring him next time. I haven't seen him in ages."

"He's in great demand, Barbara – and his social diary is fuller than mine," he added, with a hint of self-pity.

Bishop Bob eventually emerged from his study, closely followed by Amanda Leonard, the power behind the throne, who treated Tedesco to a tight little smile before scuttling off in her six-inch heels.

He pitied whichever churchwarden, rural dean or parish priest she had in her sights.

"Sorry to keep you waiting, John," said the Bishop, "a couple of problem parishes – you remember them?"

"Of course, still not paying their share into the diocesan coffers, I suppose?"

"How did you guess? As usual, it's the wealthy ones who object the most. Oh well, *plus ça change*."

Bob guided him to the now-familiar window seat overlooking the Cathedral.

"Before you bring me up to speed, John, I may have something useful about Richard Swain."

Tedesco smiled. "Is it linked to his time in Salisbury, by any chance?"

"Yes, it is. Dan attended the annual Deans' Conference in Oxford last week. In the light of your investigations, I asked him to try and snatch a word with Jane Le Prevost, to see if she remembered Swain."

"And I assume she did?"

"She visibly recoiled at the mention of his name and then told Dan that Swain had actively campaigned against her from the moment she arrived in post."

"Bob – I will stop you there. I've already heard about this from the Registrar up there."

"I would expect nothing less. But did you know that Swain moved here after Jane effectively vetoed his history of the Cathedral?

"Jane also told Dan that Swain had achieved some short-lived notoriety in the pages of *Private Eye*."

Tedesco's eyes lit up as he gestured for the Bishop to continue.

"As I am sure you know, Swain worked at Porton Down. *Private Eye* got hold of a story a while back – pretty nebulous, I gather – anyway, they spoke to a disgruntled whistleblower, who fed them some grand conspiracy theory about dark dealings by the top brass.

"Jane's view was that the piece – very brief – betrayed some scepticism on the part of the editor, but that there may have been a kernel of truth in some of the less wild accusations. No names were mentioned in the article, but the word on the street was that there were various clues in the piece which pointed to Swain."

"And from what I know of him, Swain wouldn't want this to come out years later," said Tedesco, before summarising the latest developments in the Canford case as succinctly as he could.

"We still need some concrete evidence, though, Your Grace," he concluded, "and a murder weapon would help."

"I'll pray for one – and for you and Lynne as well."

*

Tedesco was just in time for a Jenks sandwich, tuna mayo on white, and was back at base struggling with his crossword when Lynne returned from her speed walk.

"How was my favourite bishop?" she said.

"Rushed off his feet, but he had some interesting news from the Dean of Salisbury, via Dean Dan."

"To do with Swain, I guess. He'd been a real pain to her, I know."

"Indeed. He is still seething about her interference with his book. This is new information – apparently there was a small piece tucked away in *Private Eye* a few years ago."

"Go on…"

"They'd got hold of some rumours of a cover-up, dodgy management – there were no real details – at Porton Down."

"Swain worked there – and Aglionby as well."

"And they both knew Canford, of course…"

"John, are we actually getting somewhere at last, or are we heading down another rabbit hole?"

"Well, I did ask Bob to pray for a breakthrough, or at least a murder weapon."

Tedesco spent the afternoon updating the counsel's notebook. This usually helped him to order his thoughts.

Lynne searched online for old copies of Private Eye *and any media references to Porton Down. She was still in two minds about going to London – it would give her the chance to mention Swain's name to Aglionby, but would that be such a smart move?*

At ten past five, Tedesco, acting on a whim, decided to visit the Cathedral; the musical balm of Choral Evensong might just help to open up his mind, as his updating had failed to do, and if he dropped Barker off at home now, he should still be just in time for the service…

*

The boys' choir was conducted by the Master of Musick.

Ginny was to be found in her normal place in the Quire, having led the crocodile over from the Cathedral School.

Dean Dan led the service, and the Precentor, Wilf Drake, took the prayers of intercession. The lesson readers were Liz Gerrey and Richard Swain.

Tedesco looked up and saw a beam of late-afternoon sunlight pierce the stained glass, illuminating the nave. On the surface, Rhyminster had returned to calm normality. But all alone in the vestry, Colin Scopes was biting his fingernails, seemingly close to tears.

FORTY-TWO

Tedesco had a brief chat with Wilf Drake on his way out of the Cathedral, then continuing with the theme of impulsiveness, he decided that it looked like another perfect evening for a drive, so he called Nicky as he walked home.

"What is it this time?"

"Rude! I just wondered how you were."

"You can tell that to the Marines. I assume this is about Canford."

"Am I that shallow? Don't answer that. Look, it won't take long, but I don't want to do this on the phone."

"Okay – I've got a window for an hour before Chag gets back."

*

As he turned over the ignition key, Tedesco couldn't decide between Paul Simon or Joni Mitchell, so he opted for Radio 3.

It was an oboe concerto, Vaughan Williams perhaps. If only his knowledge of classical music matched his niche expertise on seventies singer songwriters!

Never mind, whatever he was listening to matched his mood and the surroundings.

As he turned into Crane House, he saw Jack and Ella hurling a rugby ball at each other.

Barker approached the stationary oval-shaped ball with some trepidation, before sniffing it and wandering off towards the house.

"Don't worry, Barker," Ella said. "I'll fetch you a tennis ball."

As it was just about warm enough to stay outdoors, Nicky brought out a jug of lemonade, and they sat at a rattan table, which had migrated from the conservatory to the patio.

"Right then – this isn't a social call," Nicky said.

"You hard-bitten journo! Okay, I'll be equally direct. That picture of the red Fabia you sent over – it could be the car that we think was used to collect Canford from the station on the night he went missing."

The *Searchlight* veteran looked bewildered. "Hang on – are you suggesting that one of Chag's guys picked him up?"

"No. We are pretty confident that one of the vergers at the Cathedral was the driver."

"That's ridiculous. As I've told you, that car is just used by Aspirational staff."

"Okay, could the verger have borrowed it?"

"Of course not! They never lend cars out like that."

She fell silent. Tedesco waited patiently for her to continue.

"Wait a moment... wait a bloody moment. My lovely husband did let slip, after several pints of Stoat's Arse or whatever, that Liz Gerrey had persuaded him to let her borrow a little runaround for a few days. Her Merc was in dock, and she hadn't been organised enough to book a hire car."

"Why would he agree to that?"

"Wake up, John! He probably fancies her."

"Really? Bit old for him, I'd have thought. Nicky, I really don't want to drag you into this—"

She butted in. "If you are expecting me to cross-question Chag about which car he lent her, forget it. I shouldn't be telling you how to do your job, but why don't you persuade Lynne to ask Liz about it? They get on well, I gather."

His silent drive home was followed by a quick supper of pasta and pesto sauce – Essential Waitrose, of course – then he rang his partner.

"Sorry to call on a school night."

"That's okay. I decided to bin out of book club and watch some property porn on Channel Four instead. I was going to call you later."

"Do tell."

"Jools Tagg let me know that they're calling Scopes in for a formal interview. He's got himself a lawyer. He's due over there at three tomorrow."

"It looks like my timing is perfect – I've just been over to see Nicky again. Chag Wills was seduced into lending your friend Liz a little runaround while her Merc was off the road."

"And you'd like me to ask her about its colour, I'm guessing."

"And I thought my sister was the cynic!"

"Don't worry. I'll think of an excuse. I'll try and ring her during the next ad break."

An hour later, the Sousa theme rang out.

"John, it's me. She was engaged for ages, but I got through to her a few minutes ago. The car she borrowed was a red Skoda."

"Wow! How did you worm that out of her?"

Lynne laughed. He imagined her throwing her head back as she giggled, and that lovely smile.

"Easy. She'd already gushed to me about the charming Mr Wills, so I said that I was calling to thank her so much for recommending Aspirational Cars.

"I waffled on about how I had been thinking about a change of wheels – I told Liz that I'd dropped her name to Chag's colleague, which went down well, and that they had already come up with some ideas.

"Then she let slip that she had been in touch with them the other day – so I naturally asked her why. Her Merc was having work done, and Swain can't ferry her about while he's serving a ban, so she needed some wheels for a few days. The lovely Mr Wills and his staff lent her their pool car."

"Are you going to share this with Jools?"

"Already have."

FORTY-THREE

A solitary pedestrian was painstakingly completing her second circuit of the Close as Tedesco and Barker left St Budeaux Place for another day at the office.

An hour later, in Exeter, Paula Fordham's PA interrupted her boss as she was busy revising a complex matrimonial consent order.

"Sorry to disturb you, Ms Fordham – but there's a call for you. He says it's extremely urgent."

"Bloody hell, Karen – you know that I've got to drive all the way down to Rhyminster later – take a message!"

"It's about Rhyminster. It's your client. He says that he no longer requires your services."

*

At Minster Precincts, fifteen minutes later, Sally Munks was interrupting Tedesco.

"It's the Dean's PA. Can you get down to the Deanery as soon as you can? It's really important."

"Blast!" he said, almost losing his footing on the steep staircase.

After turning into the Close, he had to shove his way through a group of slow-moving French tourists, prompting a sarcastic "*Pardon, monsieur!*" from their young tour leader.

Tedesco felt a keen pang of guilt as he remembered how Canford had earned his keep before his disastrous move down here.

He was momentarily startled by Jo's appearance as she opened the Deanery door; she had ditched the frizz for a fetching pixie cut – Crystal Tipps had been regenerated as Zoe Wanamaker.

She blue-lighted him into Dan's study, where he found a sorry-looking Colin Scopes being comforted by the Dean.

"Good to see you, John," Dan said, gesturing towards a comfortable–looking armchair.

"I found Colin in a state of distress during morning prayers, so I brought him here for some breakfast. He was very keen to see you, John. You want to tell us something, don't you, Colin?"

Scopes looked as if he was on the brink of a complete meltdown.

"I expect that what you are about to tell us will be very hard for you, Colin," Tedesco said.

He paused, then he continued, gently. "I have all the time in the world, and I am sure the Dean does too."

Dan nodded in agreement, his simple gesture somehow reflecting his natural compassion.

"Thank you, Mr Tedesco. I wanted you here because I trust you. You have always been kind to me."

"Take your time."

"Thank you. I just can't live with this anymore." He looked down at the floor, as if the Dean's Moroccan rug was an oracle, then he gradually looked up again, struggling to get his words out.

"I know who killed Mr Canford, you see."

The distraught verger started to weep. As Dan offered him a tissue, Tedesco said, "I know it's early, Dan, but perhaps Colin could use a brandy."

As the Dean went in search of some strong liquor, Tedesco put a soft hand on Scopes' shoulder.

"You are doing absolutely the right thing, Colin. We will help you all we can."

The Dean returned with a glass containing a generous measure of malt whisky. "I'm afraid this is all I've got."

Colin took a tentative sip. "I have never tasted anything like this before."

They let him compose himself.

"I realise that everyone thinks that Mr Tantum did it, but I know the truth. I don't want the wrong man to go to prison."

"Of course not," said Dean Dan. "You are a good man, Colin. A man of faith. We can both tell that you have been wrestling with your conscience. What do you want to tell us?"

"The thing is – it's someone I know, someone close to me."

"Is it Mr Swain, Colin? Was Richard responsible for this?" ventured Tedesco.

Scopes wiped his eyes. "No. It wasn't Richard. It was Roy Baird."

Tedesco and the Dean turned to each other. They both looked completely stunned. After a while, the detective spoke.

"This is very serious, Colin. Are you absolutely sure?"

"I was there. I saw it all. Roy was protecting me."

Tedesco excused himself momentarily.

Stepping into the corridor, he reached for his smartphone and called Lynne. After she had heard his brief summary, she headed off to the Cathedral to make sure that Baird was still in the building, calling Bloomfield as she crossed the Green.

Once he was back in the study, Tedesco asked Scopes if Roy knew that he was going to the Deanery.

"I don't think so – but he will wonder where I am."

Dan turned to him. "Colin. You will need to tell all this to the police. When are you seeing them?"

"This afternoon. But I have cancelled my solicitor – now that I have told you who did it, this changes everything, doesn't it?"

Tedesco explained, as kindly as he could, that Colin would still be asked why he had taken so long to speak out – and he would need to set out the full facts – so it would be advisable to seek help with the interview.

"Please would you come with me, Mr Tedesco?"

"Colin, I am no longer practising law, and haven't dealt with criminal work since my early days.

"If I do go with you, it would be as a supportive friend – but I think you should seriously think about reinstating your counsel."

"I don't think I can. Richard is paying for her, you see, and now that I have disobeyed him, he won't want to cover the cost of my lawyer – and I can't afford it."

The Dean turned to his verger. Noticing that Colin's face was watermarked with tears, he softened his voice.

"Colin. Why don't you start by telling us what happened to Oliver? In your own words…"

Paula Fordham called Swain to let him know that she had been sacked by her client. He would still have to pay for her time.

Lovell and Tagg arrested Baird, who went with them without demur. Wilf Drake took temporary charge of the vestry, arranging for the caretakers to help Izzie with any verging duties.

*

"Okay, Colin," said Tedesco, narrowing his eyes, "when did you see Roy kill Oliver?"

He still found it incredible that Roy Baird could have done this. The genial hobbit-like verger transformed into a killer – really?

"It might help if I started at the beginning. As you know, Richard Swain has become a great friend over the last few months. He knew that I was worried about driving again, and so he offered to help me. He even borrowed a car for me, and we went out for drives together, usually to Rhyminster Down."

"And one of these drives was to the station, after you had cleared up after prize-giving?"

"Yes. Richard called me after the service and suggested that as he had to give the car back soon, this would be the ideal opportunity to see how I coped with driving at night. He explained to me that he had agreed to meet Oliver off the late train, but he was still technically banned for speeding and so that's why he needed me to drive."

"Were you alone, Colin?" Dan asked.

"Oh no – I would have been too frightened to drive without Richard's supervision. It was raining as well as dark."

"Didn't you find Richard's request rather peculiar? Couldn't he have told Oliver to get a taxi, say?"

Colin's silence confirmed their suspicions that he would do pretty much anything Swain told him to do, no questions asked, so Tedesco resumed the soft interrogation.

"Where did you meet Richard?"

"He met me at the car, which I'd parked in Rounsevell Lane. He seemed quite tense and was really cross with me when I struggled with the Close Gate."

"Of course – it's locked by then," added the Dean. "So did you have to unlock it again when you drove Oliver back?"

"No – Richard said we would only be five minutes, so leave it open."

"Okay, so you picked up Swain, and then you went to the station. Was Oliver waiting for you?"

"No, we were a bit early so Richard told me to check and see if the train was delayed. He told me to wait until I saw Oliver and then offer him a lift. While I was looking at the arrivals board, I spotted Mr Canford and explained that I could give him a lift home."

"And how did he react to this?" asked the Dean.

"Well, he looked a bit surprised, to be honest, but it was pouring with rain, and so he was very glad of the offer."

"I'm sure he was, Colin, but if he was anticipating a lift from Richard, wouldn't he have mentioned it?"

Scopes looked helpless – "I don't know. I just did as I was told. I'm not even sure if Mr Canford was expecting Richard."

"Colin," said the Dean, "how do you think Richard knew that Oliver would be on that train?"

Tedesco stepped in. "I'd been wondering about that. Swain would have been studying his routine – and Oliver didn't exactly keep his visits to London secret, did he? Swain might have overheard something, or Liz might have mentioned Canford's choir to him. Once he knew that Canford went up to London on Wednesday evenings, Swain could have guessed that he would take the last train back."

He signalled to the crestfallen verger to continue with his narrative.

"When I went to let Mr Canford into the car, I couldn't see Richard. I panicked, but then I guessed that he might have gone to see how I was getting on.

"I let Mr Canford wait in the passenger seat while I went to look for Richard. When I got back, I couldn't believe what I found – Richard was crouched behind the passenger seat, and Mr Canford was slumped forward, as if he were asleep. Richard was wearing his driving gloves – I hadn't noticed that before."

"Carry on, you're doing really well," said Tedesco.

"It was like a bad dream. Richard shouted at me and told me to drive off, which I did."

"So Oliver was unconscious?"

"I assumed so. He had something in his mouth which smelt medical, but I was too terrified to take it all in. When we got to the Close, Richard told me to park near the Dean's entrance. He had a huge torch, which he used to help me find my keys and unlock the door.

"Then he shone the beam towards the side aisle and led me to the Rhyme Chantry. He already had the key for it in his coat. He must have taken it from the vestry."

"Of course," said Dean Dan, "he knew where it was. What did he do next?"

"He pulled out a large roll of lino – we keep all kinds of junk in there – and asked me to help him unfurl it, then we put a pile of heavy old hymn books on each end to stop it curling up again."

"Let me see – then he asked you to help him move Canford into the Chantry," said Tedesco.

"He told me to, yes. He said that if I didn't, he would leave me there and tell the police that I had kidnapped Mr Canford."

"I don't think they would have believed him, but even so, that must have been frightening for you. Dan, do you want to ask any questions?"

"Yes, John – so, Colin, you and Richard went back to the car and manhandled the body into the Cathedral. That must have been difficult. Wouldn't someone have heard the commotion?"

"Richard had planned everything. I can see that now. He knew where we kept the sack trucks – we use them for moving chairs – and so he took one of them outside with us so we could use it to wheel the body. Richard had some strap things in the boot which he used to tie the body to the truck."

Like Hannibal Lecter being wheeled off the plane at the start of Silence of the Lambs, thought Tedesco.

Colin then described how they moved the body up to the Chantry gate, where they released the straps and carefully placed it in the unfurled lino.

Swain rolled the lino over Canford's prone body, removed the hymnals and sealed the ends with some black tape. Then he told Colin to lock up the Chantry and to return the key to the vestry in the morning. It would be too risky to do it then.

"He warned me to speak to no one until I had done this, or else I would be joining Mr Canford in the Cage."

"What a nasty thing to suggest. What did Swain do after this?" asked Tedesco.

"He went back to the car and got a bottle out of the boot. It must have been a cleaning liquid. He gave me a cloth and told me to wipe down the sack truck. Once he was happy with my work, he took the cloth from me and put it back in the boot with the bottle. He must have gathered up the old hymn books while I was wiping down, as they were already in the boot. He said that no one would miss them.

"Then he made sure that I had locked the Dean's door before he drove the red car out of the Close Gate, which I had left open. He said that the car had to go back in the morning."

"I thought he was still banned?"

Colin shrugged; a gesture of total defeat.

FORTY-FOUR

While Colin was hunkered down with Tedesco and Dean Dan, Richard Swain was urgently weighing up his options, reviewing the situation like Fagin in *Oliver!*

As Colin has ditched the burner phone, I need to find another way of contacting him.

Scopes has fired Paula, so he might have pressed the panic button and told the police – that cute little DS, probably – or, knowing Colin as I do, I could just imagine him kneeling to make his humble confession to Almighty God, or to one of his feeble representatives on earth, like that Jesus freak of a Dean or the sandal-wearing Precentor.

Either way, I need to get to my puny accomplice before it's too late – otherwise, I might have to lie low for a while.

Visiting the Cathedral this morning would look suspicious, as I don't have any volunteering duties today. And I need to take that bloody Skoda back to Aspirational Cars, and to make sure they valet it quickly and thoroughly.

I'll get Liz to find Colin.

As luck would have it, the Merry Widow was already on her way to the Close when he reached her – she had booked to go on a rare tour of the Treasury, which was for volunteers only, followed by a talk by an academic.

Liz, noting the clear note of panic in his voice, unquestioningly agreed to check on the whereabouts of Scopes and to get back to him before she joined the tour group.

*

At the Deanery, Tedesco and Dan continued with their gentle probing.

Colin, growing in confidence, admitted that he had been intimidated into going along with Swain's plans.

He told them that Swain's aggressive threats in the Rhyminster Arms the previous evening had resulted in a sleepless night, followed by an early-morning walk by the river, during which he had prayed for guidance.

Tedesco leaned towards him and spoke in a firmer tone.

"Colin, I think it's time for you to tell us how Oliver met his death. Are you ready?"

Colin took a deep breath and then he recounted the final moments of the Bishop's lay assistant, clearly relieved to be shedding the burden.

"I was petrified after leaving the Cathedral that night. I didn't sleep at first.

"My plan was to get to work early the next day and see if I could wake up Mr Canford and let him out before anyone noticed. Unfortunately, once I did manage some sleep – at about four, it must have been – I didn't wake up again until gone seven.

"So when I arrived at the Cathedral, Roy was already there. We were on the early shift. Izzie had the morning off.

"As I crept past the Chantry, I could hear muffled noises. I turned around and was horrified to find that Mr Canford

233

had somehow managed to struggle to his feet while still rolled up in the lino. I think he must have got a hand free and pulled himself up by grabbing at one of the steel bars. Anyway, he moved towards the iron gate of the Chantry and started barging into it, so I decided to let him out.

"I still had the key, remember. Roy could hear the racket by now, so he came running from his office."

"Have another sip, if it helps," said Tedesco.

Colin grimaced as the peaty tang of the Islay hit the back of his throat.

He continued: "Mr Canford was still struggling to free himself from the lino when Roy got there. As I unlocked the Cage, Oliver fell on top of me, still partly wrapped up in the lino – but he was able to grab my throat with his free hand. He was like a wild animal."

Tedesco and Dean Dan nodded at each other – who wouldn't be wild after being rendered unconscious, only to wake up in a medieval iron prison, rolled up in an old floor covering?

"I thought I was going to die. I couldn't breathe." Colin went on, "And then Roy stepped in."

He took another sip of the single malt.

"I heard a firm thud and a terrible cracking sound – then I realised that the lino was being rolled off me, with Oliver still trapped in it, and I could begin to breathe again."

"So Roy rescued you?" Dan said.

"Yes. Once I'd recovered my senses, I saw him standing over Mr Canford, holding the verge."

Tedesco briefly considered the irony of the ceremonial stick being used for its original defensive purpose, before asking Colin, "So, was Mr Canford still alive when you came to?"

"He was dead – I could tell. Roy told me to help him to roll the body back into the lino, taking care not to allow any blood to seep out onto the floor or to get on my clothes, then he got me to put up the 'No Entry' signs in the aisles so we could manhandle the body back into place before anyone saw us."

The Dean chipped in: "Why on earth did you and Roy do this – didn't you think of calling 999?"

"We were in total shock. After we had locked the Chantry, Roy sat me down in his office and told me that no one would find the body for ages, and that when they did, they would never suspect either of us."

"What about fingerprints? Weren't you worried?" Tedesco asked.

"Roy had thought of that – we had both been in the Chantry before, don't forget, and we would have moved the lino back after the Earl's last visit. I had wiped the sack truck, and Richard had taken the hymn books with him."

"So you could explain your prints in the Chantry – once Barker found the body, you and Roy unfurled the lino to reveal the corpse. Sounds like the perfect alibi."

"I don't remember thinking about it that way, Mr Tedesco. I have been sick with worry ever since Richard got me into this."

"Understood – but I must ask you, as the police will, what happened to the murder weapon?"

"Roy wiped the verge down and put it back in its place. As chance would have it, the Holy Dusters were due to carry out their monthly silver polishing that day."

Tedesco and the Dean both knew that the energetic handiwork of that particular group of Cathedral volunteers would have eliminated every tiny trace of evidence from the silver stick.

235

"Colin," the Dean asked, "I completely understand that you would have been frightened by Richard Swain. John and I have been looking into him for a while now, and we have found out that he has a temper and bears grudges. But why would Roy of all people seek to cover this up?

"He may have been correct in his view that neither of you would face charges, but an innocent person could have been convicted."

"I know. That's why I couldn't keep it to myself anymore. Roy just said that he would be retired by the time anything came to light, and that what goes around, comes around."

"But Roy could have been the hero – he saved you," said Tedesco.

"Even if he was sent down, can you imagine the uproar?" added the Dean.

"Free the Rhyminster one!" said Tedesco. "Stupid man – he's landed himself in serious trouble."

"Should I go to the police now?"

"I'm afraid so," said the Dean, who suggested that he take him to the station straightaway.

*

As he wandered back through the cloisters, Tedesco pulled out his phone and called Bloomfield, who confirmed that Baird was awaiting the duty solicitor.

The sooner Colin made a statement, the better. Tedesco would get him a solid lawyer from his old firm – it would be a whole lot cheaper than Paula Fordham, who in any case was tainted by her association with Swain.

Tedesco was then distracted by a familiar drift of Chanel

as Liz Gerrey sashayed into the Cathedral, clearly on a mission.

Spotting Lynne, who was leaning on the visitor desk chatting to one of the guides, he signalled to her, headed to the Refectory, and within a few minutes she had joined him at their usual table.

After listening open-mouthed to the abridged version of Colin's long story, Lynne said that she'd spoken to Julia Tagg – the police had got hold of the deceased's bank records.

Oliver Canford had been receiving regular credits from what looked like an offshore account – the only reference was 'INTRABACS118'.

These amounts were not life-changing, but they would have gone some way towards assisting the late lay assistant with his flamboyant lifestyle.

"So what are they thinking, Lynne? Was he bribing someone?"

"That's the clear inference – but as this case has shown us, nothing is as obvious as it first appears."

"Granted. But if Canford was involved in blackmail, who was his target?"

FORTY-FIVE

Swain had just set off again in the Skoda when Liz called. He pulled into a cul-de-sac on the edge of town.

"No sign of Colin, I'm afraid, but one of my colleagues has just seen him being driven off by the Dean. Most peculiar, don't you think?"

He ended the call abruptly. He was on his own now. No point returning the Skoda – he needed to extend the loan period indefinitely.

As he reached the Trago Mills roundabout, he signalled and took the exit marked 'Okehampton A30'.

*

Tedesco and Davey decided to put in an appearance back at the office.

He had already arranged for Sally to take Barker home today; he kept a spare key for number 17 in his desk for such eventualities.

Lynne, having decided not to go up to London, as it was all kicking off in Rhyme, wanted some quiet time to think through the bribery idea – who would Canford be blackmailing, and why?

Tantum? Swain? One of his ardent female admirers? All of the above?

*

Richard Swain hadn't been to the cottage on the moor for several years. It had come to something when this was his choice of refuge.

His grandparents had bought it in the early 1930s as a holiday home for the exclusive use of the extended Swain family.

All of his childhood holidays had been spent there. The rest of his family regarded 'the Cottage' as a sacred space, and they all wanted to be buried in the churchyard of the nearby hamlet.

Swain didn't share these halcyon memories – in fact, he had grown to hate the place with a passion bordering on the insane.

His sister had inherited it – she was more than bloody welcome to the dump – and had decreed that nothing should ever change. Apart from an inefficient central heating system she had put in during the eighties, nothing had been altered since before the War.

Even the mattresses felt, and smelt, as if they predated the rise of Hitler.

So, while Swain could never understand their upper-middle-class embrace of extreme discomfort, he was silently blessing his forebears as he turned off the A30 and entered an impenetrable latticework of single-track roads, with grass growing in the middle of them.

Good luck with finding me here with no mobile reception, he thought to himself as he parked in the field below the cottage.

It was a few minutes' walk through the woods before the five-bar gate appeared.

He located the front-door key, still kept hidden from sight under an old milk churn, and having struggled with the rusted lock, he entered the main room.

It contained two wooden benches, a rickety old card table, an inglenook fireplace and a couple of ancient rocking chairs.

Bang on cue, a blackbird flew down the chimney. Welcome to the Dartmoor Hilton...

*

Back at the Cathedral, Liz had been enthralled by her tour of the Treasury.

She had no previous knowledge of the range of artefacts kept there, which included various goblets, chalices and the like held on permanent loan from some of the remote parishes in the Diocese.

It was stifling in the Treasury, so she stepped outside during the coffee break to get some welcome fresh air and to look at her messages.

Aspirational Cars had tried calling, and then they texted her a reminder to return the little hatchback she had borrowed for Richard.

Nothing from him, though – why had he been so off with her this morning?

And why hadn't he taken the car back? She tried calling him – straight to voicemail.

After a quick coffee in the refectory, she headed back to the Treasury. She would deal with Richard later. She wasn't going to give up on the chance to hear Professor Imogen Scott deliver her fascinating talk about the Woolford Trove.

*

"I need to pick your brain, John," said Lynne, as he followed her into the meeting room, signalling to Sally to hold all calls.

"Okay," she started. "Let's look at what we know. Baird will admit to killing Canford once he's seen his solicitor. He won't contradict what Colin said."

"Agreed," Tedesco answered. "Colin is incapable of lying."

"So, we have the killer, but the real villain is Swain.

"He could try to challenge Colin's story, on the basis that it is Colin's word against his – and his prints wouldn't appear on the linoleum, let alone the body. He was wearing his driving gloves when they moved Canford from the car, remember."

"And Chag's guys will valet the car to death."

"I assume Swain has returned the car – perhaps I'd better check with Liz."

"Good idea, Lynne. Otherwise, we need to establish that it was Swain who was being blackmailed. That would give him a motive for kidnapping Canford."

"I don't think Colin can help on that – he wouldn't have the wit or the balls, frankly, to ask Swain why he was being asked to help him dispose of poor Oliver.

"Any bright ideas?"

Tedesco sighed and got up to study the rooftops.

"Swain is an obsessive, and holds somewhat controversial views."

"You mean that he is a sexist bastard, John."

"Well, I would take issue with him on the role of women in the church, certainly. Let's just imagine that Canford got wind of the story about the Dean of Salisbury spiking the publication of his history of the Cathedral—"

Lynne interrupted. "I think I see where you are going. The last thing Swain would want is for the same thing to happen here. The powers that be in our Cathedral get wind of his anti-women agenda, and a campaign to prevent publication of his blockbusting history of Rhyminster soon gains traction."

"That's it, in a nutshell. But would that be enough to make Swain pay Canford to keep quiet? There must be something else."

"Okay, bear with me on this. I looked up the old *Private Eye* story, as you know. It was opaque, to put it mildly. I discovered that the journalist responsible, Clive Green, is no longer with us, so I thought we had drawn a blank on this."

"Go on," said Tedesco, his face a mask of deep concentration.

"Let's apply some lateral thinking. The choral link is still out there, and now we have a university connection."

"That's right. Tantum, Aglionby and Maxwell Patrick shared the same Cambridge college."

"And Canford. He was a Cambridge man – different college, I think."

"Correct, Trinity Hall. The others all went to King's. What are you thinking, Lynne? Dastardly Establishment plot?"

"Don't be daft. Listen, Aglionby must have been aware of the piece in the *Eye* – even if he hadn't been at Porton Down when it appeared, he would still have heard about it."

"So what are you saying?"

242

"Humour me for a second. What if Aglionby – knowing that Canford, a fellow Minstrel and a Cambridge man to boot, was going to work for Bishop Bob – decided to slip Swain's name into a conversation?"

"From what I saw in Pimlico, the Minstrels love a drink and a gossip."

"So Aglionby decided to tell Canford that he knew someone in Rhyminster – Swain – and, by the way, he was rumoured to be the target of an unnamed whistleblower in a long-forgotten piece of journalism in a satirical magazine?"

"Put like that, it does sound implausible, but do you have any better ideas?"

Tedesco frowned. "I hope you are not thinking of going to London to confront Aglionby?"

"No. I think it could be dangerous – but I assume you'd be happy for me to see if Jimmy Bloomfield wants to explore my little theory?"

*

On Dartmoor, Swain had to think quickly. He'd managed to get the electricity going. It was on a meter, and the last visitor had left a small supply of 50p coins. He'd need more, and some candles for back-up.

He could do with a change of clothes and some food. If he paid by card, then this was traceable, but withdrawing wads of cash from a machine would be equally suspicious. He checked his wallet. He had a couple of hundred in notes.

And what about the car? It was invisible from the road, so probably no need to move it once he'd stocked up. He could always cover it with some of the putrid old dust sheets from the cottage.

FORTY-SIX

The Head of the Cathedral Guides proposed a vote of thanks to Professor Scott for her informative talk, and to the Treasurer for the tour.

Striding out of the Cathedral after the lecture, Liz Gerrey stopped to check her messages. Another call from Aspirational Cars, nothing from Richard. Lynne Davey had called – what did she want this time?

Liz got straight through to the car showroom. Richard hadn't returned the Skoda.

"He probably just forgot. He's got a lot on his mind, poor thing."

Where the hell was he?

She tried Lynne Davey on her mobile – perhaps she had some news about Richard.

Lynne took the call and put Liz on speakerphone so that Tedesco could hear.

"Liz. Thanks for calling back. Listen, not sure if you can help, but I need to get hold of Richard. Nothing worrying, but he might be able to help us with Oliver."

Liz took her time before responding. "I saw the Dean driving Colin Scopes away – do you think Richard is involved? He and Colin are thick as thieves."

"I'm not saying that, but if you could let him know I called."

"Lynne, the truth is that I can't reach him either. He was supposed to take a car back to Chag Wills for me this morning, but the garage haven't seen him. I don't know where he is, or the wretched car. I wish I'd never let him talk me into borrowing it."

Tedesco leaned in. "Liz – it's John Tedesco – I'm afraid I was earwigging. Do you have any idea where Richard would go if he wanted to get away from it all?"

"Let me think – he has mentioned a decrepit old cottage up on the moors. I said how lovely it must be, but he just laughed and said that the spa facilities wouldn't be up to my standards."

"Think, Liz," said Lynne, "this could be important. Did he mention where it was?"

"I think it's near Okehampton – he pointed out the turning for it when we were driving that way, on the way back from Exeter, if I remember."

"Liz – any names spring to mind? How about Lydford? Sourton?"

"No, sorry. Something like 'Trowel' perhaps. I really don't know."

Tedesco tried to visualise his walking map – "Throwleigh?"

"Yes! I'm sure that's it. But I gather that this hovel isn't in the village – it's in the middle of a field."

After thanking Liz and telling her not to worry, Lynne turned to her partner.

"I know the Rural Dean, Lucy Renton. Leave it to me," Tedesco said.

It was DCI Jimmy Bloomfield's big moment. Selected local media had been invited to a short-notice press briefing at the Bristol Road station.

Bloomfield was introduced by Luke Barnard, and he strode to the podium, immaculately dressed as ever, his trademark bow tie in British racing green.

Nicky Tedesco represented the BBC, and as it would have made Julie Stringer mad not to have been invited, the local legend sat in the front row.

"Thank you all for coming. I wanted to brief the local media in advance. I am delighted to say that we have made an arrest in the Oliver Canford case. We are holding a sixty-five-year-old man, who has confessed to the killing, and charges will follow. I can take a few questions – Nicky."

"Thank you, Jimmy. Two points – can you give us a name? And secondly, you referred to a killing, without specifying murder. Should we read something into that?"

"Nicky – nice try, you know that I can't release any names yet. I suggest you curb your enthusiasm until formal charges are laid.

"The same applies to the nature of the offence."

Julie reminded Bloomfield that the post-mortem had revealed that Canford had been unconscious before he was struck. Could DCI Bloomfield comment on whether the man they were holding was both the kidnapper and the killer?

Bloomfield, under the watchful gaze of Barnard, gave a suitably nuanced answer. The media liaison officer allowed himself an approving smirk.

"I think we can take that as a no," Julie whispered to Nicky.

While the press conference was wrapping up, Swain drove into the market town of Okehampton.

Although it boasted a Waitrose, he thought that the Lidl would be less conspicuous.

He stocked up on survival rations – tins of soup, a kilo of pasta, milk, tea and coffee, and some ridiculously cheap wine, as well as a couple of weeks' supply of loo rolls and soap.

After dithering over some disposable razors, he decided that he'd go unshaven while he was lying low.

There was still a traditional menswear shop in Fore Street. They were having a half-price sale, so he got some underwear, a couple of lumberjack shirts and a pair of red cords.

Swain knew that he was being reckless, but he had a head start on the Neanderthal local force, and while he had more respect for Tedesco and his dreadful feminist sidekick, they'd never find him either.

He realised that the Skoda would be reported as missing, but even if some local yokel had spotted it in the town, he remained confident in the inaccessibility of the cottage.

Allow a couple of weeks to let the beard grow, abandon the car in Exeter and catch an early-morning train to London. Plenty of safe houses there, assuming he'd still need one by then. Given time, he might even be able to hook up again with Liz.

*

The press conference was followed by a brief statement on the force's social media pages, but Julie had already spread the word. Champagne corks were soon popping at The Pelistry, and in the chambers of Maxwell Patrick, QC, MP.

However, Tantum's mood soon swerved from ecstatic relief to petty vindictiveness.

"Max!" he yelled down the phone at Patrick. "Well done all round! And thank Mr Turbani when you see him!"

"Of course I will. Although it's Mr Purbani, actually," drawled the leading counsel.

"Listen, Max. Now I'm no longer public enemy number one, I need to clear my name. It is beyond outrageous that the spineless morons of the Devon and Cornwall constabulary had the temerity to enter my premises, threatening not only my good self, but my wife, and Aldhelm and Osmund as well. On top of that, my stellar reputation in this fair city has been impugned. I demand serious – I mean, punitive – reparations!"

Ginny suddenly entered the room, seething with years of pent-up frustration as she turned on her husband.

"Charles! Just shut up! Now! You have always behaved like an idiot, and that's what landed you in this mess. Just thank God that's it over and move on. Or else I will!"

Never had Tantum's flabber been so comprehensively gasted.

He abruptly ended the call with Patrick, before staring at his wife. Was this really her?

"I hear you, Ginny. I truly couldn't function without you. I'll try and keep quiet, I promise."

"You could never be quiet, Charles. Just stop being such a pompous ass."

*

Tedesco had left several messages for Lucy Renton, team vicar of the NorthMoor group of parishes. He knew that she would be busy ministering to her small flock spread around a vast swathe of the moors, so he was pleasantly surprised when she called him.

"I'm just on my way to a christening preparation, but I can give you five minutes. Anyway, how are you, Mr Registrar?"

"Oh, you know, medium rare," he said, before getting to the point.

"Lucy – I need your help. You know your patch as well as anyone. Have you heard about the Canford case?"

"The body in the crypt?"

"Yes, that's the one. Anyway, I was hired by Bishop Bob to look into things when Canford first went missing and, to cut an exceedingly long story short, one of the key actors in this drama might have holed up in your neck of the woods."

"Sounds intriguing. You haven't been reading *The Hound of the Baskervilles* again?"

Tedesco grinned to himself. "No time for Conan Doyle, I'm afraid. Lucy, this could be serious. We think this person may be hiding in a small cottage near Throwleigh. We don't have a house name to go on. All we know is that it is some way from the village, set in the middle of a field, and that it has been in the same family since the thirties."

"I see. Can you give me the family's name?"

"Yes, it is the Swain family. I know you will use it carefully."

She took a deep breath. "Wow. This is going to be difficult. Leave it to me – one of the churchwardens has farmed near there all his life – Will Heath. If anyone knows something, he will.

"Oh, and John?" she added as an afterthought.

"Yes, Lucy."

"I still think about you whenever anyone mentions Plymouth Argyle."

*

"Any luck with the Rural Dean? One of your fan club, from what I gather," said Lynne.

Tedesco ignored the tease. "She thinks that one of the churchwardens might be able to locate the cottage. How are you getting on?"

"The hot news is that Bloomfield has made an announcement – local press, then a formal release."

"So it's all over town?"

"Julie was there…"

"Poor Roy. I hope they go gently. It will be manslaughter, and he's got bloody good mitigation, assuming he pleads guilty – although he will need to answer some awkward questions about why he left the body there until Barker stepped in."

"John, Barbara has been chasing you. The Bishop wants a word – he will pop over to you at nine this evening. Barbara said she will assume you can make it unless you get back to her by close of play. And she mentioned that Bob would be bringing something from Jos Elsted, whatever that means."

"An episcopal bribe is what it means! Good old Bob. I do need to catch up with him – he is my client, after all."

"He's probably just missing Barker…" teased Lynne, before adding, "I'll try and speak to Jimmy."

"Good idea. As well as seeing if you can find out more about Roy's immediate future, I'd like to know what they're doing about Colin."

FORTY-SEVEN

Bishop Robert Dwyer arrived at Tedesco's front door at 9.30, looking totally exhausted.

Barker greeted him effusively, and Tedesco gratefully accepted the promised sample from Jos Elsted – a 2015 Château La Mothe Bergeron.

"Tough day, Bishop?"

"Uncork that bottle and I will explain."

Tedesco poured out two generous glasses.

"I've been at the House of Lords all day. After hanging around for hours, I was eventually called to contribute on a debate about the refugee crisis. Then the ruddy train was late, and now I come home to all this!"

"I assume you mean the arrest?"

"The Dean has filled me in. Poor Roy – did you ever suspect anything? And now Liz Gerrey has turned up at the North Canonry in a hell of a state."

"As far as Roy is concerned – absolutely not, never close to being a suspect. We had agreed to meet for a pint at the Rhyminster Arms after Canford first went missing, but it never happened – I wonder if he would have taken me into his confidence."

"You can't beat yourself up about that. If he had wanted to talk, he could have found you easily enough."

"I expect you are right," said Tedesco, pausing before going on. "Turning to Liz, I assume she is worried about Richard Swain. He's gone missing now, so I am not surprised that she is distraught."

The Bishop got up, walked around Tedesco's small kitchen, then sat down again.

"Hilary is reprising her supporting role from when Roddy died. Liz is naturally composed, but this has knocked her for six. Just as she was getting her confidence back! She will blame herself for allowing Swain to use her, of course. What a dreadful man he is, preying on the vulnerable.

"So, John – why do you think he has gone missing?"

Tedesco patiently took the Bishop through Colin's evidence.

"You always had your suspicions, John, but I still struggle to understand why Swain would want to kidnap Oliver, and in such a macabre setting.

"And I fail to see why Colin meekly went along with it. It sounds as if he had no real clue as to why Swain wanted to imprison Canford."

Tedesco nodded, then answered his client.

"Lynne and I have some ideas about motive.

"One, Swain had issues with Oliver over his relationship with Liz. Two, we think that he may have been blackmailed by him."

"I think I need some more of Jos' excellent claret. Why on earth would my lay assistant be blackmailing one of the Cathedral guides? It makes no sense at all, does it?"

"Bob, some interesting credits have appeared in Ollie's bank account. The police can't prove a direct link with Swain, but they will be asking him about it once he turns up. Remember when we discussed Jane Le Prevost and the business over Swain's proposed History?"

"Of course. He was going to abuse her in print, and so she got the publication pulled – wait a minute – you aren't seriously suggesting that Oliver used this to extract money from him?"

"Well, he could hardly afford his champagne lifestyle on what you were paying him!"

The Bishop affected to ignore the barb, so Tedesco picked up his thread.

"Just suppose that I'm right about this – can you think how Canford would have heard about the feud with Jane?"

The Bishop swirled his glass.

"The Bishop's chaplains – and lay assistants – have an informal trade association, called the Slope Society. They meet for an annual dinner. Canford might have picked up some gossip from the Bishop of Salisbury's chaplain, I suppose."

"Entirely possible, I would have thought. Lynne has another theory."

"Does it concern that blasted choir, by any chance?"

"How did you guess? The concert secretary, apart from attending the same college as our beloved Master of Musick, was a high-ranking civil servant. He knew Swain a little when Richard was at Porton Down. You told me about the little story that appeared in *Private Eye* which might have related to him—"

"And," interrupted the Bishop, "the concert secretary would have known about it."

"Indeed. Aglionby, that's his name, could easily have mentioned Swain to Oliver. You can just imagine it: 'When you start work in Rhyminster, young Canford, you may come across one of my old colleagues who has moved down there.'"

"'And by the way, we crossed swords over an article in *Private Eye*.'"

"You and I both know how the British Establishment floats on a sea of intrigue and tittle-tattle – and that Canford had the guile to take full advantage of any scraps than fell from the table," said Tedesco.

"I'm with you so far, John. But even if you are right – that Swain was paying Canford to keep quiet about his book and the *Private Eye* story – this doesn't really explain the kidnap plot."

"Swain was in the Chantry when Tantum loudly suggested that it would make the ideal place to leave a body. So his ears would have pricked up – not only had the idiot Charles suggested a superb hiding place, but Swain knew that Tantum had in doing so made himself the obvious suspect – added to which, Tantum had animus with Canford over the rumours about Ginny, and over their musical differences.

"Only Swain knows what finally persuaded him to put Charles' crime venue theory to the test, but you can imagine how he might have longed to scare the living daylights out of Oliver, while getting Tantum put away into the bargain."

"And now Swain has gone missing."

"We spoke to Liz about it – she mentioned a holiday home that Swain's family kept in a remote spot up on the moors."

"I hope you contacted Lucy Renton."

"I did – and she thinks one of the old wardens might know where this place is."

"Good. And what are the police doing, apart from charging Roy?"

"One of my former colleagues went to the police station with Colin – he confirmed to them all he had told Dan and me. They have let him go for now.

"And Bloomfield is on the tail of Aglionby, as well as organising a posse to track Swain down. Lynne messaged me to say that there may have been a sighting of him in Okehampton."

As Bishop Bob got up to leave, Barker trotted in to see how the meeting had gone.

"Thanks as ever, John. What a business. I blame myself – if only I'd listened to Hilary when we were in Venice."

"You can't think like that, Bob. Remember what you said to me about not blaming myself for Roy? Just look at how many people were taken in by Oliver. Go carefully."

"God bless – and thank you for being such a calming presence. That applies to you as well, Barker."

Over in Water Lane, Lynne was on the phone to Julia Tagg.

The interview with Colin had been difficult for all concerned, but, with the help of his solicitor, Colin just about held it together.

"The real villain seems to be Swain," Julia said. "Poor old Colin never stood a chance."

"Yeah, it makes me sick. The way Swain offered the hand of friendship to a desperately lonely individual – classic grooming tactics."

"Anyway," Julia added, "I have some better news. Jimmy has spoken to Mr Aglionby, who has agreed to help us with our enquiries. And there has been another sighting of our friend Richard in Okehampton."

FORTY-EIGHT

Geoff Pooley, Chag Wills' number two at Aspirational Cars, felt the full force of his boss's anger.

"Where the hell is that bloody Skoda! That bitch is fobbing us off."

"She told me that her friend was going to return it, but it had slipped his mind. She seemed really embarrassed. I trust her – she and her husband have been good clients."

"If that pathetic little excuse for a car isn't back by this afternoon, I'm getting hold of the police. And we won't be doing any more favours for glamorous widows, will we, Geoff?"

The car in question was to be found parked up in a lay-by off the A30, obscured from the road by noise reduction planting. Swain had driven there to get some mobile reception.

Checking his messages, at first he thought he had nothing to worry about. He couldn't give a toss if Aspirational Cars were hassling Liz over the Skoda. She would just have to deal with it.

She'd been trying to call and text him, of course. Much as he felt for Liz – he genuinely liked her – the main attraction for him had been the financial stability she offered.

But now the silly cow could ruin everything if she started looking for him. He didn't think she could find the cottage, but he had, stupidly, told her about it...

Perhaps he should be worried after all. Time to move on...

*

Another day unfolded in Minster Precincts. On the surface, it seemed like a routine one. Tedesco had eaten his breakfast while listening to the *Today* programme, he enjoyed his usual walk around the Close with Barker, and Sally Munks had doorstepped him about his training regime for the Walk for Wards.

But this wasn't going to be a typical day. Somehow, he knew it, and he sensed that Lynne was of the same opinion as she made her ritual energetic ascent of the stairs.

He let her settle before inviting her to join him in the meeting room.

She gave him the heads-up on the sighting – the red car had been spotted in a Lidl car park, but no real description of the driver, beyond "a bit scruffy, know what I mean?"

"I wouldn't describe Richard as scruffy," said Tedesco.

"Perhaps he is a master of disguise. Anyway, what about your lady vicar?"

"Are you referring to the Rural Dean, Lynne? She has rejigged her diary and is going over to see Will Heath, the old farmer, this afternoon. Oh, and my sister called. Her delightful husband is spitting tacks because Liz hasn't returned the Skoda."

"What a pity. Anyway, the DCI tells me that he is getting house-to-house under way in the villages – the initial feedback seems to be that no one has heard of the Swains, but there are so many second homers round there that Jimmy wasn't that surprised – and he is sending Jools up to London to see Aglionby – she will keep me posted."

*

At one o'clock, while Tedesco was waiting to be served at Jenks bakery, Lucy Renton was haring around the narrow, high-banked Devon lanes on her way to meet Will Heath at his cottage in Gidleigh – a hamlet near Chagford, birthplace of Tedesco's brother-in-law, Jeremy 'Chag' Wills.

"Good afternoon, Vicar," said Will Heath as he greeted Lucy.

The elderly churchwarden walked with a pronounced stoop, but he had retained the alertness of the true countryman. His nephew ran the farm now, and Will had moved into the cottage after his wife died.

He got straight to the point. "The Swains, you say. I do remember them. They bought an old place over towards Buttern Hill. The postman used to live there."

"What do you remember about the family, Will?"

The old man shut his eyes for a moment, as if in deep thought, and then continued: "They were a funny lot. Of course, nowadays, you can't move for people coming down here and buying up everything. I know plenty of folk who moan about it, but at least these second-home people keep the place alive.

"Anyway," he went on, "back then it was rare for people to buy a first home, let alone a holiday place. The cottage – The Bothy, it was called – was pretty much derelict, and there's nowhere else for miles around.

"They used to come down by train to Okehampton, and Maurice would pick them up – he had a car that he used as a taxi in those days – and then no one would see much of them until they went back."

"Were they what we might call 'back-to-nature' types, do you think, Will?"

"Something like that. The dad seemed pleasant enough, if you saw him in town, but the mother was a terrifying-looking thing, just glared at us lot as if we were a load of bumpkins."

"What about the children?"

"I don't remember much about them. Two boys and a girl, I think. Two of them were polite, but one of the boys was a rude bugger. Took after his mum."

"Who stays there these days?"

"The family still own it – I think they let friends stay there sometimes. I remember an author living there for a few months, nice chap, needed some peace and quiet to help with his writing, he said."

"What about the family? Do they still visit?"

"The parents are long gone, but the daughter and one of the boys used to come down with their nippers. The awkward bugger – Dickie, I think he was called – we never saw him again. His brother once told me that he hated the place."

"Will – you've been incredibly helpful. You were asking me on the phone what this was all about. I don't know much, but the police are looking for someone who might be hiding there – of course, they have no idea how to find the place. How do you fancy a little drive out?"

*

Aglionby was waiting by the gate when DS Julia Tagg's train arrived at Paddington.

He had told her that he would be wearing a carnation in his buttonhole, and she soon found him.

'As smooth as a Jazz FM presenter' was how Lynne had described his voice, and she was spot on.

"How lovely to meet you. I always want to help the police, but I'm not sure what I can usefully offer about young Canford."

He suggested a branch of Pret in Praed Street. It was before the lunch crowd descended, and so they could still find a quiet corner.

"Mr Aglionby," she started, "you knew Oliver Canford for some years, I think, as a fellow choir member."

"Yes, that's right – and please call me Hugh. He was a bit of a lost soul. Frightfully bright fellow Cambridge man, of course, but didn't have a real career until he moved down to your patch – unless you call escorting groups of dim-witted pensioners around Europe a career, haha."

She let him conclude his mirthless laughing, before adding, "Do you ever come to Rhyminster?"

"I've been there, of course, but it's such a long way from anywhere. But have you heard? I'm working with the Cathedral to try and bring the Minstrels – that's my choir – down there for a memorial concert. The Master of Musick is a splendid chap. We were at the same college, don't you know."

Tagg bit her tongue. If 'splendid chap' was upper-class code for 'total jerk', then she would agree with his designation.

She swiftly changed tack. "Hugh, I think you know Richard Swain, one of our Cathedral guides."

"Gosh, you've been doing your homework. Yes, I knew him briefly when I was at Porton Down. I heard that he had retired to Rhyminster."

"Hugh – think carefully. Could you have mentioned him to Oliver?"

Aglionby narrowed his eyes. "It is possible. I was wondering if I knew anyone down there who Ollie could latch on to, get him started in a new place. I may have mentioned Swain in passing, I suppose."

"Okay, Hugh. And could you have mentioned that Swain had been obliquely referred to by a whistleblower?"

The urbane charm swiftly evaporated. "Now look here!" he started.

"I hope you weren't going to say 'young lady'," interjected Julia.

"You agreed to assist with our enquiries, and so I suggest that you consider my question."

"Of course. Sorry. Yes, well, there was some gossip about Swain, and I suppose I might have mentioned it to Oliver – we normally adjourn to a nearby hostelry after rehearsals, and so I guess that I could have told him. Why does this matter? This doesn't have anything to do with Canford's death, does it?"

"Well… dangerous talk can cost lives. Look, Hugh, what I can say is that Canford knowing this about Swain might fill in a gap in our investigations. I don't want you to beat yourself up about it – but I will need you to make a statement."

What a peculiar world, she thought as she headed back to Paddington. *There are, apparently, still people who wear buttonholes and adjourn to hostelries.*

She was looking forward to swapping Aglionby-related notes with Lynne Davey when she got home to Rhyme, but

Bloomfield's call quickly brought her back to the present.

She filled him in on the gist of Aglionby's remarks, which seemed to satisfy his immediate curiosity.

"Well done. It confirms what we thought Canford was up to. Aglionby's indiscretion was stupid but probably not deliberate. We need a good look at Swain's finances now – see if we can link the mystery BACS payments that appeared in Canford's account to him."

*

Back in Devon, Will Heath's memory had served him well.

He guided Lucy Renton to the woods beneath the cottage. She was able to take a passable photo of the run-down hovel by using the zoom function on her recently upgraded phone.

She'd have to wait until she had a decent signal before trying to forward it to John Tedesco.

*

Andy Toms was feeling totally knackered after a hard day of emptying septic tanks.

As he made his way back to the depot, he was forced to stop in a greenway. He carefully manoeuvred into a passing place, as he could tell that the oncoming driver wasn't a local, and so would have no idea how to pass on a single-track road. Bloody grockles.

All of a sudden, he was thrust forward as his load of excrement was struck at speed.

A small red car had appeared from nowhere, hurtling down from the woods, into the lane and straight into the tanker.

The grockle was anxiously trying to call the emergency services on a mobile, but Andy could have told him there was no signal.

Extricating himself, he was relieved to find that he was okay – the tanker had been stationary, and the impact was on the other side from him.

He couldn't say the same about the driver of the red car.

Andy remained at the scene, with what he assumed was a dead body, telling the tourist to call the police as soon as he got back to a main road. He'd find reception on the A30.

*

Driving back towards Okehampton minutes earlier, Swain had seen that there were police patrolling the area. Time to go back to the cottage, gather his stuff and get out of Dodge.

As he found the gap in the woods, he was shocked to find a car in his familiar parking place – and a woman was using her phone to take pictures of the cottage. Someone had found him. Probably Tedesco or his sidekick, although from here the woman didn't look like Lynne Davey.

In any event, he had no time to gather his stuff. He couldn't get to the cottage without being seen now, so he turned the car around, not an easy feat in the woods, and took off at speed.

His last words as he drove into the Ten Tors Drainage Services tanker were grimly appropriate: "Where did that come from! Shit!"

FORTY-NINE

FIN

As he strolled through the water meadows towards the welcoming lights of the Kingfisher, Tedesco was remembering the last time he'd taken this path.

It had been back in September, on his way to meet his sister Nicky after returning from his course in Bristol. As ever, he instantly remembered what he had been tuned into on his inner soundtrack that evening – *Home Thoughts from Abroad*.

But after a gruelling case involving a kidnapping and the violent deaths of Canford and Swain, his musical mood was a shade darker this time, and he almost felt the plangent piano chords of Don McLean's *Crossroads* wafting into his brain.

As he got within sight of the foodie pub, his mood lifted at the prospect of meeting Lynne for supper.

It had been her idea – they were both free on a Friday evening, and they could do with something to mark the end of the investigation, in the spirit of reflection rather than celebration.

Tedesco had booked out the following morning, a Saturday, to complete the casebook.

He would write a single word – '*Fin*' – to close the file, turning over the blue cover of the counsel's notebook for the last time before filing it away in the office safe.

As a shy teenager coming of age in a provincial city, he had been beguiled by European style, music and, most importantly, cinema.

He would drift away during Maths lessons, imagining himself hanging out with Sophia Loren and Marcello Mastroianni between takes at Cinecittà, or sitting outside a Parisian café, sipping Ricard and smoking Gauloises with his best mates Alain Delon and Jean-Paul Belmondo.

He no longer smoked Gauloises, but he did drive a Lancia…

Investigations were a bit like French films of the late fifties and early sixties – you were never quite sure when they had ended until those three letters appeared at the bottom of the screen, and, in the same way, an investigation wasn't really concluded until he had closed his book – hence his beautifully inscribed 'Fin'.

*

As he ducked to avoid the beam at the front door of the inn, he noticed his business partner sitting at a candlelit table overlooking the river.

There were occasional moments when the sight of her made his heart jump like a spring lamb, and this was one of them.

She wore a loose cream cardigan over her trademark black designer jeans, the bottoms of which were tucked into a pair of retro Chelsea boots.

Lynne waved him over, but just as he was about to join her, Sally Munks appeared, wearing what appeared to be a miner's safety lamp.

"Fancy dress night, is it, Sally?" said Lynne.

"No! This is to help with my night vision. We've just popped in for a drink at the bar after training."

The penny dropped – "Of course, the Walk for Wards!" said Tedesco. "How could I forget!"

"How is your training going?" Sally asked.

Lynne suggested that perhaps they could compare training regimes at the office on Monday.

Sally grinned. "I see. You don't want to be disturbed. Mum's the word."

Tedesco pointedly ignored the comment, and Sally joined her fellow walkers.

"Ooh, Mr Tedesco, it will be all over the office now," teased Lynne.

"Good job that the office just consists of Barker and Sally then."

They avoided the subject of Oliver Canford until they had ordered their seafood. John Dory for him, Lyme Bay plaice for her.

Deferring to Tedesco's expertise, she let him choose the wine, a greenish Chablis.

They clinked glasses, somewhat shyly for two such long-standing friends and colleagues, and then Tedesco asked her if she thought that they had been successful.

"Did we really make a difference, Lynne? Did I do enough for Bob? Should I have pushed Bloomfield harder on my gut feeling about Swain? And what if I'd gone for that drink with Roy?"

He took a deliberate sip of the Chablis.

"And if we'd got to Swain earlier, Jimmy could have questioned him about those suspicious bank transfers."

"Whoah! Wait a minute, partner," said Lynne.

"Our little agency has triumphed again. Great teamwork. Barker found the body, you smoked out Swain by using your clergy contacts, my research skills led me to linking Aglionby to both Canford and Swain. And Jimmy would never admit it, but he knows that he owes us big time."

"He's certainly come out smelling of roses. I wish I could say the same for the Cathedral. Wilf Drake tells me that their marketing people are so desperate that they have suggested a special ghost tour, with the last resting place of Oliver Canford as the highlight."

"I'd heard about it from Liz – perhaps they could time it to fit in with Tantum's wassail party – do the tour, then watch one of the main suspects in roaring action."

Tedesco broke into a grin, which morphed into laughter.

"Seriously, though, they need a lot of healing. Roy is staying with his brother in Lee-on-the-Solent as part of his bail conditions. Whatever happens on sentencing, we've seen the last of him in Rhyme.

"Poor old Colin is still employed pending sentencing. He's getting counselling and there will be the inevitable safeguarding review. Colin was a vulnerable person so I hope and pray that he won't get a custodial sentence. The Dean and Chapter are standing by him, which should help."

"I should jolly well hope so – how is prison going to help Colin? He's as much a victim as anyone in this awful business."

"In the meantime, Izzie has been promoted as acting Head Verger, with Wilf as her mentor, so at least she has something to look forward to – and there's poor Liz, of course."

"She's another victim of Swain. But on the bright side, I've gained something," Lynne said. "A great new yoga class, and a good mate in Jo. I know you think she's the ultimate hippy chick, but there's a lot more to her.

"By the way, she told me that she and Dan thought they should invite Charles and Ginny round for supper, to show there were no hard feelings.

"Dan approached Tantum after morning prayers, and he eagerly accepted, so Dan asked him if there was anything he didn't eat. Can you guess what Charles said?"

"I give up."

"Weasel."

Tedesco laughed again. He hadn't enjoyed an evening out like this for ages.

After a brief debate, they decided against a second bottle – he wanted to keep a clear head for his written conclusions, and she had Park Run in the morning – so they opted for the decidedly safe option of two black americanos.

While they waited for the coffee, Tedesco asked Lynne if she had received an invitation from Barbara Battershill, on behalf of the Bishop and his wife.

"Indeed I have – to supper. And, Mr Tedesco, I was called by your sister the other day, inviting me to dinner. She suggested that you could give me a lift."

"What do we do? Plead a subsequent engagement?"

It was Lynne's turn to laugh. "You old misery. We have just proved that we can socialise. Wouldn't it be fun to keep them guessing?"

When the bill eventually appeared, which Tedesco insisted on paying, he asked the waiter to order a taxi.

They didn't have long to wait. The driver was the Halloween lantern-faced Mickey Hunn.

"DS Davey! And Mr Tedesco, I assume? Hop in. What a business at the Cathedral, eh!"

After waiting at Water Lane to make sure that Lynne got indoors, Tedesco asked Mickey to drive him home through the Close – the gate was still open at that hour – and he gave him a generous tip when they reached St Budeaux Place.

Barker, awakened, rushed to the door. "Sorry to leave you, old friend. You look like you could use a snack before bed."

The terrier made short shrift of the contents of his bowl, while Tedesco boiled a kettle. The coffee at the Kingfisher hadn't met his exacting standards.

Tedesco poured his coffee, then moved towards his CD player. He decided that Nick Drake, as so often, would fit his mood.

Barker joined him on the sofa, appearing to agree with his master that *Time of No Reply* was an overlooked gem.

Tedesco stroked the dog gently. "What do you think, oh wise one? Could Lynne and I be more than friends?"

Barker responded by yawning, and then moved slowly in the direction of his basket.

FIFTY

Morning in Rhyminster

Tedesco and Barker were up early for their traditional Saturday-morning walk to the paper shop.

It was just about warm enough, in early October, to enjoy his coffee outside while he skimmed the headlines, but the Review section would have to wait until he had finally put his casebook to bed.

After promising Barker that they would go on their usual yomp after lunch, he retired to his study, where he worked for three solid hours, and had just inscribed '*Fin*' when the dog alerted him to the arrival of the post.

He gathered up the small pile of mail. All junk, as usual.

As he was about to chuck the rubbish into the blue recycling bin, his heart froze. There was a letter – a real handwritten letter – and he had almost thrown it out.

He recognised the writing immediately. No one, not even himself, could write so beautifully.

He held the letter, examining it as if it were part of a Japanese tea ceremony, taking in the quality of the stationery, and the postmark:

Republic of Ireland. Cork.

"But why now?" he said aloud.

It wasn't Christmas, or his birthday. They had written long letters to each other twice yearly since his early days in the law.

Using his father's old paper knife, he carefully slit open the envelope.

After slowly taking in the contents, he grabbed his mobile and called Crane House. Ella answered and, correctly sensing that this was important, fetched her mother.

"Nicky – I need to go away for a few days. Could you take Barker?"

"It must be serious, Bro. Is it her? Sorcha?"

"It is. I need to see her before it's too late."

"Go. Go now, you idiot. You can't mess about. Do you want me to call Lynne for you?"

"No, thanks – I'll ring her from the road."

He opened up his laptop and searched for flights to Cork.

ACKNOWLEDGEMENTS

So many people have encouraged my writing over the years, but I would like to specifically mention Mr Horsler, my English Master at Sutton High, Plymouth. Some of us are lucky enough to have had an inspirational teacher, and he was mine.

More recently, thanks to everyone who has urged me to get published; I hope I have proved worthy of your support.

I should also mention my fellow volunteers at Salisbury Cathedral. Unlike those at Rhyminster, they are universally lovely – not a murderer, kidnapper or bloodthirsty musician among them.

Finally, those who know me best will not be surprised at the final dedication.

My generation has been blessed to have grown up in a golden age of singers and songwriters. As well as providing us with a lifelong soundtrack, their words and music have given comfort and hope, and kept us sane when trouble has struck.

In the context of this book, I'd like to thank Ralph McTell for writing his beautiful song *Fin*, which indirectly inspired John Tedesco's trademark sign-off to his casebooks.

If Tedesco does nothing else, I hope that readers will take him up on his musical recommendations.